HER AMERICA

HER AMERICA
"A Jury of Her Peers" and Other Stories
by Susan Glaspell

EDITED BY
Patricia L. Bryan and Martha C. Carpentier

University of Iowa Press
Iowa City

University of Iowa Press, Iowa City 52242
Copyright © 2010 by the University of Iowa Press
www.uiowapress.org
Printed in the United States of America

Design by Sara T. Sauers

The University of Iowa Press is a member of Green Press
Initiative and is committed to preserving natural resources.

Printed on acid-free paper

Library of Congress Cataloging-in-Publication Data
Glaspell, Susan, 1876–1948
Her America: A jury of her peers and other stories /
by Susan Glaspell; edited by Patricia L. Bryan and
Martha C. Carpentier.
     p.   cm.
ISBN-13: 978-1-58729-864-6 (pbk.)
ISBN-10: 1-58729-864-3 (pbk.)
I. Bryan, Patricia L., 1951–   II. Carpentier, Martha
Celeste.   III. Title.
PS3513.L35H47 2010
813'.52—dc22 2009041593

Contents

 Acknowledgments

WE GREATLY APPRECIATE THE careful work of Mika Chance and Caitlin Womersley in helping us to ensure accurate transcriptions from the original periodicals. In addition we thank Mary McAleer Balkun, chair of the Department of English, Seton Hall University, for her generous support, both financial and intellectual. We had invaluable assistance from the library staff at the University of North Carolina Law School, particularly the research by Dean C. Smith. We are also grateful to Valentina Cook, executor of the estate of Susan Glaspell, for her permission to reprint the stories in this collection.

HER AMERICA

Introduction

SUSAN GLASPELL (1876–1948) WAS one of the preeminent American writers of the early twentieth century, and she was particularly remarkable for her success in three different literary genres. She wrote fourteen groundbreaking plays (including *Alison's House*, awarded the Pulitzer Prize in 1931), nine novels, and some fifty short stories, producing a body of work that was critically acclaimed and widely read during her lifetime. Her novels were reviewed in the *New York Times*, with several listed as best sellers; productions of her plays were nationally publicized; and her works of short fiction reached audiences throughout the country, appearing in the most influential literary magazines, such as *Harper's* and *McClure's*, as well as in those with the greatest circulation numbers, such as the *Ladies' Home Journal*.

Born in Davenport, Iowa, Glaspell began writing and publishing very early in her career. While in high school, she contributed to the *Davenport Morning Republican* and then published a column titled Social Life in the *Weekly Outlook* from 1896 to 1897. After graduating from Drake University in Des Moines in 1899, she took a job as a reporter for the *Des Moines Daily News*, where she covered the legislature and wrote a weekly feature, the News Girl, interspersing lighthearted social commentary with serious suggestions in favor of women's rights, educational programs, and prison reform. In 1901, she reported on her first criminal trial, which was also her last assignment for the newspaper. Glaspell returned to Davenport, committed to writing short fiction. As she later remarked, "[At the *News*] I was always running into things I saw as short stories, and after less than two years of newspaper reporting I boldly gave up my job and went home to Davenport to give all my time to my own writing. I say boldly, because I had to earn my living."[1]

Glaspell thus joined some of the most distinguished writers—Poe, Harte, Bierce, Twain, Crane, Lardner, and Cather—whose careers as journalists fed directly into the development of American short fiction in the late nineteenth and early twentieth centuries, bestowing economy, precision, and the personal, distinctive narrative voice on the short story form.

Glaspell's early stories reflect her state legislature beat and her critical view of the political system, but a term she spent at the University of Chicago provided a new setting that further inspired her developing craft. She began shifting her point of view from male to female and from jaded governors to young women like herself, migrants from midwestern towns to the alienating city, as her stories gained in psychological realism. Reflecting also the influence of socialism and literary naturalism, Glaspell's stories from 1902 to 1912 portray the Midwest as "the new battleground between preservation of the land and humanism on the one hand and the steady encroachments of industrialism and mechanization on the other."[2] It wasn't long before the talented young author was making her living by her writing. In 1902 and 1904, she submitted to the periodical *Black Cat* two stories that won substantial cash awards, and she began consistently publishing in magazines of wider circulation, such as *Youth's Companion* and *Booklovers*. In 1912, with two well-reviewed novels under her belt, Glaspell reprinted thirteen stories with the Frederick A. Stokes Company under the title *Lifted Masks*. Praised by the American Library Association for its "well constructed stories of decided originality," the collection was also recommended by the *Boston Evening Transcript* as a book "that holds one's breathless attention"; and according to the *New York Times*, the selections were "full of human tenderness and human laughter," with some of them "among the best stories of the sort that have appeared for a long time."[3]

During the next ten years, after moving to New York's bohemian Greenwich Village, summering in Provincetown, Massachusetts, marrying, and starting the theater group Provincetown Players with friends, Glaspell wrote more than twenty short stories, including eleven featured in this collection. Nearly all were written from 1915 to 1920, the most fertile time in Glaspell's career, when she was producing innovative plays, novels, and short fiction simultaneously.[4] These mature stories display an exceptional range of skills, from realistic and dramatic narrative to deft and comedic satire, and they reflect Glaspell's deep concerns about political and ethical issues prevalent then and today: the country's participation in foreign wars, mounting political conservatism, anti-intellectualism, economic inequality, and women's rights. Until now almost all of these stories have been inaccessible to modern audiences, located only in the archives of the original periodicals.

Over the last three decades, the feminist literary critical movement has contributed to a resurgence of Glaspell's reputation. Scholarly interest in her has grown explosively, with the appearance of books such as Barbara Ozieblo's *Susan Glaspell: A Critical Biography*, J. Ellen Gainor's *Susan Glaspell in Context: American Theater, Culture, and Politics, 1915–48*, and Linda Ben-Zvi's *Susan Glaspell: Her Life and Times*. Many have focused on Glaspell's profound impact on American drama as cofounder, with her husband, George Cram Cook, of the Provincetown Players in 1915 and on the plays she wrote, which include some of the finest produced by little theater companies in America. Readers familiar with Glaspell's drama will find fascinating echoes in several of the stories collected here, for her most famous play, *Trifles*, and its short story version, "A Jury of Her Peers," are not Glaspell's only exploration of similar themes, plots, and characters in two genres. "Unveiling Brenda" is a short story version of her play *Close the Book*; "A Rose in the Sand" develops further her earlier one-act play *The Outside*; and "Pollen" clearly inspired two of her greatest full-length plays, *The Verge* and *Inheritors*.

"A Jury of Her Peers," published in 1917 and rediscovered in the early 1970s, is Susan Glaspell's best-known short story today. Based on a murder trial she covered as a journalist for the *Des Moines Daily News* in 1901, in which a woman was accused of killing her abusive husband,[5] Glaspell's story was lauded in 1986 as a "feminist classic," raising issues of women's oppression and gender differences in perception.[6] Now the story is regarded as an American classic, widely anthologized in introductory and American literature textbooks and taught to students in high schools, colleges, and law schools across the country. "A Jury of Her Peers" has also become familiar to readers outside of academia, publicized to contemporary audiences by its reprinting in two different volumes celebrating the finest short works of the twentieth century: *The Best American Short Stories of the Century*, edited by John Updike, and *The Best American Mystery Stories of the Century*, edited by Tony Hillerman.[7] Despite this story's contemporary prominence, little has been written about the details of its publication in 1917 or about its wide circulation then, nor has the extent of Glaspell's reputation as a short story writer been realized. In fact, "A Jury of Her Peers" initially reached an audience of at least one million, a remarkable number at a time when few popular periodicals could boast higher figures.[8] The story first appeared on Sunday, March 4, 1917, as part of a syndicated Sunday supplement published by Associated Sunday Magazines, Inc. Local newspapers relied on competing magazines of this type to sell their more expensive Sunday issues, with the supplements typically featuring colorful cover art by well-known illustrators and fiction by popular authors. In 1917, the Associated Sunday Magazines' supplement was distributed along with six major newspapers: the *Boston Post, Buffalo Courier, Detroit News-Tribune, Minneapolis Journal, Pittsburg Post*, and *Washington Star*. Circulation was reported to be eight hundred thousand.[9]

But "A Jury of Her Peers" had an even larger audience in 1917 than reflected by that figure. Since 1915, a stand-alone version of the Associated Sunday Magazines' supplement had been sold on newsstands on Mondays under the name *Every Week*, a unique venture launched by the publisher to increase market share. Modeled on popular penny weeklies in England, *Every Week* was offered at three cents an issue, a price well below that of its competitors, and it took most of its material directly from the Sunday supplement. When the idea of the Monday version was conceived, the publisher hired new editors, including Bruce Barton, from *Collier's*, as editor in chief and Edith Lewis, Willa Cather's lifetime companion, from *McClure's*, as his assistant, and they had enhanced the magazine's visual appeal, experimenting with innovative changes in format. From the beginning, longer works of fiction were a significant part of *Every Week*, making up about one-third of each issue, and it was hoped that one story each week would be by "a writer of reputation."[10] The Monday magazine was quickly a success, reporting a circulation of nearly two hundred thousand in 1916 and increasing to the half-million mark during the next twelve months. Although wartime paper shortages

4

brought it to an abrupt end in mid-1918, *Every Week* was exceptionally popular throughout its short life and proved to be a fortuitous placement for Glaspell's story.[11] Combining circulation figures for the Sunday supplement and *Every Week*, it seems likely that well more than one million copies of "A Jury of Her Peers" were distributed in March 1917.

Early the next year, its audience was increased still more, when "A Jury of Her Peers" was selected as one of twenty works to be reprinted in *The Best Short Stories of 1917*. This collection was the third in a series edited by Edward J. O'Brien, a project he had initiated in 1915 with a specific goal: to focus attention on "the significant position of the American short story," a distinctive and evolving genre that offered American writers the chance to earn much-needed respect as well as income from magazine publication.[12] O'Brien understood the potential economic gains for writers, with the burgeoning media eager to supply an increasingly literate middle class with fiction for casual reading, but he warned that commercial incentives could result in the production of work that was less compelling and imaginative. O'Brien hoped to reverse that trend with his series, where he would reward literary craft over formulaic writing, encouraging authors and editors to maintain high artistic standards. For his first volume, O'Brien read more than two thousand published short stories and ranked them all on a scale of zero to three, with the highest grades awarded to those most distinguished in style, imagination, and narrative substance. The system was one he would continue, with each yearly collection including a lengthy annotated index with his rankings for all stories, statistical evaluations of American magazines based on the quality of their fiction, and his "Roll of Honor," typically reserved for fewer than 125 stories deserving of the greatest recognition for their literary excellence.

Stories by Susan Glaspell were regularly awarded honor roll status, and almost all of them appeared in magazines that, in O'Brien's opinion, published the finest literary works.[13] In 1917, both "A Jury of Her Peers" and "A Matter of Gesture" were on his Roll of Honor, and in his notes on Glaspell, O'Brien commented that "few American writers have such a natural dramatic story sense." Two more Glaspell works earned places on the Roll of Honor the following year, with O'Brien describing "Beloved Husband" and "Poor Ed" as "the best she has done, with the possible exception of 'A Jury of Her Peers.'" In 1919, three of Glaspell's stories ("The Busy Duck," published in November 1918, and "Pollen" and "Government Goat," in 1919) were on O'Brien's Roll of Honor, a list that also included contributions by Sherwood Anderson, Theodore Dreiser, Jack London, and Mary Heaton Vorse.[14] Just as in the two previous years, Glaspell was one of the few authors who earned O'Brien's highest praise for more than one published story, and he again chose a work by her as one of the twenty for the annual collection, with "Government Goat" appearing in *The Best Short Stories of 1919*. O'Brien's repeated approbation shows that, although Susan Glaspell was one of many American writers in the early twentieth century who took advantage of the new market for short fiction to pay the bills, she did not compromise the quality of her work to conform to the formulaic demands of the mass media.

The original version of "A Jury of Her Peers," from March 4, 1917, is reprinted here for the first time. Previous reprints of the story, in all of the many anthologies where it appears, were derived from the 1918 version published in O'Brien's *The Best Short Stories of 1917*. Readers familiar with "A Jury of Her Peers" may be surprised to notice that this version includes a different ending, in particular a concluding sentence that we believe reinforces Annette Kolodny's well-known interpretation of the story as a "semiotic analysis" in which men are excluded from reading the nonverbal signifiers of the female "conceptual and symbolic world."[15] It is impossible to know when or why Glaspell revised the ending, but scholars, critics, and students of her work may enjoy comparing the two and discussing the many implications of this difference.

As the publication history of "A Jury of Her Peers" indicates, the readership of Glaspell's short fiction was far wider than has been realized, and this holds true for the other stories reprinted here as well. Their publication ranged widely throughout the three-tier structure of magazines, which by the early years of the twentieth century dominated the market: mass media, middle-range "highbrow" periodicals, and radical little magazines. While Glaspell sometimes published in mass-circulation magazines ("Looking After Clara" appeared in the *Ladies' Home Journal*, which by 1900 had a circulation of nearly one million), she also published in the noncommercial little magazines that sought aesthetic experimentation and political radicalism, and usually had small readerships.[16] But the venues that most often published Glaspell's short stories were the middle-range American magazines, such as *Munsey's*, *McClure's*, and *Harper's*, which "offered a consistent outlet for established writers of quality" and cultivated a discerning, literate, influential readership.[17]

It is a testament to the high esteem in which Susan Glaspell's short fiction was held, and to its consistent quality, that the majority of it during these years was published in *Harper's*, including six of the stories reprinted here. Founded by the Harper brothers in 1850, *Harper's Monthly Magazine* was addressed "to the educated reader, not to a broad or popular audience." In 1853, *Harper's* initiated the Easy Chair, an editorial column that for over one hundred years informed American opinion, from the tenure of its founder, George William Curtis, through that of William Dean Howells, the publicly acknowledged "Dean of American Letters" and its voice from 1899 to 1920. Along with Howells, Henry Mills Alden, editor of *Harper's* from 1869 to 1919, changed the focus from British to American fiction, and according to Lewis H. Lapham, "Alden crowded the magazine with short stories, sometimes as many as eight or ten in a single issue, by authors of the quality of Mark Twain, Willa Cather, Stephen Crane, Edith Wharton, [and] Henry James," and "by 1895 Alden's magazine and the publishing house of Harper & Brothers passed as synonyms for the highest grades of American literary ore."[18]

Glaspell's stories were published during the editorial regime of Alden and Howells, and it is no wonder that her fiction appealed to their sensibility. A midwesterner like Glaspell, Howells always revered his Ohio roots, and both Howells and Glaspell were informed by a reverence for Lincoln and a love of New England transcendentalism, particularly Emerson and Thoreau. Howells published Twain and James during his editorship of the *Atlantic Monthly* (1871–1881), becoming a personal friend of both and a vocal proponent of American realism, a style Glaspell consistently employs in her short fiction. While her drama was influenced by European expressionism, Glaspell did not favor the modernist Chekovian epiphanic form of the short story and always remained closer in her technique to native and regional generic traditions. Stylistically she followed in the footsteps of two great American forefathers in the genre, Poe and Twain, particularly in her use of the grotesque and in her development of a humorous, satiric narrative voice. The short story genre offered Glaspell the opportunity to express her playful wit and acerbic, though ameliorative, social satire.

The association of humans with animals is fundamental to both the grotesque and the satiric fable. "A Jury of Her Peers" is far from the only story in this collection in which an animal (the infamous dead canary) plays a significant role. Animals serve the same narrative function in her fiction as they do, for instance, in Poe's "The Black Cat" and "The Raven" or in Twain's "The Celebrated Jumping Frog of Calaveras County," "What Stumped the Blue Jays," and "A Dog's Tale": whether comically or tragically, animals provide a window into the human soul and reflect the foibles and terrors of humans. Like Poe's black cat, the "government goat" in Glaspell's story of that name bears the full weight of Joe Doane's despair as he screams helplessly at his nemesis, "Go to *hell!*" Professor Peyton Root in "Unveiling Brenda" realizes the depth of his love for Brenda only as "the stronger became his desire to be sharing Scraps's experience"—Scraps being her "fat, yellow dog with a corkscrew tail . . . quivering with happy excitement" as he looks adoringly at his mistress. And it is Mrs. Paxton's gesture of compassion, providing water at the pump for an old horse "life had no use for," that creates "A Rose in the Sand," which in turn inspires her rebirth.

Glaspell's image of the pig eating one of its babies in "The Nervous Pig" is a brilliant rendering of the Bakhtinian grotesque. According to Bakhtin, the essential principle of grotesque realism is "the lowering of all that is high, spiritual, ideal, abstract . . . to the material level, to the sphere of earth and body . . . to acts of defecation and copulation, conception, pregnancy, and birth. Degradation digs a bodily grave for a new birth; it has not only a destructive, negative aspect, but also a regenerating one."[19] In the young scholar Horace's dawning realization that he and the pig are "the same thing," a realization that "draw[s] him into that main body of life from which he was holding away in order to pursue his studies," we see the deflation of intellectual pretense and pedantry at the heart of Menippean satire, a mode shared by many of these stories, especially "Looking After Clara," "Poor Ed," "Unveiling Brenda," and "The Busy Duck." From Horace's acceptance of his common mutability with the pig, it is but a short hop to his announcement while eating roast pork at the dinner table: "War is civilization eating

her own little pigs." Even in this lighthearted farce, Glaspell connects
American consumerism and capitalism with its involvement in World
War I, while stories such as "The Manager of Crystal Sulphur Springs"
and "Beloved Husband" explore more seriously the corrosive effects of
materialism on American society and family.

In *The Gruesome Doorway: An Analysis of the American Grotesque*,
Paula Uruburu discusses "the crucial, unresolvable conflict embedded in
the American mind and experience which makes their vision grotesque.
It is the inevitable confrontation between Adamic innocence and terrible
self-knowledge, between a realistic and an idealistic view of life."[20] It was
Poe in his preface to *Tales of the Grotesque and Arabesque* who first claimed,
not only for himself but thereafter for American letters, a grotesque style
that is "of the soul" rather than simply an expression of physical fecun-
dity and abnormality.[21] The paradox fundamental to the grotesque—a
disturbing fusion of the laughable and the horrifying, the comic and the
tragic, the ideal and the real—became, as Baudelaire said of Poe himself,
"an impersonated antithesis" in which an inner, personal truth melds
incongruously with an outward manifestation or personification.[22]

Sherwood Anderson carried on from Poe, advancing a similarly American interpretation in "The Book of the Grotesque," his introduction to
Winesburg, Ohio, by writing that "it was the truths that made the people
grotesques. . . . The moment one of the people took one of the truths
to himself, called it his truth, and tried to live his life by it, he became a
grotesque and the truth he embraced became a falsehood."[23] Uruburu
states that both Poe and Anderson suffered from the "terrible awareness
of being isolated from their countrymen because of the depth of their
poetic vision" (57). This is a quality in Anderson, whom Glaspell knew
from their heady Greenwich Village days in the first two decades of the
twentieth century, that she deeply sympathized with. Both writers lived
with this sense of isolation as outsiders, midwesterners on the fringes
of an already marginalized cultural group, artists, in the "refined" and
often—from the point of view of midwesterners—privileged and preten-
tious East. After Anderson's death, Glaspell wrote the following notes:

> Reading Sherwood Anderson's letters to V.W.B. [Van Wyck
> Brooks]—the feeling of how Brooks failed him (though

perhaps Brooks couldn't help it, they were too different, in region, in culture & temperament.) But realizing how lonely Sherwood was in the very times I knew him as gay at parties. . . . Sherwood had hunger—exposed hunger— & perhaps this didn't seem refined to V.W.B.

I read the letters last night with sorrow & understanding. I am sure I did understand them, as S— & I came from about the same time & same kind of place. He would say, "It is lonely out here" & I knew what he meant—Lord, yes. And I understand, as not all would, that deference for the "cultivated man"—the master—the man of letters in the East.[24]

Glaspell was part of a whole generation of midwestern writers and artists, including Sherwood Anderson, Sinclair Lewis, Willa Cather, F. Scott Fitzgerald, Ernest Hemingway, and many others, who migrated east and spearheaded, as Thomas Gullason has written, "a revitalized short story in the 1920s" (74). These "emerging writers of the Midwest were a godsend," according to Gullason; "self-reliant and tough-minded . . . closer to the pulse and beat of past traditions, the heritage of America," they were able to capture "with remarkable fidelity the native American values and colloquial speech patterns" in their short fiction (Ibid).

Yet like many of her fellow midwesterners, Glaspell retained a deep ambivalence toward her native region. While she revered the midwestern pioneer and agricultural traditions she remembered from her youth and celebrated the region's honest, unpretentious values of common men and women, she had migrated east to escape its provincialism and narrow-minded conventionality, which she parodies in her "Freeport" (Davenport) stories. Taken together, these stories (including "Finality in Freeport," "The Manager of Crystal Sulphur Springs," "Unveiling Brenda," "Poor Ed," "Beloved Husband," and "Pollen") constitute a significant contribution to the "revolt against the village" mode, or thematic movement, in American literature of the first half of the twentieth century, which embraced works ranging from Twain's "The Man That Corrupted Hadleyburg," a "relentless" satire of the "piousness and hypocrisy of small-town America,"[25] to Sinclair Lewis's *Main Street* and many others. Indeed, Lewis paid tribute to Glaspell's influence when an unconventional character in *Main Street* wants to outrage the town by performing Glaspell and Cook's play *Suppressed Desires*, and Lewis further acknowledged her in the dedication of his novel *Our Mr. Wrenn.*

This volume features several of Glaspell's satiric gems from 1914 to 1920, stories that "reflect the sense of isolation and loss of innocence which the nation as a whole experienced after World War I" (Uruburu, 71). Similar to Anderson's, Glaspell's stories are peopled by isolated grotesques whose lives are destroyed or saved by some inner truth they bear, characters such as the senile entrepreneur of "The Manager of Crystal Sulphur Springs," the pretend revolutionary of "A Matter of Gesture," the sacrificial capitalist of "Beloved Husband," the nativist father of "Government Goat," the Faustian farmer of "Pollen," or the misanthropic divorcée in "A Rose in the Sand."

But whereas Anderson's spare tragedies sometimes seem to hit the reader with a brick, Glaspell's deft satires seem to tickle with a feather. Colette Lindroth has discussed Glaspell's use of "techniques of indirection—irony, understatement, metaphor, the juxtaposition of opposites, and especially the weapon of humor" to make her points "subtly but unmistakably."[26] According to Lindroth, much of Glaspell's effect is achieved through the genial narrative voice that establishes a "tongue-in-cheek transaction ... a privileged relationship between author and reader, who is in on Glaspell's jokes" (260), and it is this humorous persona that marks her legacy from Twain. In "How to Tell a Story," Twain wrote the following: "The humorous story is American, the comic story is English, the witty story is French. The humorous story depends for its effect upon the *manner* of the telling; the comic story and the witty story upon the *matter*."[27] For Twain, the emphasis of the American writer of humor should be on the narrative persona, the teller of the tale, and "Twain is such a humorist, for ... the trust that readers have customarily placed in Twain derives in part from some sense of the author's affably earnest character ... and in part from his self-evident contempt for pretense and sham.... The cogency and popularity of it depended upon a perceived sense of the author's upright moral character coexisting with his sense of good-natured fun" (Quirk, 12).

It is just such a narrative voice that Glaspell cultivates, for example, in

"The Nervous Pig," which opens with a question: "If you were writing a book on the comparative civilizations of ancient and modern India, how would you like to have a young woman come bounding up to your window to tell you that the neighbor's pig had eight little pigs?" Here is the affable, good-natured omniscient third-person narration, the "amused tolerance, mingled with protective compassion" that seduces the reader into sympathizing with—yet how mockingly!—Horace Caldwell, the pompous young scholar struggling to resist the charms of his girlfriend.[28] Further, Glaspell's direct address to her audience with the second-person pronoun immediately places the narrative within the Western tradition of tall-tale telling that Twain transferred so successfully from the oral to the written medium.

Glaspell was adept at playing with point of view. "The Busy Duck" is a masterpiece in the use of unreliable first-person narration for satiric purposes, as Glaspell skewers the supercilious teller of this tale, a college professor who is unsuccessful at both writing and wooing despite his high opinions of himself. Like other modernist writers, Glaspell could manipulate third-person narration into a form of stream-of-consciousness that reveals a character unbeknownst to him- or herself, as in "Poor Ed," where we sense right from the opening that another self-important, self-deluded writer is headed for a fall:

> How many times he and Henry had sailed down the river! His eyes blurred, though as he cleared them he thought he would write an essay on "Going Back." He would make it a tribute to poor old Henry. Yes, he would be glad to do that. It would be something that would remain from Henry's life. And, who could say? It might be one of the best things he ever wrote. Success interpreting failure—and with gentle understanding.

"Feminist humor is NOT the obverse of male humor," write Gloria Kaufman and Mary Kay Blakely.[29] Unlike the misogyny typical of male satires about women, dating from Juvenal through Jonathan Swift and Alexander Pope to many of today's stand-up comics, feminist satire does not rely on gendered stereotypes, and it avoids jokes in which "laughs come from a perceived superiority of the hearer or reader to the character ridiculed" (16). In feminist satire, Kaufman and Blakely assert, "we do not laugh *at* people, we *bond* with them" (16). While this may not be applicable to all women satirists, it is certainly true of Glaspell's stories. The objects of her satire are men, but their pretenses and failings are exposed with sympathy, and in the more serious stories, such as "Government Goat" and "Beloved Husband," with pathos. In "Unveiling Brenda," Brenda herself exemplifies Glaspell's satiric method, as she wittily and lovingly mocks her young English professor in the essays she writes for him, which indeed cause him to love her in return.

Often the male protagonists are shown to be more vulnerable, insecure, and emotional than they want to appear, exemplifying a theme of play-acting that is common to much of Glaspell's work in other genres, in which people act roles in order to preserve their illusions about themselves. In "Looking After Clara," for example, Mr. Blatchford strives to project the image of efficiency and responsibility expected of men even as he struggles to hide his anxieties, both about the task he's been assigned by Dorothy and about her feelings for him. He worries constantly about how he's perceived by others, whether as the strong and dignified figure he'd like to be or as someone who inspires suspicions or laughter. The male protagonists in "The Busy Duck," "Unveiling Brenda," and "The Nervous Pig" present themselves as intellectuals with a single-minded focus on higher knowledge, and yet the reader, privy to their inner thoughts and feelings, observes how frequently they are distracted by their emotional reactions to members of the opposite sex, their focus on their own clothes and outward appearance, and their concerns about how others are judging them.

Glaspell portrays gender expectations for men and the ways they internalize these roles tragically as well as comically. Many of her male characters suffer from their attempts to keep up appearances in a society that does not recognize their individuality. Mr. and Mrs. Peters in "The Manager of Crystal Sulphur Springs" ask themselves "What harm does it do?" as they protect and even foster the illusions of Bert Groves that enable him to survive, a pretense that seems benign enough, but only as long as they are in charge and can keep the real world at bay. Play-acting proves just as harmful and even dangerous in other stories, such as "Pollen," in which Ira Mead's pretenses, a cover-up for his sense of inferiority, end up merely isolating him, for "when you are apart from others, what you do has to be superior to the works of others, else—why are you apart from them?" Harry Ruhl's grandiose play-acting in "A Matter of Gesture" eventually proves fatal, and Amos Owens, another man who cannot successfully act the part expected of him by his family or by society, is finally driven to a desperate act by his obsessive fears and isolation in "Beloved Husband." Joe Doane, the protagonist of "Government Goat," constantly cracks jokes to hide his feelings of unworthiness, and yet his shame and his sense of failure as the provider for his family nearly end in his death.

Glaspell's women, also outsiders seemingly without power in the accepted hierarchy, often draw on unexpected reserves of strength and take action that goes against the expected course. They rebel in quiet ways, subverting expectations and acting in accordance with their own ideas about compassion and true justice. The four works in this collection that feature female protagonists—"The Manager of Crystal Sulphur Springs," "A Jury of Her Peers," "A Matter of Gesture," and "A Rose in the Sand"—raise many of the issues, such as empathy, crime, and punishment, that have inspired so many discussions of "A Jury of Her Peers." Like her namesake in "A Jury of Her Peers," Mrs. Peters in "The Manager of Crystal Sulphur Springs" faces a similar quandary involving empathy and legal ethics. Empathizing with Bert Groves, the now bankrupt former owner of Crystal Sulphur Springs, Emma Peters understands that he has been rendered obsolete by capitalism's single-minded pursuit of profit, just as she herself has been. Yet her inaction at the end, knowing full well that Bert Groves is dying, can be seen both as an act of compassion and as an unsanctioned euthanasia. A jury of one, she makes a decision over life and death, and Glaspell ends this story with a rhetorical question because she wants her readers to try to answer it for themselves, or perhaps to realize that it never can be definitively answered.

Similarly, the maternal narrator in "A Matter of Gesture" rejects a judgment that she sees as unfair and narrow-minded, writing her own narrative to stand in opposition to the more simplistic explanation of Harry Ruhl's recantation, which had been accepted as "the verdict of the majority." As so often happens in Glaspell's works, the protagonist's initial attempts to understand lead her to broader questions of causation and responsibility, with the narrator in this story pondering the morality of keeping Ruhl in prison, once it became clear that he did not have the moral fiber to rise to the occasion. As she says, "There is something not to be borne in that idea of exacting of living things that which is immeasurably beyond their strength." Does the punishment fit the crime? In an era in which teachers, students, writers, laborers, and common people of all kinds were being imprisoned for simply speaking out, Glaspell was deeply concerned about the suffering caused by confinement and isolation—whether in a prison cell, in an abusive marriage, or in a society that ruthlessly expects conformity.

In "A Jury of Her Peers," Mrs. Hale cries, "Oh, I *wish* I'd come over here once in a while! . . . That was a crime! Who's going to punish that?" Similarly, "A Matter of Gesture" poses the question of the responsibility of the whole community for the individual's crime. Although she condemns Harry Ruhl's weakness, the narrator alone, among all the characters, feels responsible, even guilty, as she concludes, "Oh, yes, I think there's a good deal to blame ourselves for." In "A Rose in the Sand," Ellen Paxton, abandoned by her husband and stubbornly clinging to the safety of her isolation, is brought back into human communion through the compassion of her servant, Allie Mayo, just as she herself finally adopts an orphaned child. And Ira Mead, in "Pollen," learns that he cannot keep his perfect corn to himself because the wind "blew and carried seed. Winds blew and brought the life that changed other life."

While Glaspell's deflation of her characters' illusions and self-deceptions is in some stories comic and in others tragic, all her protagonists learn that people are deeply interconnected in ways that can't be controlled and that are ultimately saving. Again and again, Glaspell explores the conflict between innocence and self-knowledge, between arrogance and empathic understanding, between conformity and individualism, while always emphasizing the importance of collective responsibility. Gathered here and reprinted for the first time, these superb examples of her short fiction show how cohesive a body of work it is and how true it is throughout to Glaspell's vision of "Her America."

In reprinting and presenting Glaspell's stories to today's readers, we have added a number of clarifying footnotes and have corrected obvious typographical errors. We have generally regularized and modernized archaic spellings, particularly hyphenated words that have since become spelled as one word. In addition, we have eliminated space breaks between paragraphs that we believe were editorial insertions to suit the stylistic demands of periodical publication. We let stand, of course, the frequent use of long dashes and occasional neologisms that are part of Glaspell's inimitable style.

NOTES

1. Qtd. in Linda Ben-Zvi, *Susan Glaspell: Her Life and Times* (New York: Oxford University Press, 2005), 49.
2. Thomas Gullason, "The 'Lesser' Renaissance: The American Short Story in the 1920s," in *The American Short Story, 1900–1945*, ed. Philip Stevick (Boston: G. K. Hall and Company, 1984), 74.
3. *A.L.A. Booklist: A Guide to the Best New Books*, vol. 9 (Chicago: American Library Association, September 1912–June 1913), 125; *Boston Evening Transcript*, October 19, 1912; "Simple Stories and Good," *New York Times*, September 29, 1912.
4. Susan Glaspell's success in all three genres for a long time prevented critical categorization of her work. Other factors contributed to her virtual disappearance for nearly three decades from the American canon: first, gender bias in the New Critical construction of a male-dominated canon to represent the United States as a world power during and after the wars; second, growing political conservatism that increasingly found Glaspell's adherence to the liberal values of the Progressive Era dated; and third, an inconsistent publication history because, in the case of her plays, unlike her cohort Eugene O'Neill, Glaspell did not move from Greenwich Village to Broadway, and in the case of her novels, her publisher, Frederick A. Stokes, went out of business in 1941. When Lippincott bought out Stokes, the company donated the metal from the plates of Glaspell's novels to the war effort, thereby silencing her largest body of work. Today only two of Glaspell's novels are in print, in paperback editions from Persephone Books in the United Kingdom.
5. For more on the murder trial that inspired "A Jury of Her Peers," see Patricia L. Bryan and Thomas Wolf, *Midnight Assassin: A Murder in America's Heartland* (Chapel Hill, NC: Algonquin Books, 2005; Iowa City: University of Iowa Press, 2007).
6. Elaine Hedges, "Small Things Reconsidered: Susan Glaspell's 'A Jury of Her Peers,'" *Women's Studies* 12 (1986): 89–110.

7. "A Jury of Her Peers" has also been translated into cinematic form. Now distributed by Women Make Movies, the movie version of "A Jury of Her Peers" was produced and directed by Sally Heckel in 1980 and received an Academy Award nomination in the category of best dramatic live-action short films.

8. While the circulation of the *Ladies' Home Journal* exceeded one million in 1904, only a handful of other periodicals, including *Collier's*, *Cosmopolitan*, *McCall's*, and the *Saturday Evening Post*, reached that figure prior to World War I. Theodore Peterson, *Magazines in the Twentieth Century* (Urbana: University of Illinois Press, 1956), 56.

9. N. W. Ayer and Son, eds., *American Newspaper Annual and Directory* (Philadephia: N. W. Ayer and Son, 1917), 649.

10. William R. Kane, *1001 Places to Sell Manuscripts: The American Writer's Year Book and Directory to Markets for Manuscripts* (Ridgewood, NJ: Editor Company, 1915), 291 (describing *Every Week*). A longer description of *Every Week*, including the roles of Bruce Barton and Edith Lewis, may be found in Melissa J. Homestead, "Edith Lewis as Editor: *Every Week Magazine* and the Contexts of Cather's Fiction," *Cather Studies* (2010). Homestead cites several sources that describe the active role of Edith Lewis in the creation and design of *Every Week*, and we are most grateful to her for sharing her research with us.

11. N. W. Ayer and Son, eds., *American Newspaper Annual and Directory* (Philadephia: N. W. Ayer and Son, 1917), 656 (reporting *Every Week*'s weekly circulation of 177,473 for 1916); N. W. Ayer and Son, eds., *American Newspaper Annual and Directory* (Philadephia: N. W. Ayer and Son, 1918), 787 (reporting weekly circulation of 542,401 for 1917). The announcement in January 1918 that the publication of *Every Week* would end six months later came as a shock to many in the industry, given its dramatic success in becoming in such a short time "one of the most popular magazines of the eastern United States." John A. Ferrall, "Shall It Suspend Publication? Magazines in General and the Volta Review in Particular," *Volta Review* 20, no. 1 (1918): 450.

12. Edward J. O'Brien, ed., "Introduction," *The Best Short Stories of 1915 and the Yearbook of the American Short Story* (Boston: Small, Maynard and Company, 1916), 3–11.

13. In the years 1917 to 1919, for example, when Glaspell was publishing many of her stories in *Harper's*, O'Brien consistently ranked that magazine as one of the most selective in terms of literary excellence. At least sixty stories appeared in *Harper's* annually, and in all three years, O'Brien included more than two-thirds of them on his Roll of Honor. He also consistently ranked *Pictorial Review* (which published "Government Goat" in 1919) among the most selective magazines.

14. Edward J. O'Brien, ed., *The Best Short Stories of 1917 and the Yearbook of the American Short Story* (Boston: Small, Maynard and Company, 1918), 487–505 (Roll of Honor), 535 (notes on Glaspell's stories); Edward J. O'Brien, ed., *The Best Short Stories of 1918 and the Yearbook of the American Short Story* (Boston: Small, Maynard and Company, 1919), 336–51 (Roll of Honor), 377 (critical summary of Glaspell's stories); Edward J. O'Brien, ed., *The Best Short Stories of 1919 and the Yearbook of the American Short Story* (Boston: Small, Maynard and Company, 1920), 355–63. Seventy-eight different authors were represented on O'Brien's Roll of Honor with the one hundred best works in 1919, but only three authors (including Glaspell, Wilbur Daniel Steele, and Mary Heaton Vorse) had three or more stories on the list.

15. Annette Kolodny, "A Map for Rereading: Or, Gender and the Interpretation of Literary Texts," *New Literary History: A Journal of Theory and Interpretation* 11, no. 3 (Spring 1980): 451–67.

16. The publication history of "Poor Ed" provides another interesting example showing the broad appeal of Glaspell's short fiction across class and cultural boundaries. It originally appeared in March 1918 in the first issue of the *Liberator*, founded by *Masses* editor Max Eastman and his sister, Crystal, a leading feminist political writer, with Floyd Dell as assistant editor, to be the successor to the radical leftist magazine the *Masses*, which had been shut down by the Justice Department during World War I. All of these people were well known to Glaspell, especially Floyd Dell, who was a close friend from Davenport days, and she shared many of their progressive political views, particularly their avid support of women's rights and of the workers' movement. It is fascinating to see "Poor Ed"— basically a city mouse/country mouse tale of two brothers, one a writer and the other a farmer—printed right next to John Reed's impassioned description of "the triumph of the Bolsheviki" and the transcription of his interview with Trotsky. Then, nine years later on February 18, 1927, "Poor Ed" was reprinted in *Time and Tide*, a British weekly political and literary magazine founded by Lady Margaret Rhondda in 1920, also a left-leaning publication that supported feminist causes. Here Glaspell's very American story may well have appeared alongside work by such writers as Vera Brittain, Robert Graves, D. H. Lawrence, Rose Macaulay, George Orwell, Emmeline Pankhurst, Olive Schreiner, George Bernard Shaw, Rebecca West, or Virginia Woolf.

17. Philip Stevick, "Introduction," *The American Short Story, 1900–1945: A Critical History* (New York: Twayne Publishers, 1984), 8–10.

18. Lewis H. Lapham, "Hazards of New Fortune: Harper's Magazine, Then and Now," *Harper's Magazine* 300, issue 1801 (June 2000): 57–72.

19. Mikhail Bakhtin, *Rabelais and His World*, trans. Helene Iswolsky (Bloomington: Indiana University Press, 1984), 19–21.

20. Paula Uruburu, *The Gruesome Doorway: An Analysis of the American Grotesque* (New York: Peter Lang, 1987), 3.

21. Edgar Allan Poe, "Preface," *Tales of the Grotesque and Arabesque*, vol. 1 (Philadelphia: Lea and Blanchard, 1840), 5–6; see Edgar Allan Poe Society of Baltimore, http://www.eapoe.org/works/misc/tgap.htm.

22. Qtd. in Uruburu, p. 58.

23. Sherwood Anderson, *Winesburg Ohio* (New York: Modern Library, 2002), 6.

24. Susan Glaspell, holograph notes on reading Sherwood Anderson's letters to Van Wyck Brooks, 3 pages, unsigned and undated, Henry W. and Albert A. Berg Collection of English and American Literature, New York Public Library, Astor, Lenox and Tilden Foundations.

25. Tom Quirk, *Mark Twain: A Study of the Short Fiction* (New York: Twayne Publishers, 1997), 12.

26. Colette Lindroth, "American Unmasked: Cultural Commentary in Susan Glaspell's Short Fiction," in *Disclosing Intertextualities: The Stories, Plays, and Novels of Susan Glaspell*, eds. Martha C. Carpentier and Barbara Ozieblo (Amsterdam and New York: Rodopi, 2006), 259–60.

27. Twain published "How to Tell a Story" in October 1895 in *Youth's Companion*, a magazine in which Glaspell published three stories from 1903 to 1906. The essay is reprinted in Quirk, 150–54.

28. The quotation comes from the *New York Times* reviewer John Chamberlain, probably one of the most astute readers of Glaspell's fiction. In a review of her novel *Ambrose Holt and Family*, Chamberlain wrote: "And because she treats them with the amused tolerance, mingled with protective compassion, that one would accord a household pet, she is the best person in the world to act as mediator between the idealist and the rest of humanity." "A Tragi-Comedy of Idealism in Miss Glaspell's Novel," *New York Times*, April 12, 1931, BR3.

29. Gloria Kaufman and Mary Kay Blakely, eds., *Pulling Our Own Strings: Feminist Humor and Satire* (Bloomington: Indiana University Press, 1980), 15. See also *In Stitches: A Patchwork of Feminist Humor and Satire*, ed. Gloria Kaufman (Bloomington: Indiana University Press, 1991).

Looking After Clara

WHEN YOU OPENED THE DOOR which bore the lettering, "Bureau of Statistics of the Allied Societies for Social Betterment of the City of Boston," and Mr. Stephen Blatchford turned in his chair and looked at you, you felt that the figures you were about to receive would be both accurate and important. Nor was this alone because young Mr. Blatchford wore tortoise-rimmed glasses. Efficiency and responsibility also breathed from the chair in which he revolved. Mr. Blatchford was one of those persons who are constantly thanking Heaven that they have a sense of humor, and as he said it you had the feeling that he would the next instant turn to "Sense of Humor" in the card index. He was an utterly worthy young man, and there seemed every chance that he would receive the headship of the "Bureau of Statistics" when his chief, Mr. Snow, left the following month to assume the editorship of "The Social Good."

But this morning, after the second mail came in, Mr. Blatchford was guilty of a little dallying over the "Unmarried Women" table which he was revising. The second mail had brought a letter from Miss Dorothy Ainsley, the southern girl he had met during his vacation at Gloucester. Mr. Blatchford, speaking from the depth of his social researches, had always maintained that a man should marry. It was not until he heard the soft voice of Dorothy Ainsley that the idea seemed related to something other than social responsibility. When they were sailing, and the breeze fluttered her brown hair before her brown eyes, young Mr. Blatchford had had a disturbing sense of himself as something more than a member of society.

He had written her two letters, drawing a painstakingly humorous picture of himself as immersed in dry figures—with a little side note questioning his figure of speech—and expressing longing to be back in the "bully outdoors" of Gloucester. In reply had come only a picture postcard of the harbor, saying, "Lingering on here for a time longer." Now came the letter saying Miss Ainsley would get in that day at noon; she trusted that she did not presume too greatly upon their friendship in asking him to meet her at the North Station; this, she boldly confessed, that she might still further presume upon their friendship in a very great favor she was going to ask of him. She concluded: "There is no one else of whom I cared to ask it."

Mr. Blatchford dwelt upon this, as, arrayed in the new autumn overcoat which he wore with a gratifying sense of its impressiveness, he waited before the iron gate: No one else of whom she cared to ask it! And she knew Bob Graham, a Boston fellow. She had been more with Graham than with him; but it was not to Graham she turned now! Of course he would see much of her in the few days she had said she would be in Boston and vicinity. He was just a little sorry that it came at the time Mr. Hennesey wanted to go over things with him. It was Mr. Hennesey who would have the deciding voice as to the place left vacant by Mr. Snow's assuming editorship of "The Social Good." But then, should there be a time when he could not keep an engagement with her, she would understand. Might it not be that, as things developed, she herself would be greatly interested in those very meetings with Mr. Hennesey? Such, together with a warm feeling of self-congratulation in having just the day before received his new overcoat, were Mr. Blatchford's roseate considerations as the Gloucester train neared Boston.

An hour later, as they were finishing luncheon in the staid dining room he had taken her to—having gently turned her from the frivolous basement cafe of her suggestion, with the protecting remark that he did not believe he cared to take her there—he asked that he now hear of the little favor she was going to do him the honor to ask of him.

"Oh, do you know," Miss Ainsley began meaningly in her caressing southern voice, "now that I come right to it, I fear it would be asking too much?"

"I think not," said Mr. Blatchford, looking into her brown eyes as a strong man looks.

So, leaning confidingly across the table, Miss Dorothy told him. She was on her way home to Virginia; but a dear friend was in school out at

Wellesley; she could not go through without a little visit with Stella. So, that afternoon, after a little shopping, she would go out to Wellesley, there to remain a couple of days, then come in and take the boat for New York. But there was one thing that greatly troubled her; her brown eyes beautifully clouded in the thought of it. She paused, looking over at Mr. Blatchford in timid appeal. "I wonder," she said, tremulous, troubled and yet trusting, "if you *would*—look after Clara?"

"Look after Clara?" uncertainly murmured the efficient Mr. Blatchford. She nodded, soft eyes all the while timidly, trustingly imploring. "But who," inquired the bewildered and reddening young man, "is Clara?"

She looked surprised. "Oh! Why, didn't I have Clara when you were there?"

"I do not recall—Clara," said Mr. Blatchford.

"Why, Clara," confided the lovely Dorothy, "is my cat." And then, as she looked into the face of young Mr. Blatchford, she threw back her head and laughed.

Mr. Blatchford, who felt momentarily affronted, pulled himself back to the fact that—Heaven be thanked!—he had a sense of humor. He laughed too—less lightly, but efficiently.

"I *knew* you had a sense of humor!" Dorothy cried in triumphant gratitude. "It just helps one through everything, doesn't it?"

"It certainly does!" vigorously agreed Mr. Blatchford.

He was never more desperately in earnest about his sense of humor than when he entered the express office where they would unbox Clara and deliver her into his keeping. He had pictured a soft, fuzzy, frolicsome kitten, probably Angora: such a cat might constitute one of the feminine foibles of a Dorothy Ainsley. Picture then the astonishment with which he peered through the slats at just such a cat as the alleys of Boston abounded in—the undistinguished, mottled gray, not kitten, not fine, big cat—for all the world just another one of those animals which constitute one of the problems of a humane municipality.

Sense of humor ebbed; face reddened; back grew stiff. But Dorothy was cooing: "Nicest Clara! Nicest Clara! Was her lonesome? Oh, was her scared?" She turned to him, sweetly grave. "I realize," she said, "that Clara at first may not seem an especially attractive cat. But, you see, it's her—ways."

"There was no one else I was willing to trust her to," she murmured while Mr. Blatchford was engaged with his first attempt at adjusting himself to Clara's "ways," Clara seeking escape from his arms by way of his neck. He had suggested taking her home in the box she had arrived in, but Dorothy could not bring herself to the idea of again shutting Clara up in a box. Poor dear Clara was frightened, but if he petted her there would be no trouble. Why couldn't he just tuck her under his overcoat? The very thing! Clara would snuggle under it—oh, just as cunning!

A more painfully disturbed young man never descended into the subway at Scollay Square. His slightly loosened coat was covering Clara; but Clara was squirming about, so he must keep one arm planted firmly against her, the other hand from time to time making hurried passes at his overcoat. To get out his nickel he had to hold Clara so tight that he heard a distinct spit and felt a clawing within him. To soothe her as he threw out his nickel he murmured, "Nicest Clara!"—dulcetly repeating, "Nicest Clara!" Then he chanced to look up at the feminine person within the cage. She was the picture of affronted virtue. As he stumbled on, appearing to be clasping himself to his own breast, he caught: "Those fresh guys!"

Waiting for his car, arm planted firmly across the breast of his bulging coat, he looked up to see a policeman regarding him. It was the first time a policeman had ever evinced official interest in Mr. Blatchford. He tried to lose himself in the crowd, then realized that that was the worst thing he could have done. Well he wasn't used to being taken for a criminal, he somewhat bitterly reflected, giving Clara a left-arm pressure which made it necessary that he instantly murmur, "Nicest Clara!" The woman crowded close to him edged away. He saw her looking back nervously.

Mr. Blatchford distinctly did not like the position in which he found himself. He had always moved freely and frankly among his fellow men. He had never been called a "fresh guy," nor suspiciously eyed by a policeman, nor edged away from by women. He had always stood—firm and not unimportant—among those enlightened and upright members of the community who are keenly alive to their responsibilities toward persons to be eyed with suspicion and edged away from. Now he sat as far as possible from his fellow passengers, stick between knees, left arm across his breast, right hand pressed, it would seem, over his heart.

Occasionally, crimson face rigid, he patted his heart, as though he were attached to that organ.

Gloomily he looked into the immediate future. What was he going to say to Mrs. Lily, his landlady? What would they all think of him— bringing a cat home? He hated to think of all the silly things Charlie Morse, his roommate, would say, though Charlie was his great hope; he had recently sprained his ankle and had to stay at home. That was almost providential. Of course he would look after Clara.

Mr. Blatchford looked up to see that a woman sitting not far away, facing him, was staring. He shifted his position a little; so did Clara. She squirmed around as if preparatory to settling down. The woman had spoken to another woman and both were staring. Clara had chosen a place just over his stomach. He folded his arms over it and tried to look loftily unknowing; but he was conscious of the moving of his arms. Those vulgar women seemed to be going into hysterics! They had their handkerchiefs out and were laughing into them. They were saying things to each other and went into new convulsions at the things they said. It was disgusting. What was so funny? he'd like to know. Clara continued to squirm about and every time she moved there were renewed gasps of laughter.

The car came to a stop—not his stop; but, as sedately as circumstances permitted, he rose to leave.

This was intolerable. Those vulgar women had made him feel most uncomfortable; he knew that his face had been flaming as he left the car. Even now, as he turned toward his boardinghouse in St. James Avenue, the breast to which he pressed Clara was a tumultuous one. Why could not the young women of Wellesley College have looked after Clara quite as well as he? Did they have any more to do than he did? That very instant he should be at his desk, completing that "Unmarried Women" table. And what was he going to do with Clara when he got home? What would Mrs. Lily say? As he rounded the corner of St. James Avenue Mr. Blatchford was thinking of all that man has endured for woman.

He felt it was not just the moment for revealing Clara to Mrs. Lily. He could carry the situation better when he had himself a little more in hand; so with great difficulty he let himself in, softly cooing a final, "Nicest Clara!" as the key turned, and, with glances of fear to right and left, he stole stealthily up the stairs he had never before ascended with anything but manly tread.

He gained his room unseen. He addressed no word to his roommate, sitting there in the Morris chair, reading. Unfastening his overcoat he let Clara spring to the floor. He then sat down in weary and bitter silence.

Clara began at once on the usual feline tour of investigation. "Thought it would be nice to have a cat, did you, Steve?" mildly observed Charlie, his blue eyes dancing.

"Nice to have a cat!" bitterly murmured Mr. Blatchford. Then brusquely he explained: He was keeping her for a friend, a young lady; they would have to keep her several days; young lady very attached to her; she had come to their cottage in Gloucester; couldn't bear to abandon her; taking her home to Virginia.

"Awfully kindhearted girl," said Charlie.

Mr. Blatchford, who was trying to pull his new overcoat back into shape, vouchsafed no reply. About to depart he said shortly: "Well, it's a lucky thing that you're staying at home."

"Act of Providence," murmured Charlie.

Mr. Blatchford stood with his hand on the knob. "You'll look after her for me, Charlie?" he asked in humble appeal.

"Sure," cheerfully replied Charlie. "I like cats all right; she'll be company for me." He reached over and deftly pulled Clara to his lap. "Nice pussy," he soothed, stroking her. "What's her name, Steve?" he asked.

"Clara," briefly replied Mr. Blatchford.

"Cl–ara!" ejaculated Charlie. "How'd they happen to name her Clara?"

"How should I know?" sharply retorted Mr. Blatchford.

"I think she's hungry," said Charlie. "Better ask Lily-white for some milk."

Mr. Blatchford moved uneasily. "I—I haven't mentioned her being here yet," he said.

"I see," said Charlie in his mild way that was sometimes perturbing.

It ended with Mr. Blatchford being sent to Boylston Street for milk. The first dairy place he went to had none. With set teeth he strode to another. Late to his work! Mr. Hennesey might come in! Nice thing to tell him he had been out getting milk for a cat! On his way home he spilled milk on his overcoat. It gave him a feeling of acute resentment toward the whole of Wellesley College.

And then Mr. Stephen Blatchford eagerly turned a worn face toward that seat of decorum, the Bureau of Statistics of the Allied Societies for Social Betterment of the City of Boston. He returned that night to find a newspaper clipping, "Care of the Cat—How to Keep Your Pet Healthy and Happy," pinned on the inside of the door.

"Did you ever know anything more fortunate," Charlie began brightly, "than my running across that in today's paper? I've read the newspapers all my life, and this is the first time I ever remember coming across an article on the care of the cat. Sort of weird, don't you think?"

Mr. Blatchford was examining the milk spots on the overcoat he had just taken off, and made no reply. Clara came rubbing against his legs, swaying toward him in ingratiating cat fashion, flourishing her tail and purring as if they were on the best of terms.

"It says," remarked Charlie, "that you want to cultivate their love for open-air exercise."

Mr. Blatchford's face set to grimmer lines, but again he made no reply.

"And, if there's lettuce for dinner, I think you'd better try and pass a leaf into your pocket." Charlie hobbled to the door, and from the clipping solemnly read: "'Occasionally chop a lettuce leaf and mix it with chopped raw meat to keep their digestive systems in good order.'"

"I am glad you find this amusing, Charlie," said Mr. Blatchford with the cold forbearance of a superior person.

As the evening progressed Mr. Blatchford himself was finding it less and less amusing. He had not enjoyed his dinner. He was not enough at home in the surreptitious to be happy in the smuggling in of a cat. Nor had he ever sufficiently indulged in disorderly conduct to face with equanimity the prospect of that infringement upon dignity likely to ensue from the discovery of Clara. He had never at any time been a young man given to doing questionable things. He had led an orderly life. Until this unfortunate episode there had never been a time when he could not look all the world in the face. Now he could not look Mrs. Lily in the face. He had gone down before dinner intending to tell her, but found her in conversation with Miss Earle, the "Care-of-the-Scalp" lady. So he had eaten his dinner in guilty and miserable silence, ears wretchedly alert for cat noises from above.

And all through the evening, every time he started to tell Mrs. Lily, there was some reason for not doing it. Charlie, on the other hand, reveled in the concealment; he would hear someone coming, make a lurch for Clara—greatly imperiling his sprained ankle—and smother her in cushions while he talked with open countenance to the maid, or whoever it might be, at the door. The atmosphere that Charlie threw around it grew more and more distasteful to the honorable Mr. Blatchford. And his thoughts were not happy ones. He was not spending the evening with Dorothy Ainsley; he was at home looking after Dorothy Ainsley's cat. And what evening was he to spend with her? He could not see that there was going to be an evening. She had taken his office telephone number—that she might call up to inquire for Clara. He was to meet her for tea on the day of her departure—that he might deliver Clara. He considered again that there was no one else of whom she cared to ask it. But—ask what? With gloomy eye he watched Clara rolling on her back, twisting herself into meaningless feline shapes. An ugly doubt was trying to get into his mind. He banished it in the memory of her soft eyes as she asked this of him, the color fluttering in her cheeks, her tender, laughing mouth. She had come to him in her difficulty. He would not fail her and she would come to him again—for something different. His was not the only love that had been put to a great test. Mr. Blatchford dreamed of days to come.

Meanwhile his roommate had hobbled out for a visit in another room, and presently Mr. Blatchford decided that he was very tired and was going to bed. He was about to lose the cares of the day in sleep when his ears were outraged by a shriek that brought him instantly to the floor. Again it came and again, a piercing, frantic, feminine shriek of terror. Pulling his bathrobe about him he rushed into the hall. Others were rushing into the hall, fully clad, clad in bathrobes, lesserly clad. Mrs. Lily was crying: "Oh, what is it?—where?—what?"

From the bathroom came a piercing series of "Cat! Cat! Cat!"

Mr. Blatchford longed to be transported into another world.

Mrs. Lily was speaking against the bathroom door. "It couldn't be a cat, Miss Earle. There is no cat."

"There is a cat!" screamed the indignant as well as distracted inmate of the bathroom.

"She has the cat fear," murmured a young woman to Mr. Blatchford. "It's just terrible. I've often chased them away from her on the street and places. They affect her something awful, like rats do me."

"She's climbing into the tub! Go 'way! 'Way!" There was a splashing of water, evidently used as a weapon against Clara.

Mrs. Lily looked around at her informally clad guests. "Did anyone bring a cat into this house?" she demanded.

Stephen Blatchford's throat was dry; his hands were cold; so were his bare feet. There was an instant of faltering; then he chanced to look up and meet the eye of his roommate. He was gathering himself together for a manly "I did!" when all proving of manhood was deferred by a series of shrieks.

"She won't get into the tub, Miss Earle," soothed the distraught landlady, who was trying to see through the keyhole. "They never get in water. And she really won't hurt you a bit. It's just that you think she will. Now if you can just bring yourself to get out and unbolt the door—"

"She's between me and the door," sobbed the lady in the tub.

"Kitty! Kitty! Kitty!" began Charlie Morse.

"This is not funny, Mr. Morse," snapped Mrs. Lily.

"No, indeed," said Charlie; "I should say not. I thought maybe we could induce her to climb up over the transom."

Then through the chaos came a voice of command—the firm voice of a strong man, a voice to inspire confidence in any truly feminine person, dispelling weak terrors. "Miss Earle," commanded Mr. Blatchford, "simply get out of that tub, walk to the door, unbolt it and allow Mrs. Lily to take the cat out."

"I tell you I have the cat fear," sobbed the weak woman. "Dr. Weir Mitchell wrote about it!"[1]

"We can't help it if he did!" thundered Mr. Blatchford. "Simply—" But new resources were at his command. He went nearer the door and yelled through the crack: "Where's your sense of humor?"

At the suggestion of a sense of humor the lady abandoned herself to complete hysterics.

"Something must be done at once!" cried Mrs. Lily.

The door was whittled—Clara mewing nervously the while—and the bolt slipped from without. A friend went in to minister to Miss Earle— and out walked Clara.

Mrs. Lily seized her by the neck and held her accusingly aloft. "Who brought this cat into my house?" she demanded in fearful tones.

Mr. Blatchford tried to get his feet under cover. "I did," he said, looking as manly as a bathrobe will permit.

Mrs. Lily dropped the cat. "*You?*" She could only repeat: "You?"

"I will endeavor," said the utterly miserable young man, "to explain."

The next morning a fresh, sweet young voice called the "Bureau of Statistics" from Wellesley College: "She's all right? And does she seem happy?"

Mr. Blatchford replied that he thought Clara was reasonably happy.

"And you're sure she's not a bit of trouble?"

He did not instantly reply. He had raised a weary hand to an aching head. "Oh, that's all right!" he said in a voice a little bedraggled.

Miss Ainsley went on to speak warmly of how she appreciated it, what it meant to her, how there was no one else of whom she would have cared to ask it.

Mr. Blatchford then asked if she would come in that night and go to dinner and the theater with him.

She deeply regretted that it would be impossible; but they were going to meet for tea next day—weren't they?—he bringing Clara, and then she would *try* to tell him how she appreciated all he had done.

That evening Clara was nervous. Perhaps she felt that her position in that household was not all a cat could ask; she mewed at the closed door; she kept walking about the room, switching her tail; she jumped up in the window and peered through the screen down the fire escape. She did not settle down and purr that evening.

Nor did Mr. Blatchford settle down and purr. Again he was not spending the evening with Dorothy Ainsley; he was at home looking after

Dorothy Ainsley's cat. And his position in the household had entirely changed. There were frowns for him now—and titters. Never before had he been treated like an offender—or like a ridiculous person. He had had to humble himself before the landlady, who had always treated him with deference; had been compelled to plead and promise. And for what? That he be permitted to keep a cat! Everybody in the house knew that he was keeping a cat! Memories of the night before, when he had stood there in his bathrobe explaining, embittered his soul. And now it was, "How's the cat?" "What's her name?" "Where'd she come from?" "Like cats?" until it seemed, if they went on talking about cats, that he would take leave of his senses.

In the dead of night, awakened from a sound sleep, he sat up in bed. What was that noise? Was someone trying to get into the room? Then returning consciousness made known to him that far worse than someone getting into the room would be someone getting out of it. Instantly acute he switched on the light. What had awakened him was the sound of a falling screen—and there was no cat in the room!

Mr. Blatchford crept out on the fire escape and softly called: "Kitty, kitty, kitty!" Then: "Clara, Clara, Clara!" He peered up and down the alley. He thought a half block away he saw two cats. More loudly he called: "Clara, Clara, Clara!"

A window across the alley went up. Hastily Mr. Blatchford drew back into his room. Then back he stole to the fire escape. Again a little way down the alley he saw two cats. He was afraid to call again. He went back into the room and looked at his watch. Three o'clock! He would go back to bed—and when he met Dorothy Ainsley for tea next day!

He got into some clothes; down the fire escape he crept, through the alley he stole, like the abandoned character it seemed he had come to be. He drew near the two cats, softly calling, "Clara, Clara, Clara!" He thought the one nearest him was swishing her tail in a familiar way, but when he was right upon them both fled—through that alley, down a deserted street, into another alley. There again he called: "Clara, Clara, Clara!"

"Clara's not here, my boy," said a deep voice, "and a young man in your plight better get home fast as he can."

A policeman!

"I am hunting my cat," said Mr. Blatchford, with what dignity he could command.

"Oh, yes, I know; but better let the kitty alone now and be getting home, or I'll have to give you a lift."

Mr. Blatchford turned away. He would prowl through no more alleys. He did not have his key; he returned as he had gone forth—by way of the back fence. He feared another policeman. He tore his clothes getting over the fence. He crouched at the foot of the fire escape, fearing to ascend. Little had he ever dreamed that he would be slinking up a fire escape while a city slept!

He climbed back into his room. He went to bed, but not to sleep. He heard cat cries and went out again and called: "Clara, Clara!"

A window on the floor below went up!

At daylight he went out again and began looking for Clara. He looked down alleys; he peered over back fences; he called, "Clara, Clara!" whenever he heard a cat.

To what part of Boston would Clara go? Would she prefer the business or the residence district? Had she retreated to the Back Bay region, or was she roaming Boston Common? Once he thought he saw her sitting on the steps of the library; he pursued the wrong cat around Castle Square.

He went home to breakfast footsore and full of rage. News that his cat had escaped had spread through the boardinghouse, and he was pressed with inquiries, condolences, jokes. He ate hastily and went forth again to look for Clara. The time came when he must go to his work; indeed he was already late for his work.

In an alley, half a block from where he lived, were two small boys. They gave him an idea. He told them he had lost a cat: a gray cat; a medium-sized, gray cat. He must have her by noon. She must be somewhere in that neighborhood. Here was a quarter for each of them, and if they had her when he returned at noon each of them should have half a dollar.

It was arranged that at one o'clock they should be waiting for him in the shed door where they then stood.

And then a disheveled Mr. Blatchford turned a harassed face toward the Bureau of Statistics of the Allied Societies for Social Betterment of the City of Boston, there to arrive three-quarters of an hour late and find Mr. Hennesey, he who held promotion in the hollow of his hand, impatiently twirling in the revolving chair.

"I—I'm just a little late this morning," said Mr. Blatchford in a high, nervous voice.

"So I see," dryly replied this chief of his chief.

Mr. Blatchford was suddenly conscious of unclean hands, dusty shoes, straws hanging to his trousers. He passed a fidgety hand over his ill-brushed hair. He was not sure that his face was clean. A swift glance at a mirror showed bloodshot eyes.

"I—I was up late last night—that is, I mean to say—my sleep was rather broken in on—" He mumbled off into nothingness.

How could he explain that he had been roaming the alleys of Boston, looking for a cat?

At a little before one o'clock he was at the alley shed appointed for the rendezvous.

One of the boys awaited him outside. "Guess we've got her here, mister. Found a lot of medium-sized gray cats. Got seventeen in here."

"*Seventeen!*" gasped Mr. Blatchford.

"Yep," said the proud youth. "Hunted all morning. Got seventeen."

Mr. Blatchford staggered within. The world swam—with cats; cats mewing, cats growling; cats walking around with switching tails; cats with humped backs; fighting cats, loving cats, mouse-hunting cats; cats frightened, cats resentful, cats contented; a cat rubbed against him and purred; a cat backed away from him and spit; all known cat emotions seethed within that shed. Mr. Blatchford raised a hand to a reeling head.

"We had an awful time getting some of them," said the gratified collector, exhibiting scratched hands. "Two that we had the women made us give back. There's a woman in that house says she's going to call the Humane Society."

Mr. Blatchford leaned back against the shed door. The Humane Society! One of the Allied Societies for Social Betterment!

"I hadn't meant you to bring more than one," was his prostrate murmur.

"Yes," cried the youth, "but *which* one? There's more 'an one medium-sized, gray cat in this part of town."

"So I see," was all that Mr. Blatchford could say.

He looked about. As the boy said: *Which* one? Within that shed—doubtless—was Clara. Clara must be one of those seventeen medium-sized, gray cats. He called: "Clara, Clara, Clara!" Some came nearer; some drew farther away; glad recognition o'erspread no face. One moment he thought none of them was Clara; the next instant all were Clara—the shed was filled with Clara become seventeen. He could not transport these seventeen cats to the tea room where he would meet Dorothy Ainsley; he could not invite Dorothy Ainsley to an alley shed to inspect seventeen fighting, misbehaving cats. His tongue grew large and dry.

He must pull himself together and meet the situation. He would attack it by a process of elimination. He inspected a cat trying to climb the wall. It had a yellow streak down its back. He drew a real breath; perhaps many of them on examination would have something that marked them as not Clara.

"This cat can be thrown out," he said to the boy.

The cat who was not Clara had gained a high beam. "How?" asked the boy.

Sweat broke out on the brow of Mr. Blatchford. A collection of cats was indeed no simple thing to deal with. Another cat had a white foot; he himself bravely got her by the neck and threw her out. Then panic seized him. *Didn't* Clara have a white foot? Did she? Didn't she? White foot? Gray foot? His brain reeled. Another face was too white; another had a black circle around her eye; one had a yellow undertone; one was too light; one too dark—at least he thought so. *Was* Clara light?—dark? Bigger than this cat?—smaller than this one? Was her tail striped like this?

By the process of elimination the cats had been reduced to five. Some of the rejected had been evicted; others crouched in corners with glaring eyes. There was one cat who, to his dazed brain, seemed to be Clara. She allowed him to pick her up. He decided to take her over and show her to Charlie; Charlie, bringing to it a fresh mind, might know whether or not it was Clara.

Charlie thought it was; then he doubted. It seemed Clara, yet it didn't.

Humbly Mr. Blatchford waited on Charlie's decision. Charlie wished that his foot would permit him to go over and view all the cats. He could not go to the cats; couldn't the cats come to him?

Mr. Blatchford hastened back to the shed. He selected two others. One he put in a gunnysack which the small boy had found useful in making the collection, the other he bore in his arms.

Mrs. Lily saw him through the window. She met him in the hall with blazing eyes. "This has gone far enough, Mr. Blatchford! I finally give in that you may keep *one* cat; now you come into my house with *armfuls* of cats!"

"It's only temporary," stammered Mr. Blatchford. "I—I shall not go on doing it," he assured her humbly. "I'm having great difficulties, Mrs. Lily."

The cat in the sack grew unpleasant, and also Mr. Blatchford feared for his own emotion. He hastened up to his room.

Charlie, upon seeing the other cats, was convinced that the first one was Clara. She had been acting like Clara, he said; she walked to the same places in the room; she rubbed her back against the wall just like Clara. The more he looked at the other two the more it assured him that the first one was Clara.

Charlie evidently saw that it was no time for levity. He was a true friend in the tenseness with which he met the situation. And his confidence that it was Clara who had been selected was calming to the well-nigh distracted Mr. Blatchford. He breathed again. He saw light ahead. Natural things were emerging from a swimming world of cats.

He bore the rejected cats out of the house and set them loose, Mrs. Lily watching from the window. He was even so heartened that he was not greatly distraught when the frightened small boy said the woman next door had sent for the police. After his recent experiences sending for the police seemed a small matter.

He had tea with the girl to whom he wished to offer his hand and heart; there seemed no opportunity for offering them then, but she was to be in New York in the winter. He said that he had been intending to go to New York himself; they would see each other there. Mr. Blatchford saw the future opening out from that. In the glow of her presence the terrors of the immediate past fell away. All of that was over now, and happiness banished the last faint doubt.

Clara was waiting at the checkroom in the South Station in the superior box he and Charlie had made for her. He would at this moment say nothing of the horrors he had endured for love's sake. Sometime he would tell her and he could fancy her eyes deepening in new love.

She spoke gently—was it not tenderly?—of what he had done for her. Her smile for him, as they stood before the check window, was sweet beyond his dreams.

Box in his hand, they stepped back to a bench.

"Nicest Clara!" the girl was cooing to the cat behind the slats. "Was Clara scared? Was her?" She poked a playful finger through the slats. Swiftly she withdrew it—scratched.

Amazed, she looked through the slats, saying Clara must be terribly frightened. She bent closer. She peered. She looked up at Mr. Blatchford. She looked back in the box.

"This—is—not—my—cat!" she said in terrible tones.

The miserable man stood there limp, speechless.

White, angry face, blazing eyes, she stood before him. "Is this a joke," she choked, "or an insult?"

He tried to say that it was neither.

"And where *is* Clara?" she cried. "Where *is* she?"

Fifteen minutes later he slunk out of the station, abandoning a boxed cat. The girl who had kindled love in his breast had as cruelly abandoned him. She made it plain that she never wished to look upon his face again. Certainly it wasn't very *much* she had asked of him! She had supposed that he was one of those methodical, reliable persons, just the person to be entrusted with the care of a cat!

His explanations only kindled new rage against him. In his attempt at self-defense he made an unfortunate remark about Clara's disposition to go forth into alleys. He was told that Clara had never been that kind of a cat when she was with *her*.

Two hours later he opened the door of his boardinghouse. In those two hours he had been walking about, seeking command, seeking healing. He had stopped at the office, hoping for solace in work, and Mr. Snow had gently asked him if he drank. Mr. Hennesey feared that he drank. Because of that Mr. Hennesey was inclined to put a woman in the place to be left vacant by Mr. Snow's resignation.

After that he had again gone forth into the streets, his cup of bitterness running over.

When he stepped into the hall at his boardinghouse Mrs. Lily came forward and addressed him in frigid tones: "A lady has been waiting here for an hour to see you, Mr. Blatchford."

"I want my cat!" snapped a shrill voice right behind her. "Young man, I want my cat!"

He at last escaped from her tongue-lashing, her threats. But he had an awful feeling that he was about to be sprung upon by sixteen other women each demanding that he instantly produce a cat.

He made his way past Mrs. Lily, past Miss Earle, whose repressed triumph was more bitter than the hard things just said about his accumulation of cats.

He reached his room. He was glad to find Charlie not there. He could bear nothing more. He leaned back against the door too prostrated to advance. His wild eye roamed the room. At the window off the fire escape it became fixed—it became glassy.

Sitting just outside the window, confidently waiting to be received back—was Clara!

Originally published in the *Ladies' Home Journal* 31
(August 1914): 9, 35–37

NOTE

1. Dr. Silas Weir Mitchell (1829–1914) was an American neurologist and very successful "nerve specialist" who became famous for developing the "Rest Cure." This treatment prescribed total bed rest and inaction, isolation from family and friends, overfeeding, and massage. Patients, usually middle-class women, were not permitted to read, sew, converse, feed themselves, or get out of bed, as a form of "moral medication" to induce them to control their illnesses and return to their household duties. In 1887 Mitchell treated Charlotte Perkins Gilman (then Charlotte Stetson) in his sanatorium, who wrote that she "came perilously near to losing my mind" as a result and went on to publish her story about the treatment, "The Yellow Wallpaper," in 1892. Glaspell was very likely familiar with "The Yellow Wallpaper," and she may have met Gilman at the Greenwich Village feminist Heterodoxy Club to which both belonged.

The Manager of Crystal Sulphur Springs

THE ARRAY OF TURNOUTS AWAITING the noon train seemed testifying to the prosperity of Freeport. It was an array calculated to make the transcontinental traveler, looking languidly from his window, stroll out and ask the porter, "What town is this?" Glossy limousines panted in the proud new concrete causeway recently built for the overhead tracks, and the very baggage wagons somehow suggested a Boosters' Committee a few blocks away.

The jaded pair of bony farm horses which turned in there a couple of minutes before train time seemed to know they bore an equipment which would not serve the Boosters' Committee as the "Golden State Limited" went through. They bore what in its brilliant past had been called a closed carriage. Once it had carried the society of the town to weddings and parties; when too scuffed for festivity it had a long time of somberly taking its place in the funeral procession. But that day, too, passed, and then it came to be called a hack, and met trains for a third-rate hotel until it occurred to the management that the hack perhaps kept away more people than it brought, when once more it was deposed, this time to be sold for the office it now filled. It filled that office limpingly, wheezing as the aged wheeze.

The young boy driving it surveyed the backed-up line diffidently. How could he ask any of them to move over and make room for the hack from the Poor-farm?[1] A woman opened the door and peered out, anxiously. "No room here, Johnnie?"

But the driver of the proud new bus from the Hotel Freeport hastened to make it plain that he was not one to crowd out the lowly. "Room enough, Mrs. Peters," he called. "Back right in here, John. Them expressmen don't need the earth," he added, with a dark look for menials from a rival hostelry.

"Expectin' someone for the Farm?" he asked, sociably, as the woman alighted.

She nodded, shaking out her skirts and moving as if cramped by long sitting. Then she looked up and said, in the manner of one telling no ordinary thing, "Expectin' someone who never expected to end his days at *that* place. Well, no," she hastened to amend, with a growlingly significant manner, "never expected to end 'em in the poorhouse, is what I mean." Then, "It's Mr. Groves—it's Bert Groves that's coming," she said, looking at him to see if he got all that it meant.

His long, low whistle told that he got some of it, at any rate. "So *that's* what those fellows I heard talking at the hotel last night—" He did not finish it, but said, instead, "Why, my father knew him well!" He repeated it, as if it were one of the important features of the whole thing. "Drove him time and time again. And to that same place that boy'll be driving him to now." He stood there darkly surveying the new bus from the Hotel Freeport, as if contemplating the possible fate of even the driver of that. "Wasn't there nobody to do for him where he went?" he asked, in a tone of incredulity.

She shook her head, but just then a whistle sounded, and, "There she comes!" broke in the bus driver, stepping forward quickly, all alert for his own job. But the woman stepped back and stood waiting beside the rusty hack, as if depending upon it to identify her with an institution the Boosters' Committee had not yet reached.

She might not have been so sure it was he—it was about thirty years since she had seen Bert Groves, and he was an old man now—if he had not been straightening the lapel of his coat as they got off the train. Bert Groves always was one to put up the best front.

She had a few hurried words with the man who had brought him—a kindly man going through, who had consented to act as traveling companion. While they talked, Mr. Groves stood a little apart, uncertainly watching the talking, laughing people getting into the shiny equipments. She wondered if he knew what town it was.

The man who had brought him spoke of that. "Pretty—" He tapped his own head. "Oh, not really gone, you know, but doesn't get things straight. He'll know a thing one minute, and not know it the next. But you needn't worry about him being hard to look after. He's been handed

40

around too much for that." The conductor called, "All aboard!" and, taking a hasty leave of the man who was not going on, he turned back to the train.

The old man stood looking after him, as if not wanting to be left. But he took only a step, then stood there uncertainly.

She touched his arm. "This way for us," she said, kindly, then stood at the door of the sagging old hack, waiting for him to get in. He looked in at the lumpy, leaky upholstery, then stepped back and surveyed a motor car nearby, took an uncertain step toward it. "In here, Mr. Groves," said the wife of the superintendent of the Poor-farm, not unkindly, but firmly.

She saw at once that what the kindly man had said was true. He would not be one to give trouble. He had been "had" too much for that. He moved uneasily on the unfriendly springs, but as if trying to conceal the fact that he was moving. She saw him looking covertly at her. Several times his lips started to move, and then he would not say anything. But at length he asked, in a whisper, as if afraid of what he was doing, "Where am I going now?"

Mrs. Peters claimed she got along in her office, and helped other people get along, by making the best of things. Making the best of things was her great phrase. As she looked into the troubled face of this broken, helpless old man—this *meek* old man—and remembered the Bert Groves she had known, she had—if nothing else—to help herself out of it by answering: "Why, you're going home, Mr. Groves! To the old Groves place," she added, as he looked quite blank. After an instant's hesitation she finished, "To the Springs—to Crystal Sulphur Springs."

It was as if she had flicked something before his eyes; then he moved so restlessly, there was such a strange, excited look in his eyes, that she went on in a matter-of-fact, soothing voice: "See? This is Freeport we're going through now. In a little bit we'll turn down the river road—to the Springs."

He looked from the window, turned and looked at her, then edged a little away from her. He would steal covert glances out at the town, back to her. But he soon closed his eyes as if too tired to bother more about it—as if it had passed.

She sat there wondering just what it had meant to him, wondering how he would "take it" when they turned in at the old place. She was fluttered, more than a little awed, by her own part in so strange a thing. She sat there trying to realize it, telling herself she didn't realize it. "If this can happen," she said to herself, "*anything* can happen!" Riding along with Bert Groves now, her mind went back to the times she had seen him on that very road. The Groves place was the big farm of the neighborhood, and her father a small farmer nearby. He worked for the Groveses part of the time. They were not like other farmers, for they were more city folks than country people, having a house in town and only living in the country a part of the year. One of the first things she could remember was watching Bert Groves ride past the house. He had a fine horse and rode down from town a great deal. From her father's farm she could see the Groves place. She was fascinated by their comings and goings. They had a great deal of company down from town; her mother, who would sometimes go over there and work, would report on the gay doings.

Bert Groves was in the real estate business in town; his brother Edward was a doctor; the father ran the farm. And then one day when they were boring for oil—oil was suspected in the neighborhood, and Bert Groves, always one to take up with a new thing, always believing in things, insisted that they try for it on the Groves place—they found, not oil, but the "Crystal Sulphur Spring," a strong artesian well of sulphur water. It startled everyone to find it there, and, as the town said, it set Bert Groves crazy. What Crystal Sulphur Water did to his imagination made life a different thing for the whole Groves family. Emma Peters—then Emma Haines, a girl of about sixteen—remembered very clearly the talk of those days. There were excited people who believed it was true that Bert Groves was going to make the fortune of the entire neighborhood, and there were plenty of skeptics to scoff at the believers.

The first thing he started was a bottling works. He was going to ship Crystal Sulphur Water to the farthest bounds of the country. All the thing needed, she remembered him emphatically saying when he stopped at their place one day to get her father to come over and work, was pushing.

So he proceeded to give his time to pushing it. It was said that he spent the whole year's crop in advertising. She remembered her father and another farmer sitting before their kitchen stove and laughing over a pamphlet that told the story of the final discovery of the spring of eternal youth. They said, "The old man'd better look out."

But the previous stir was as nothing to the excitement there was the day it was told that Bert Groves and his brother, the doctor, were going to turn the Groves place into a kind of hospital, a place for people to come and rest and build up on Crystal Sulphur Water—a sanitarium, they called it. People got together and contributed what they had heard. Why, there was to be a lower *and* upper veranda round the whole house! That had its brief day, but paled before the later knowledge that there would be a *fountain* right in the middle of the house!

Old man Groves died during the commotion of the remodeling. People said it was just as well; later they declared it was Providence. Bert had talked him over, and he died believing.

The father's death sobered Bert, they said, but he went right ahead like what they called "a house afire." She stole a glance at the old man beside her and tried to realize that this was the man who had kept everybody on the move that summer they made the Groves place into a sanitarium. Her father was working there, so she would be back and forth on errands. She would loiter around all she could, thrilled by the excitement. And everlastingly Bert Groves was telling men a thing could be done when they were saying it couldn't; he was behind everyone, making things move, keeping everybody livened up. Her father would come home and say, "That boy may be crazy—but he's a wonder, just the same."

And then the next spring there was a grand opening—all the town people down and dancing—gay carryings-on. And Bert Groves was behind everything that night, too, beaming on everybody, his face shining as he showed people around, a spring in his step, and his voice so glad and sure.

Emma Haines was engaged to work at the Springs as a chambermaid. There were a number of chambermaids, and for the most part they spent their time keeping empty rooms freshened up. "Oh, you'll be busy enough later on," Mr. Groves would call as he passed a group of them loitering in the halls because there was nothing else for them to do. She wondered just how long he kept on thinking that. Most of the people there were friends of the Groveses, but there were a few sick or tired-out people who had read the pamphlets and really came to drink the water. Mr. Groves would beam upon them as they sat round the fountain. "And how are you feeling this morning?" he would ask in a courtly way as they came down to breakfast.

43

But the house did not fill up, and they let some of the help go, the manager assuring them they'd want them all back a little later. But the beaming look began to fade, his eyes to look pulled together in a worried way; there were times when he spoke sharply to the help, though it took only the arrival of a new patient to make him beam again. "Why, you can't expect the thing to start off all in a minute!" she remembered him saying jubilantly one night when two patients arrived after a long period of no arrivals.

They said afterward that the wonder was it lasted as long as it did, that Bert Groves had about hypnotized folks or it couldn't have been done. But there came a day when he could no longer hypnotize anybody into lending more money for Crystal Sulphur Springs. Of course, the place had been mortgaged at the first, money borrowed right along. The crash came.[2] Crystal Sulphur Springs was closed. The Groveses had lost everything.

She was there the last night it was open. After the reduction of help she did various things, and she waited at Mr. Groves' table that night, though, as a matter of fact, it was the only table in the dining room. But there were two guests at it, and he went on talking to them in that pleasant, courtly way he had with the guests. But when she passed things she noticed how awkward he was about helping himself, and when he laughed it was hard to keep her place by the table—she wanted so to run away.

After that they did not see Bert Groves on the road between town and the farm any more. For a little while he went on with his real estate business in town, but she heard a man tell her father that deals couldn't be swung without any money to draw on, and that Groves wasn't making a living—that he had lost his snap, anyway. In town one day she passed him on the street. He did not see her, for he was looking straight ahead, his face drawn, driven-looking. She turned and looked after him, and what made her feel the worst was that she could see he was trying to walk in the old way.

He went away from Freeport soon after that; people said they guessed he'd rather be a poor man in some other town. One of the farmers who went to the state capital saw him a couple of years later behind the cigar stand of a farmers' hotel. He said Bert looked as if he wanted to drop behind the counter when he spoke to him, but he pulled himself together

44

and they had quite a talk. Groves said then that all the thing had needed was pushing; the trouble was they hadn't given him time to push it.

Then they heard nothing about him for a long time. Edward Groves, whose practice had been hurt by the sanitarium craze, died about ten years later. There was no near relative left. Things changed; no one seemed to hear from Bert Groves. The place for a long time was a white elephant on the hands of the creditors. They rented the farm, but who wanted that great building which Bert Groves had believed was going to be crowded with people coming from far and near to drink Crystal Sulphur Water? A woman tried it for summer boarders, but Bert Groves' hopes had been too high; it was on too big a scale. For years it stood there deserted; and so, when with the growth of the town "The Farm" as well as other things needed bigger quarters, the Groves place was eagerly offered for consideration. It was run down; it could be had very cheap. And so at last a use was found for the sanitarium.

And so, too, it came about that Emma Haines went back to work at the old Groves place. She had married Henry Peters, who from working the farm at "The Farm" managed to get the place of superintendent. Twenty-five years elapsed from the time she waited on Bert Groves' table that last night the sanitarium was open until she went there as wife of the superintendent of the Poor-farm. She had seen queer things in what she called "our business," but one day Henry came into the kitchen with a scared sort of look and said:

"Who do you suppose is coming here?" He sat down weakly as he said it, and sat staring at her, his mouth a little open.

"For the land's sake," she had replied, flurried with something she was doing, "how do I know who's coming here?"

"Bert Groves is coming here," he told her, and she dropped the cup she was measuring with, and stood staring at him.

He had to tell her all he knew about it before she would believe there was any truth in it, though he didn't know a great deal—just that the commissioners had had a letter from the wife of a cousin of the Groveses, from Simpson County, in the west of the state. She said she had "had" him for two years and could have him no longer. She was poor herself, and he was getting in his dotage. It wasn't as if she were a blood relation. There was nobody left who was a blood relation who could have him.

45

So the county he came from would have to do for him. Emma Peters and her husband had a very late supper that night; for a long time they could do nothing but sit there gaping at each other.

They had wondered with something akin to bated breath how he would "take it." At first there was no way of telling how he was taking it. Mrs. Peters was not able to "make out" his look when they turned in at the old Groves place, could not make up her mind just what it was made him look frightened in so strange a way. It gave her what she called the creeps to see him staring up at the house he had remodeled thirty years before. And then before they reached the house he stopped looking from the window; when they pulled up at the side door he was looking straight down at his feet, hands clasped on his stick, so strangely still. She had to say, "Come, Mr. Groves; we're here." And when they went in the house he did not look around at all, but was all the while so still in that queer way. Mrs. Peters told Henry she couldn't make it out; she didn't know whether he *knew*—and *that* was why he was like that—or whether he didn't really know, and yet, in a way, did. "I think it's kind of *working* on him," was the nearest she came to a decision.

The first time she saw him in the dining room she felt, she said, as if her knees were going to let her drop. It was the same dining room in which she had waited on him as manager of Crystal Sulphur Springs. Now he sat at a long table with the other men "inmates"; when he looked up he seemed only to look a very little way, all the time so still in that way that made her feel "queer." The men who were not able to work about the farm sat a good deal on the big porch which Bert Groves had designed for the guests of the Springs.

"Out here is a nice place to sit, Mr. Groves," she had cheerily said to him the second day when she found him in a somber place back of the stairs. She took him out to a chair. After that he sat always in that same chair, as if he had been told to sit there. But every time he sat down he edged it a little away. "Too good for the other boarders," she heard Joe Minor laugh in a rough way.

But after the first week or so he began to steal covert, frightened glances around. She would catch him looking at things—looking in a dazed, troubled way. One day she came upon him rubbing his foot in an annoyed way over a broken board in the porch floor; he even began to

46

venture away from the chair where he had seemed to think he had to sit. One day she saw him down in the yard, walking round and round on a little rise of ground. She could not make out what he was doing until it suddenly came to her that on that piece of ground there had once been, in crushed stone, the words, "Crystal Sulphur Springs." She stood and watched him rubbing his foot around on the not-very-well-cared-for grass. The stone had long before been taken up and used on the road running round the house. But some traces of it apparently remained, for she saw him pick up something and stand staring at it. Then he turned and stared up at the house. One big wing of it had been entirely taken away, sold years before to a prosperous farmer; there were other changes, and a general run-downness. It had been fresh-painted the day Bert Groves opened the sanitarium; it was a long way from fresh-painted now. A little while after she had watched him thus staring up at the house, she came upon him in the chair where she had suggested he sit. He was almost crouched there, and looked covertly out of the corner of his eyes when he heard her footsteps. He looked very old and frightened—and something more than that, something she couldn't find words for. She spoke pleasantly to him, and stood there hesitatingly. She wished she could help him; she wished she knew where he *was*, as she thought it, so she would know how to help him.

After that it became a common sight to see him about the place, looking for things that used to be there. One day she saw him hobbling round and round the chicken yard. Then it came to her that there used to be a grape arbor where the chicken yard was now. The guests of the sanitarium were to have sat out there. And always after those things he would go back to that same chair and sit there very still. In the dining room she would see him stealing puzzled, troubled looks at the others.

In the large hall before the dining room there had once been the wonder of half the county—the fountain. Now that hall had been partitioned off for the superintendent's own quarters. One day she came upon Mr. Groves in the straight hall that replaced the big, open place, staring at the partitions. This time he stepped up to her and spoke.

"Where's the fountain?" he asked, in an excited, tremulous voice.

"Why—why, they had to take it out, Mr. Groves," she faltered.

"Nobody had any business to take it out!" he cried, angrily, pounding his stick on the floor. He was trembling and his cheeks were flushed. And then of a sudden his face went colorless; he stumbled, and she thought he was about to fall. She helped him into her own rooms and hastily got a stimulant for him. The man who brought him to Freeport had told her of "attacks," of a very much weakened heart that must at times have immediate stimulant. That was not a strange thing to the people who ran the poorhouse; many of the old people were like that.

He was soon sitting out in his chair again, looking weak and yet somehow different, not *still* in that same queer way. The next day he came up to her as she was out feeding the chickens.

"Things are run down," he began, abruptly, jerking his head toward the house. "That's why we don't get a better class of people."

She was aghast, but it was her policy of making the best of things that made her answer, soothingly, "Why, maybe that's so, Mr. Groves."

"Of course it's so!" he cried, with an energy that, burning there in his frailness, made her want to cry. He hobbled away, muttering, "I'm going to discharge half the people round this place!"

That was the beginning of it—of things that soon caused everyone, not only the Farm, but the town, to know that Bert Groves did not know he was an inmate of the poorhouse, but thought he was manager of Crystal Sulphur Springs. There were people who laughed about it and people who were disposed to cry, but everyone who heard wanted to hear more. Never had the Poor-farm been so much on the public tongue as in those days of telling the story of how old Mr. Groves believed he was still running the sanitarium. The "inmates" were glad of the new excitement, of the new interest in the place, and it was easy enough to get them to tell the tale of all that went on. Perhaps it was wanting to have a tale to tell which, quite as much as kindness, made them keep up the pretense. Perhaps most of all it was the love of everyone for "play-acting" that made them humor the old man in thinking he was still running the place he used to run. There were tales of how some of the number wanted to "tell," kept threatening to tell, and how the others in turn threatened them with what would happen if they did tell. Perhaps, if they had, it would not have mattered as much as they thought, for "The Manager" was, after all, pretty well protected by that almost drawn veil which, for the most part, shut out things as they were. Had Joe Minor really said:

"Don't be a fool, or don't expect us to be fools any longer. This is the poorhouse, and you're one of the paupers, like the rest of us—no better, no worse. You ain't running a hotel. Your hotel went busted long ago. You're on the county now." Had he said it, it is probable he would only have troubled the waning mind for a little while, not likely he would have brought it really out into the hard light of facts. Doubtless Mr. Groves would only have gone to Mrs. Peters, as he did when things displeased him, and said: "I tell you we've got to get things in better shape. Then we'll get a better class of people," and she, making the best of things, would have answered: "That's so, Mr. Groves. We must do that as soon as we can get around to it." Something like that would satisfy him, for he never pushed anything very far; he would forget the next hour what he had proposed the hour before. The very cloudiness, fitfulness, of his mind safeguarded him. Often when the inmates were coming downstairs in the morning Bert Groves would be there at the foot, bowing and smiling to them, and asking, solicitously, "And how are you feeling this morning?"—and some of them would say, heartily, "Feeling fine, Mr. Groves," with a wink for someone nearby, and others would look sheepish, and some would grin, and some would grunt. "Might as well let him think so," was the feeling of most of them, adopting the good-humored attitude of Superintendent Peters. "What harm does it do?"

One day he said to Mrs. Peters: "I think I'll move into my old room. I don't want him"—jerking an elbow toward the old man with whom he shared a room—"in my room any longer."

"Well, now, Mr. Groves," she said, "if you could just let it go on that way awhile longer. We really haven't got a room for him—and it wouldn't look well to send one of the patients away, would it?" He was content, going away and sitting down by himself, dozing and ruminating in that thin, fitful shaft of light left to his brain, perhaps getting up to tell a man coming with coal where to put it, not long disturbed if the superintendent told him to put it somewhere else.

The Crystal Sulphur Water was still piped to a place outside the house, and every day he could be seen going over to get his drink of it, frequently carrying a glassful to someone else, saying, in a cracked voice, but with something of his old manner, "Don't forget that you're here to drink Crystal Sulphur Water." And the person, as the case happened to be, would reply volubly, leading him on to talk more, or good-humoredly take the water with a thank-you, or snicker, or maybe say, "What you givin' us?"—in which case he would go to Mrs. Peters and talk of ways of getting a better class of people.

It went on that way for two years. People would come down from town to see him. There were a few, a very few, of his old friends left, and a number who as younger people had known him slightly, and he would receive them in a courtly way, tell of improvements he was going to make, show them around the place, ask them to stay to dinner. By this time the inmates, instead of calling the place "The Farm," called it the sanitarium—giving the word various inflections; their little jokes about the good that Crystal Sulphur Water was doing them, and how soon they thought they would be able to get away, enlivened life for them. And all the while the old man—he was over seventy-five now—grew more feeble; the times were increasingly frequent when someone had to run fast for the drops that would persuade his heart to go on beating.

And then the Boosters' Committee, or at least the spirit of boosting, at last struck the Poor-farm. There were more people than Bert Groves who talked about things being run down.

Superintendent Peters' easygoing "What harm does it do?" with which he humored Bert Groves in the idea that he was running the place, was his policy, it seemed, about too many other things. It was a time when a great deal was being said about efficiency, and the discovery was made that Hen Peters didn't so much as know the meaning of the word efficiency. And so the upshot of it was that the Peterses were to be succeeded by a man with very efficient-looking red hair—a brisk, shrewd, decisive man. The Peterses would go back to farming.

One sunny afternoon in very late fall Mrs. Peters, after a hard day's work in the house getting things in shape to leave—the new superintendent was to come the following week—walked out across the yard, slowly pushing her feet through fallen leaves. She had come out for what she called a breath, but she walked on over to the far side of the yard—just this side of the pastureland—and stood looking at some fruit trees that had been set out a little while before. Despite her protestations that she did not mind leaving, that it was a thankless job, and anybody who wanted to be saddled with it was welcome to it, she was making a number of little pilgrimages in these days. And as she sat now on a bench by the new fruit trees which she herself had helped set out, old Mr. Groves came hobbling across the yard and joined her. He was bent, and trembled as he moved; it was strange how, being like that, he could still seem Bert Groves.

"I'm going to have a lot more of these put out," he began in a shrill, quavering voice. "There's no reason why they shouldn't run all up this line." He pointed along where he meant, then sank to a seat and sat there breathing with difficulty, as if he had moved too fast.

"Why, that will be nice, Mr. Groves," she said in her humoring tone.

He fell into the quiescence of age, but after a minute roused to say: "Oh yes—and I've got a lot of other plans. A lot of things I'm going to get right at in the spring."

"That will be nice," she repeated, a little break in her voice, for she wondered how things would be with Mr. Groves by spring.

The new superintendent said he was not going to have any such fooling after *he* took the place. There was to be an end to special privileges; there would be rules and regulations, and people would *keep* them—old man Groves as well as the rest. It was a scandal the way everybody had pampered that old man in thinking he was running the place! It interfered with discipline. First time he gave an order he would be told that he wasn't giving orders there now.

And so Emma Peters sat there, sadly wondering how it would be with Mr. Groves by spring.

She thought of the day she went to the train to meet him. He was more feeble now than then, and yet in those two years of what the incoming superintendent called "tomfoolery" he had in another sense come back to himself. He no longer looked around in that covert, frightened way. Feeble though he was, he would give an order quite briskly. And, as the deposed, too-easygoing superintendent would say, "What harm did it do?" when all he cared about was giving the order, forgetting it almost as soon as it was given. But the power to give orders had somehow brought him back to his own. In the two years he had emerged from that meekness that told the story of those years of being "had." And now? Now, at the very last, was the comfort that delusion had given him to be taken from him? Even though the truth did not actually come home to him, it would distress him, spoil the poor little peace in which he rested, send him back to that crushing sense of dependence. What would he think had happened? To whom would he turn? Where, she wondered, sudden tears blinding her, would he think *she* was? It was the thing that made it hardest to go. She wished, for the little time that was left, she could be there to shield him, just to continue to say, "Yes, Mr. Groves." What harm *did* it do? she thought with a rush of resentment against this man with the red hair whom they talked about as being so "efficient"—whatever they meant by that! Why not, as she had always said, just make the best of things?

The old man beside her again broke out in his rumination. "Well," he said, in that quavering voice, and nodding toward the house, "the old place has seen a good deal."

"It has, Mr. Groves, hasn't it?" she agreed.

"Yes—yes, seen a good deal." Then, after a pause, looking at her, "Why, I was born in that house," he said, as if telling it to her for the first time.

She nodded.

"Yes, born right there in that house. My grandfather was living there then—and my father and mother—and Ed." He sat nodding over it.

But again he roused himself. "Yes, and if it hadn't been for *me*—" He nodded wisely, leaving it unfinished. "Why, do you know," and he made a little move as if to nudge her, "my father didn't *want* to make the place into Crystal Sulphur Springs!"

"Now, is that *so?*" she murmured.

"Well, 'tis," he chuckled. "Why, I had to talk—and talk—and talk—" He stretched his legs, as if wearied beyond endurance just to think of how he had had to talk.

Then he sank back, and when once more he roused, it was as if less of him came, as if a little more of him had been claimed. He made a feeble motion as if with the idea of nudging her, and with a chuckle whispered: "And my brother Ed—*he* wasn't for it first, either. Well, he *wasn't*," he affirmed, noddingly, and sat there feebly chuckling at the joke on Edward.

And she sat there thinking of the whole story: of that house when it used to be the Groves place, the gay doings, Bert Groves riding his fine horse down the river road; thinking of Crystal Sulphur Water, of Bert Groves when he was like "a house afire," of the way he had been able to make people believe in things. Her eyes were misty again, thinking of the strangeness of life, of the hard things people had to meet. There was a wonderful sunset; the color flamed through the bare trees. It was for Emma Haines Peters one of those moments which come to all sensitive human beings of a certain mellowing sense of the whole wonder of life.

When she felt the chill of night and rose to her feet her voice was gentle as she said, "Guess we'd better be gettin' in, Mr. Groves."

He looked up at her, his eyes a little glassy; he started to get up, but fell back to his seat. "The drops!" she said, under her breath, and wheeled as if to run, as if to call to some men raking leaves up near the house. And then she did not run, did not call. She stood there still—stood mute, held.

He was gasping; she knew that his head was sinking to his chest. She had seen it before; she knew what had to be done—what must be done in a hurry. She tried to move, but something in her would not let her move. Before her was a picture—the picture of what would happen the first time Mr. Groves walked into the dining room and told the new management what to have for supper. And so she stood there with her back to the gasping old man, stood there as if *locked*, looking off at the men—their backs to her—raking leaves up near the house, looking at the wonderful sunset streaming through the bare trees. Even after there was silence—complete silence—behind her, she still stood there, hands clenched, looking at the color flaming through the dark branches. And then at last she moved—found she could move—and her lips moved then, too. "But it's *better*," she breathed, with passion. As if imploring something off there in the color that flooded the old Groves place, she breathed again, "*Wasn't* it better?"

Originally published in *Harper's Monthly Magazine* 131
(July 1915): 176–184

NOTES

1. Starting in the late nineteenth century, local governments often operated facilities to house elderly and disabled persons who could not support themselves. These accommodations, referred to as poorhouses, were typically quite sparse, with strict rules enforced. Sometimes they were located on the grounds of a working farm, and able-bodied individuals were expected to work in the fields or gardens, contributing to the farm's production. Although poorhouses were common in the United States in the early twentieth century, they disappeared soon after the Social Security Act became federal law in the 1950s.

2. The story takes place many years prior to the stock market crash of 1929, which brought about the Great Depression. Even before that, however, the economy often suffered from "boom and bust" cycles: speculation and bullish enthusiasm would inflate prices beyond realistic values, only to be followed by swift downturns. As happens even now, these precipitous declines could lead to the financial ruin of those who overpaid, especially when they discovered that they owed more to creditors than their property was worth. Creditors who were not repaid were entitled to take over the property in foreclosure proceedings, so that the original buyers, just like the Groveses in the story, would lose their entire investment.

Unveiling Brenda

GIVEN AN INSTRUCTOR IN ENGLISH who has the profile of a Greek god—and has had it for only twenty-six years—and given at his feet coeds aspiring to write, does it not follow as the night the day that the most colorful things of the school year will not be of a strictly academic nature? There was a crabbed old regent from downstate who dropped in early in the term to look things over—as crabbed regents do—and, after his eyes had rested for some forty seconds upon the beautiful countenance of Peyton Root, he said he feared this was not going to be as serious a year in the life of the university as one who had its true interests at heart could wish. The year before, Miss Stanton—fifty-two, and as serious as the crabbiest could wish—had taught English 13, and this theme course never at any time embarrassed the capacity of the classroom. But after the faculty reception in opening week, at which function the social graces of Miss Stanton's successor had excellent opportunity for liberation, it was amazing how many earnest students—largely of the militant sex—felt the year must mark an advance in their writing of the mother tongue. The second week English 13 changed quarters with Medieval History, and from that airy room looked out across the sloping campus to the river which wound through the plenteous farm country of the great middle western state of—well, as Peyton Root is a nephew of the governor, and it is not desirable to embarrass those in high station, let us say the great state of Ioda.

Peyton Root was other things than nephew of the governor. He was Mr. Root of Harvard and Heidelberg; he was Peyton Root of Des Champs—proud capital of the fecund state, a city which boasted as giddy a social life as ever scandalized a metropolis. "Peyton Root!" breathed one of the Des Champs girls. "Why, my dear, do you know who he *is?*" "It is not often," solemnly wrote an influential regent, "that a university has so great an opportunity." So great an opportunity, he meant, as to be able to get for the piteous sum the plenteous state paid its instructors one who had absorbed practically all which the greatest halls of learning had within them for absorption; one who, the influential regent expatiated, would also bring to the university the fruits of a rich social experience such as—this most tactfully put—certain other instructors were not able to contribute.

Instructor Root himself would have selected quite other things as his real contribution. Mr. Root took his soul more seriously than he did his social position or his degrees. The reason he secretly despised the U. of I. was not because it was "jay," but because it was insensitive. He wasn't "stuck on himself," as an insensitive freshman put it, because he was handsome, but because—if you really must know—he had what in the secret recesses of his consciousness he thought of as a beautiful, sensitive soul. Please do not put him down for a jackass. He really wasn't, at all. He was a nice, lovable fellow, who laughed a lot in spite of the fact that he took Walter Pater very hard.[1]

Now it was the third week, and four o'clock in the afternoon. The lads and lassies of English 13 were giggling in the corridor; their instructor sat at his desk frowning over the themes they had just handed in. How could youth be so stupid?—so banal! "What My Books Mean to Me." Good heavens!—that was from Ina Gilson, daughter of the influential regent, and—worse yet—the girl with the sunny hair whom he had danced with just the night before. He would like to suggest to Miss Gilson that she next write on, "What My Toes Mean to Me." Her toes really must mean something—dancing like that. He was about to chuck all the themes into his portfolio and start for home when his eyes fell upon a blotted page in a rather childish hand, and he was startled by the heading, "On the Pain of Teaching Dolts."

He read it through; he'd started to smile—he'd frowned. He colored; he chuckled. "There is an acute anguish in teaching dolts," he read. "One gives one's best—and leaves them dolts. Dolts will be dolts. Why should a noble soul unveil itself to dolts? 'Tis hard, and yet the pain is not without its edge of ecstasy. Is giving less because it leaves the giver dumb? All is not beautiful—but beauty lives. The God who gave us many dolts gave a few noble souls."

A girl had written it! There was a girl in his class who actually had the face to write this thing and sign it and hand it in! Brenda Munroe. Never heard of her. Munroe—Munroe; he fairly agonized in the effort to recall a student by the name of Munroe. He forgot all about his engagement to play tennis, and sat there telling himself he didn't care a hang *who* Brenda Munroe was. Munroe?—Munroe? Brenda. Queer name. He again read, "On the Pain of Teaching Dolts." Certainly he had *not* acted like that!

That night he had dinner with Mrs. Shields—wife of the head of his department, a woman wiser in the ways of the world than most of the faculty wives. Ina Gilson was there. It appeared that Mrs. Shields was much attached to this daughter of the influential regent. She was also attached to the idea of making her husband president of the university.

After dinner he very casually asked Ina, "Oh, by the way, is there anybody named Munroe in our theme class?"

"Why, yes," replied Ina; "there's Brenda."

Her blue eyes were upon him in inquiry, so he lightly asked, "What's Brenda like?"

"Poor Brenda," murmured Ina—and just then they were interrupted.

Poor Brenda? Why poor? He didn't see why anybody as brazen as that need be poor. Very well fitted indeed, he should say, for coping with the world in which she found herself. He took Ina home and was particularly nice to her; after all, she was a lady. But after he had left her at her sorority house and was cutting across the campus to his own apartment—a studio-like affair which he had astounded university circles by fitting up over a tailor shop—a sentence from Ina's theme hit him square in the face. "It is indeed impossible," Ina had written, "for me to tell all that my books mean to me." He went home and reread poor Brenda's theme—and he laughed. But after he was in bed he tossed about and couldn't go to sleep. He had *not* acted like that!

A very businesslike instructor entered the classroom of English 13 next afternoon. He was distinctly curt as for the first time that term he called the roll. As in quick staccato he progressed through J's and K's and L's, students sat up straighter, stopped rolling lead pencils and twisting paper. "James Milligan?"—and then, "Brenda Munroe?" called the brisk instructor—and looked up. There came a "Here," but he didn't locate it. "Miss Munroe?" he repeated, incisively, and an equally incisive "Present" was returned from the rear of the left wing.

He spoke of the mediocrity of all the themes; he discoursed loftily upon the cheapness of trying to pass off impertinence for ideas. He could see that on the rim of that left wing there were brown braids above a green waist, and across the area of moving heads two curiously grave eyes fixed him steadily. He found himself flushing under that speculative look, and telling himself he wasn't going to have any ridiculous thing lurking beneath the surface, "Just a moment, please, Miss Munroe," he said, as the class was leaving. The girl in the green waist—it turned out to be a whole green dress—sat down on a front seat. He was irritated by Ina Gilson's look of surprise as she passed out.

"I would be interested in knowing what governed your selection of a subject."

She looked up in a startled way that lighted her whole face. He found a peculiar satisfaction in noting that she didn't have a very good nose. It wasn't perfectly straight—Mr. Root himself had an amazingly straight nose. But there was none of that satisfaction to be had from her eyes. They were queer eyes—lights in them like the sun on old copper. She was looking at him now in an earnest, troubled way, brows knitted. But he had an uncomfortable feeling of an imp trying to break loose in those grave eyes.

"I thought we were to write of the things that interested us," she said, in a perplexed voice.

"Why, certainly!" he snapped. He couldn't very well say, "Why did it interest you?"

"I thought," she went on, as if wanting to be put right if wrong, "that we were just to write of what was in our minds."

"Certainly," he said, stiffly.

"I suppose, then—it shouldn't have been in my mind?"

"I think you must know," he began, huffily, but checked himself and said, with dignity, "That is all, Miss Munroe."

She got up. "I will try to write with more restraint," she said.

"I never said I wanted restraint!" he retorted, heatedly.

She took a step or two. "I will try to write more conventionally," she murmured, contritely—and passed out before he could say anything.

She left him fuming. He—Peyton Root—put in the position of wanting one of his students to write more conventionally!

He met Ina Gilson and walked through the campus with her. "I'm so glad you're taking an interest in Brenda," she said, gently.

"I'm not taking an interest in her," he replied, peevishly.

"I beg pardon," murmured Ina.

He colored. "I had something to say to her about her theme," he explained.

"But that was what I meant," said Ina, with patient sweetness. "A little special interest will mean so much to Brenda."

"I don't know that there's any special interest," he muttered. Irritated, he said brusquely to this author of "What My Books Mean to Me," "She writes more interestingly than the rest of the class."

"I suppose she would," murmured Ina.

He gave her a sharp look. Now what did she mean by that? It was in the "Poor Brenda" tone. But she was now talking football and he didn't want to turn her back—thus fostering the idea of "special interest."

That evening was again disturbed by this Brenda Munroe. He had not acted in accordance with his ideal as a teacher. He had found a spark and, instead of breathing upon it, he had put it out—because it was a gibe at himself. He tried to read Santayana, but was too distressed by the idea that Brenda Munroe might think he had no sense of humor.

At four o'clock next afternoon he impatiently turned over the newly received themes until he came to that queer, childish little hand. He read it through with a puzzled look, then reread it with a smile. It was as prim and immature as the handwriting that set it down. It was on "Trees."

"Trees," wrote Brenda, "are an inestimable blessing to the human race." She enumerated the utilitarian and the aesthetic reasons which indebted us to trees. It might have come from the author of "What My Books Mean to Me." Across this the cultured young instructor blue-penciled: "Cut it out. Be yourself."

Then he went over to have tea with Mrs. Shields, and boldly asked her who Brenda Munroe was. "What do you want to know for?" inquired this breezy lady, tantalizingly. He said that naturally he was interested in knowing about his students. "Then," said Mrs. Shields, "I will begin by telling you about Abigail Sears." After exhausting Abigail she began on Jimmie McGuire, saying she could see it was absolutely essential he know about all his students. And so she forced from him the admission that the student he particularly wanted to know about was Brenda Munroe. "She's original," he explained.

"Too original for university circles," replied the wife of his chief.

"Now what do you mean by that?" demanded the young man.

"She doesn't fit in," said the U. of I.'s social leader. "There's a reason."

"What reason?" impatiently pressed Peyton Root.

"Oh—" said Mrs. Shields, vaguely, and fussed with the tea things. "Her father's a milkman," she observed, and it might or might not be related to what went just before.

Peyton Root set down his cup. "Well, is this such a bourgeois place that a girl—a clever girl—an *attractive* girl— Good heavens!" he exploded, "what standards! What's the difference between a milkman and a wholesale grocer?"—the latter was the occupation of fair Ina's father, influential regent.

Instead of telling him the difference between a milkman and a wholesale grocer, Mrs. Shields observed, "Ina has lovely hair, hasn't she?"

"*Is* Brenda left out?" he demanded, waving aside Ina's hair.

"She doesn't go about it right to get in. She would have made a sorority all right, but just at the critical moment she handed in to the *Iodian* a silly little skit which the editor was unwise enough to print—"Suppose They Left Me Out!"—the tenor of which was that she might as well seek death then and there. Needless to add, she didn't get in."

"How corking!" cried he. "Why, the girl's a rebel!"

"Naturally," murmured the social leader.

"Oh, I suppose there have been milkmen's daughters who haven't been rebels," observed the delighted young instructor.

"Oh—milkmen's daughters," murmured Mrs. Shields.

He looked at her inquiringly. She seemed about to say something—but didn't.

"I am surprised," he bantered, "at your attitude toward milk—beautiful, wholesome, indispensable milk!"

"I confess I don't care for the girl," she said shortly, and added, in that vein which made him like her: "This university's no place for a rebel. Just take my word for that," she finished, dryly—"needn't try to find it out for yourself."

But the talk had fired all the rebel that was in him. He read Nietzsche till 2 a.m., and next day told his American literature class that American literature was a toddy with the stick left out.[2] This a student reporter sent to his Des Champs paper, where it made the front page. Mr. Root was advised by his chief of department to be less epigrammatic and more reverent. The crabbed old regent from downstate wrote up saying that the University of Ioda was maintained by the taxpayers of that state for the purpose of training Americans, and that the way to do it was not to teach them to despise their own literature. The secretary of the prohibitionists wrote in, deploring the content of the figure of speech; a newspaper paragrapher[3] said that possibly the stick had not been left out of the toddy young Mr. Root had before entering the classroom; and the influential regent—fair Ina's father—wrote that while he hoped they would one day sit over a toddy themselves, he did feel that all reference to these questionable things must be kept from the classroom. And as to American literature, why not speak of that which was worthy, and not too much emphasize the shortcomings? He, as a true American, would greatly prefer this course, and he felt he voiced the sentiment of many other patriotic taxpayers.

But Instructor Root was not greatly perturbed—instructors with incomes can afford their little fling in rebellion—and Brenda Munroe, who was in "Am. Lit." as well as English 13, had taken to smiling at him, and it was amazing what a long way that went in his general feeling of well-being.

But for a young man who brought to the university the fruit of a rich social experience he was finding it singularly hard to advance his acquaintance with the milkman's daughter. She wasn't at the places where acquaintances are advanced. And while there was between them a delightful little classroom understanding, as between two lively souls in a world of dolts, it didn't seem to have any tendrils out into the wide world beyond the classroom. This, Instructor Root one day decided, was a state of things which had existed long enough.

So when he was in the grocery store buying some apples he suddenly demanded of the clerk, "Do you know where a milkman named Munroe lives?"

"Joe!" the clerk bawled out to the driver at the curb, "know where a milkman named Munroe lives?"

Some of the college boys were going by; one of them stopped and respectfully told his teacher that a milkman named Munroe lived about a mile out on the Duck Creek road.

Red in the face, Mr. Root grabbed his bag and strode away, so upset he told himself he didn't care where the devil a milkman named Munroe lived. He went home and looked over the themes, and he wrote upon Brenda's: "Too loosely constructed. Watch your English. Only the writer who has mastered it has any right to take liberties."

Then he wished he hadn't written it, and tried to rub it off, making a fearful smudge. For ten minutes he sat looking at the smeary theme in deep discontent. Then he started for the Duck Creek road.

He had no business to be doing anything of the sort. It was the day before Thanksgiving, and he was going home to Des Champs. He ought to go and see Mrs. Shields, who wanted him to do something in town for her. This was playing off. For that—or some other reason—he was much keyed up by what he was doing. It was one of those bully days of late fall. He liked the day. He liked the world.

After he had gone what he thought was about a mile he was on the watch, looking for a place with a lot of cows and a girl with brown braids wound round her head. A fat, yellow dog with a corkscrew tail who was sitting by the roadside accosted him agitatedly.

"Hello, Apollo!" replied Mr. Root. "Know where a milkman named Munroe lives?"

A man with a spade in his hand stepped out from behind some trees. "I am a milkman named Munroe," said he.

Nothing in Peyton Root's social experience told him what to say next. So he had to invent something. It was, "Oh, I—was thinking of buying a cow." The milkman named Munroe looked the young man up and down. "That so?" he said, in surprise.

"I heard," lied Instructor Root, "that you had a cow for sale."

Milkman Munroe leaned his spade against the tree. "Well," said he, "I have."

The young man who had announced his quest for a cow was silent. "Want to come up and look at her?" suggested the milkman.

A cow! But he looked at the dingy brown house set well back from the road. He thought he could see someone moving about in there. He said he'd like to see the cow.

So Mr. Munroe picked up his spade. "Comin' along, Scraps?" he said to the dog.

Scraps, too, appeared to be dealing with a conflict, but decided for staying by the road. "He's waiting for my daughter," said Brenda's father. "You can't budge him till he spots her down the road."

At this it suddenly occurred to Mr. Root that the cow was for a friend, and he might as well wait till his friend was with him. Milkman Munroe grew a little peevish, and went back to digging.

Instructor Root wanted to wait with Scraps for the person Scraps was waiting for, but he felt he had made no hit with that person's father and had better move on. Perhaps he would meet her; he went over the conversation that would take place if he did meet her, but it was one of those brilliant conversations doomed to remain in the land of the spirit.

Back in town he met his friend Billy Enright from Des Champs. Billy and his big car were in front of the building which domiciled the tailor and Mr. Root.

"Hello there, Peyt!" called Billy. "Been lookin' all over for you. We've come to take you home. Goin' to drive home by moonlight."

Peyt brightened. Fact is, he was glad to see Billy. Intellectually, Billy simply wasn't there, as Peyton in an expansive moment had explained to him, but, as he had further made clear, he liked him, anyhow. They met on a gay-young-blade basis,[4] and Billy secretly scorned Peyton for what he was that Billy wasn't, quite as much as he himself was scorned for not being that thing. He was now explaining that there was a "whole bunch" had come to take Peyt home. They were over at Mrs. Shields'. Mrs. Shields couldn't understand where he was—she'd been expecting him there. He wound up with, "Where can we get a drink?"

"We can't," said Peyt.

Billy looked pained. "I know where we could get a drink of milk," his friend observed.

For the instant Billy was speechless. Then, *"Milk?"* he breathed in such an outraged tone, with such an "I-ask-for-bread-and-you-give-me-a-stone" look, that Peyton went on:

"Milk, Billy, is very nourishing. It is simple. It is beautiful. It is good." Billy's face was all screwed up.

"Say, Billy," Peyton burst out, animatedly—"tell you what! Why don't you buy a cow?"

Billy now grinned sheepishly for not having at once perceived the joke.

"I mean it!" pursued his friend. "Never have I been more serious than at this instant. I was just looking for a friend who would buy a cow. I've been out seeing about it. I've got the cow all engaged—all I need is the friend. You can well afford to buy a cow, Billy, and it will—it will give you an interest in life. Come on! Let's run out there now!" His eyes were dancing. He had stepped into the car.

Just then a gay crowd turned the corner, and, "Here they are!" called a girl's voice.

"We've come not a minute too soon," darkly pronounced Billy. "Peyt has about gone off his head in this godforsaken place. I ask him for a drink and he talks about *milk*. Says it's nourishing. Wants me to buy a *cow*. He says he's been out looking at the cow. He was insisting we shake you all now and go *back* to the cow. *That's* why he didn't come to your house," he told Mrs. Shields.

Peyton looked up to find that lady's eyes upon him in a very queer way. "I see," said she.

It seemed the cow had only led him into a blind alley, but the alley was not totally blind, after all, for a few weeks after Thanksgiving Brenda handed in a theme entitled:

On the Pleasure of Buying a Cow for a Friend
One should have every possible experience, not overlooking the experience of buying a cow for a friend. To be sure, one may have no friend, but one must not be so easily cut off from experience as to let this stand in the way. It is beautiful to buy a cow for a friend. One dwells upon what the cow is

going to mean to the friend. Will she kick? Does she hook? There is splendid adventure in it, for little does one know whether one's friend will love one more or less after the cow has come into his life. In buying a cow one always wonders why the other person is selling the cow. There is infinite field for speculation here. But the timid soul halts midway in the robust experience of buying a cow for a friend.

"Well, I'll be *darned!*" was the low-breathed comment of the instructor upon this effort.

He arose and started for the library. He told himself he was now going to take the bull by the horns—perhaps the cow suggested the figure. Timid soul? Timid soul—*nothing!* He had at other times seen Brenda Munroe sitting in the library after class. He would go up to her now and say, "How did you know it was I?" Or he would say, "*Does* she hook?" or, "Well, why does he want to sell her?" He would say *something*. One would think he had been raised in the backwoods!—or in a monastery.

But how say something to a girl who wasn't there? He looked the library through in high expectation; he looked it through in determination which petered out to disappointment; he looked it through in the sulks. Sulking, he went and stood by a window, and from that window he saw Brenda Munroe crossing the campus in the direction of the Duck Creek road. She was not alone. With her was a boy—Harry Baker, who lived out in the country somewhere, doubtless on the Duck Creek road. Undoubtedly, Instructor Root reflected, with a pang for which he did not try to account, they were boy and girl sweethearts. They stood still looking at something. Ah!—a kodak.[5] Baker—a stupid fellow, a jay— was taking her picture. She was laughing. Then he gave the kodak back to her and she took his picture. Silly performance. He intensely disliked that kodak.

He met Mrs. Shields and she asked him where he was keeping his cows. He didn't think it at all funny, and made it plain to her he didn't. He sat up very late writing a poem about love. It dealt with disappointed love and the consolations of the spirit. Next day he was very sleepy. And, being sleepy, he yawned. He yawned in class, having leisure to do so because he had put them to writing during the hour; they were writing against time—as they would have to do on a newspaper. Interesting experiment—especially valuable to sleepy instructors. He made decent attempts at suppressing his yawns, but sometimes they got the start of him. He noticed that Brenda Munroe had come down to the dictionary stand at the front of the room. He was seeking for something clever to write upon the margin of "On the Pleasure of Buying a Cow for a Friend," but the effort was too much for him. He yawned. It was an awful yawn—a writhing, twisting, tortuous yawn. It was holding the apex of its tremendous upcurve when something turned his eyes to the dictionary. On the dictionary sat a little black box. Upon the box moved the hand of Brenda Munroe. A picture of him with his mouth sprawled open like that!

In a quick wave of anger: "Miss Munroe," he said, "you may bring that here!"

The class sat at attention. The girl at the dictionary did not move.

Anger mounted with the realization of the position he was in. "I think you heard me, Miss Munroe," he said, icily.

A queer little smile on her lips, she walked slowly to the desk and handed him the camera.

That smile haunted him all through the Christmas holidays. It was a mocking smile—a maddeningly understanding little smile. And something else haunted him—the look in her eyes when she handed over the little black box—the look in a child's eyes when you take a toy away. Perhaps she didn't have very much to amuse herself with; doubtless she loved her little kodak. He wished he had been a better sport, but it is hard to be a good sport at the very instant a girl who peculiarly interests you has snapped you with your face all distorted by a sprawling yawn. And if you haven't been one on the dot, it is hard to know how to slide into being one later. So you retire into professional dignity.

Not knowing how to make a graceful return, he took the kodak home and through the gay two weeks he thought a great deal about that little black box and its owner. He considered the grave ethical problem of whether it would be honorable to have the films developed. Could developing another person's films be classed with reading another person's letters? Curiosity settled this question in ethics, as it has many another, and—also far from unprecedented—he persuaded himself that what he

66

wanted to do was the decent thing to do. To develop the films before returning the kodak would be in the nature of a light little apology. And he would show that he was, after all, a good sport by not suppressing the one of himself.

But this became a terrible test. The picture was a complete success—the acme of ridiculousness. Peyton Root looked long and ruefully at that picture. Not a bit did he like the idea of Brenda Munroe looking at it; but still less did he like the idea of that speculative look in her eyes as she contemplated the absence of it. He was on the rack of indecision. He went about to all the parties with Isabel Stephens—Des Champs' reigning girl. But the night he came home from the Christmas-eve dance he sat a long time over the fire in his upstairs library, thinking, not of Isabel Stephens, but of the milkman's daughter. He looked over the other pictures the kodak yielded. There were two of the fat, yellow dog with the corkscrew tail. In one he blissfully gnawed a bone; in the other he was looking up at someone, quivering with happy excitement. The purloiner of the picture was pretty certain it was not Milkman Munroe Scraps was looking up at. The longer he looked the stronger became his desire to be sharing Scraps's experience. He thought back to the party that night, and told himself that Brenda Munroe somehow made other girls like that toddy with the unfortunate omission. He wrote a poem on the brutalities of confiscation, and mailed it to Brenda with her pictures and kodak, keeping out a copy of the one of herself, and burning the film of that stupid jay of a Baker—who would want such a picture as that?

That she had forgiven him was early apparent by her reopening fire through the themes. Through English 13 she attacked his teaching of "Am. Lit." Not being interested by American literature, he had used it as little more than a peg on which to hang such things as did interest him. Hence this:

The Oblique Method

Great are the opportunities afforded by the teaching of
American literature, for one can consider everything that
American literature is not—a field practically inexhaust-
ible. Greek literature—the road to learning American literature does not have beauty. Russian literature—road to the

knowledge of American literature is not serious. Shelley—for would it not have been an excellent thing for America to have had a Shelley? Milton—for did not Milton very nearly sail in the *Mayflower* and found American literature? . . . Pleasant indeed to teach American literature, for the French poets are unfailingly interesting to survey.

This theme met with an accident which advanced a romance. He sometimes gave the themes out to fellow students for criticism. After class he couldn't find "The Oblique Method," which he thought he had put aside for private comment, and next day it was handed in by Ina Gilson—and with it a most self-contained look from that young lady.

"Not serious work," Ina had written. "Not carefully constructed and not in good taste. One is tempted to say, impertinent. Evidently written with the idea of drawing attention to the writer rather than the legitimate idea of advancing in the writing of English."

He was furious at himself and furious at Ina. He had meant to go and see her that night and ask her to go to the Pan-Hellenic, the big dance of the year. Now came the idea of asking Brenda Munroe instead. He didn't know why he shouldn't ask Brenda Munroe if he wanted to! He'd like to know why Brenda Munroe shouldn't go to that dance as well as anyone else! He'd show some people a thing or two about who was interesting and who was not!

So he wrote Miss Munroe a quite correct note, asking if he might have the pleasure, etc. And back came a primly written little missive, saying she would be pleased—and so on.

There was no theme-sparring in those next two weeks. Brenda was shy. He was shy himself—shyly excited, after the manner of a boy who for the first time in his life has asked a girl to go somewhere. He kept living it all over ahead.

About a week before the big night Mrs. Shields one afternoon asked him to come in and have tea with her. And as they drank their tea she told him, with the deftness of managing matrons, that Ina had not yet decided whom to go with to the party.

"That so?" he replied, with mild interest.

"I thought," she went on, "that some of us might have dinner here and go over together."

"It's a nice idea," he said, guardedly.

"Got your girl?" she asked, bluntly.

"Got my girl," he answered.

She looked a little dashed. Then, "Who?" she plumped at him.

"Brenda Munroe," he plumped back. As there was silence, he looked up. "What was it about dinner?" he asked, pleasantly, as if remarking nothing unusual in the way she was looking at him.

"Nothing about dinner," she answered.

The night came. He was ready to start for his girl. It wasn't quite time to go, and he found it hard to put in the minutes. It must be confessed that he put in some of them looking in the glass —seeing himself as Brenda Munroe would see him. As is sometimes said of the other sex, he was "all of a flutter."

There came a knock. "Carriage for me?" he demanded of the boy at the door.

"My sister said to give you this," replied the youngster, and fled.

The young man who had been about to step into his carriage then read the following:

Dear Mr. Root,—I am sorry, but I can't go to the party with you, after all.

Brenda Munroe.

Perhaps the less said about dear Mr. Root's state of mind that night the better. A record of it would not make him appear an amiable young man. He was staggered. He was outraged. He told himself it was too much. He told himself it was not amusing. He passionately affirmed that no girl in the world could treat him like that!

He did not go to the party. How could he? He took off his gorgeous raiment and fumed and sulked and swore. He thought of Mrs. Shields. He thought of Ina Gilson. He thought of Brenda Munroe! He was still awake when he heard them coming home from the party.

That was Friday night; Saturday and Sunday passed with nothing by way of explanation. Mrs. Shields said they missed him at the dance. He replied with dignity that there had been a change of plan. Monday he never looked at Brenda Munroe—addressed no word to her in class. Further, she addressed no word to him—not even after class. Rage mounted.

On Wednesday she handed in this theme:

When Someone You Loved Is Not There Anymore
Everything is different. Things the one who is gone had nothing to do with are different. Things *look* different. They are dimmer. You know that you are alone. You do not want to go home. . . . You do alone things you used to do together. That is lonesomeness.

He did not read it until evening—too late for seeing her that night. He was instantly melted to contrition, to tenderness. Someone had died. It sounded like her mother. Her mother had died the very night of the party—and he railing at her like that! He found a keen satisfaction in telling himself he was a vain, vapid cad. He longed to be with her and comfort her. How tender she was, after all. Poor, lonely little girl! A long time he sat dreaming of her.

When English 13 broke up next day he went up to her and asked, quietly, "May I walk home with you?"

"I wish you would," she said, simply.

They remained quiet as they walked through the campus and down the street that led to the Duck Creek road. She was like a hurt child. They had crossed the bridge which left town behind before he gently ventured, "I am afraid you have had trouble."

She nodded, mute sorrow in her strange eyes.

"I am sorry," he said, softly. "I—of course I wondered the night of the party," he went on; "and then your theme—"

"I was sorry about the party. I—I had wanted to go." She said it wistfully. "And I was afraid you might not understand." She looked at him shyly.

"I do now," he said.

"I suppose some people would think it strange to care so much," she said, a defiant little quiver in her voice.

"Well, they must be queer people!" he retorted.

They walked a way in silence. Then, "Perhaps you have had a dog of your own?" she suggested.

"A— I beg pardon?" stammered the young man.

"A dog of your own," she repeated, now wrapped in her own thought.

"I—oh—certainly—many dogs," he found himself mumbling.

She began talking about Scraps. He tried to make certain adjustments. A dog! . . . She had picked him up in town. Nobody wanted him. He was—well, a waif. Some people would hold that against him, she said, with a singular intensity—but there never lived a more loving or a smarter dog! Every afternoon he watched for her. That was what did it. He saw her coming way down the road—came running. An automobile—she saw it with her own eyes!

He drew nearer and took her arm and held her hand tight in his. They walked on like that to the place where Scraps used to sit waiting for her.

The upshot of it was that he was to try to take Scraps's place. He smiled over that as he sat alone that night before work he should be doing and wasn't—smiled an intimate little smile at that thought of himself taking the place of a fat, yellow dog with a corkscrew tail. It had come about quite simply. She dreaded coming to the place where Scraps was no longer waiting for her, dreaded the place where she had seen it happen. He suggested that perhaps if he came with her it wouldn't seem so bad. He said that company did help. She accepted it in a grateful little way that moved him more than he tried to understand.

And so all the rest of the term he went on trying to fill Scraps's place. Almost every afternoon he walked home with her. He did not stay in Scraps's place, but made a place of his own.

She was not like any girl he had ever known. He told himself that was what interested him. He liked the way her mind worked—her flashes, her unexpected little turns. He loved her gay scorn. What he himself had been theoretically he felt in her as an emotional reality. Defiance played through her like a lovely flame, lightly; for the most part, gaily. Well, he got on with her; after all, that was chiefly it. Before this, girls had been something apart from what he really was. She somehow cleared up what he really was. And nothing in his whole life of pleasant things had pleased him as her liking of him pleased him.

Spring came, and the homeward walks took longer. There were lingering moments still longer lingered over after he left her. It was amazing
how an hour could get away from him!

And all this time university social life was not profiting by the fruit
of his rich social experience. Brenda made university social life very flat.
His friendship with Ina Gilson had not advanced.

One day in "Am. Lit." they were talking about Poe, and Ina made a
smug remark about his heredity, which inspired her instructor to a defense of foundlings. Almost flamboyantly well-born himself, he had long
cherished a romantic feeling about waifs. Indeed, he had once written a
poem about them. And as he that day wanted to give English 13 a subject
for the fortnightly theme, he told them to write on Waifs.

Brenda was subdued going home that night. He found her looking
at him in a way that puzzled him. She remained different all that week.
She was shy, and yet her eyes were warm with a deepened friendliness.
She was more gentle, more pensive, but with it all that strange intensity,
that thing mysteriously potent—sometimes her eyes would flame in a
way that quickened his sense of the whole life of the world.

The Waif themes were handed in the next week. There were a few
laggards, and, strangely enough, Brenda Munroe was among them;
usually her themes were right on the dot. He said that all of them must
be in by the next day.

And next day all of them came in save Brenda's. Because of his friendship with her—naturally not unknown to the class—he was always
anxious not to show favoritism, and so now quite welcomed this opportunity for public mention of her shortcoming.

"Miss Munroe," he said, "I haven't your theme on Waifs."

Instantly the room was singularly quiet. He felt it was related to gossip
about him and Brenda. In order to display a lack of self-consciousness
he added, pleasantly, "I am expecting something particularly good from
you on that."

Again utter stillness; and then he had the sense of something like a
collective gasp. How absurd of them! And when he went down to the
library to meet Brenda he found no Brenda; and when he went out on
the steps, thinking she had sauntered along through the campus, as she

sometimes did, he saw her on the front seat of a wagon being driven rapidly toward the Duck Creek road.

He was disappointed and a good deal hurt. So that evening he thought he would go and see Mrs. Shields—he hadn't been there for a long time.

"I'm glad you came," she said. "I was thinking of sending for you." He murmured some inanity of appreciation.

"Do you want to know something for your own good?" she demanded.

"No," he replied, promptly, but sat down and waited for it.

"If you are fond of Brenda Munroe," she began, bluntly—"and goodness knows you appear to be—don't talk to her in public about waifs."

He stared at her.

"Because she is one," she finished.

He could only sit there, staring.

Mrs. Shields went on to tell him what she knew. A couple of years before there was a girl in the university named Mary Greene, who came from Annisville, a town where the Munroes had once lived. It seemed they had moved around several times—Mr. Munroe apparently being one of those farmers who always thought there was better land somewhere else. Mrs. Munroe herself told someone in Annisville that Brenda was adopted. And Mary Greene said the idea was current there that Brenda had something to do with a band of gypsies. She didn't know the story definitely, as the Munroes got Brenda when they lived in Dakota. So whether she *was* gypsy, or a child the gypsies had stolen— Anyway, the Munroes got her from a band of gypsies. "I had an impulse to tell you once before," she concluded, "but I decided it would just make her picturesque to you—well knowing what fools men are."

He got away as soon as he could and started for the Duck Creek road. Amid much confusion of feeling stood out the impulse to see Brenda at once. His strange girl!—his dear, wonderful little imp girl! How this explained her!—intensified her. He wanted to be with her instantly and tell her he loved her. He knew now that in all the world this was the woman soul for him. Strange, wild little thing! Dear little outsider! There was something about her gallant gaiety, something in the thought of her strange, bright aloneness made his throat tight. How he loved the untamed thing in her! He must hear her say that she loved him; her eyes let him believe she did. He wanted to talk to her about what life together was going to mean—the perpetual freshness, the spirited adventure.

But the house of Milkman Munroe was dark. He struck a match and looked at his watch. After ten. Stealthily he went nearer. If only he could call to Brenda, get her to come out. He couldn't get up the nerve to go and knock at the door at that hour. He did whistle faintly, but no response.

A long time he sat on a big stone at the side of the road—thinking, profoundly stirred. He saw Brenda as the determining thing in his life. Because of her he felt many old things slipping away; because of her he saw new things opening. He was happy, but very serious. He felt the stir of all the unknown, of all that was mysterious and wild and beautiful. It reached him through her. She made life like that.

Next morning Brenda's place in "Am. Lit." was vacant. In the afternoon she did not appear for English 13. So he set out to find her.

He had not come to know the Munroe family. Brenda had seemed to want to limit it to the homeward walks; he rather liked that, too—it somehow kept them more poignant. So he had to ask the blank-looking woman if she was Mrs. Munroe. And then he asked for Brenda.

"She's gone away," he was told.

"Gone *away!*" he gasped.

"On the morning train."

"But *where?* Where's she gone?"

"She's gone to Dakota—where we lived once."

"But *why?*" he demanded.

She looked at him warily then. "I don't know what you want to know for."

So he told her who he was and why he wanted to know. He told her that he cared for Brenda and *must* know.

She looked a good deal awed. "Well," she said, "Brenda left a note. She says she's gone to find out. Why, I never knew she knew. I meant to tell her, but I just never got around to it—and, anyway, what was the use? I thought it might just make her feel bad. But she says in this note she's known since she was seven years old. She heard me telling a woman. And then afterward a boy at school told her something—I don't know what. I couldn't make out what she was driving at last night when she asked me those questions about Waterburg—that town in Dakota where we lived when we got her. And I don't know yet what's stirred it up all of a sudden, and what she's run off like this for—spending all that money for nothing—when all she's got's what she makes on the eggs. I'd have told her everything there is to tell."

He was on the point of asking her to tell him, but something checked him. He wanted to know only what Brenda wanted him to know.

He left a note for Dr. Shields saying he had been called away. He took the night train for Dakota.

It was a horrible trip—changes and waits, and miserable, jolting cars. He thought about what he was doing: The board of regents!—his mother; his sister Margaret. He thought about the whole world he knew. He knew that everything he had been part of would be pitted against what he was doing now. And with all of that in the scale against Brenda—well, it weighed about a feather.

The middle of the next morning he saw, far across the prairie country, a town which the conductor told him was Waterburg. Sight of it flamed his imagination anew. Perhaps he was following the very path a wild, wandering little band had followed about twenty years before. He wanted to tell Brenda how he loved her for the immensity and mystery of her background. The essence of all the uncaptured life of the world reached him through her.

Then he got off, and for the first time confronted the problem of finding her. It hadn't seemed there would be any difficulty about finding any one—particularly Brenda!—in a little town in Dakota. He walked up and down the streets, and Waterburg grew larger and larger. He asked at the hotel. No such person there. He asked in a store—never heard of such a party. The post office—a new name to them. And then, after two anxious hours, on an outer street that marked the town off from the prairie, he saw, walking slowly toward him, head down, the girl he had come to find.

He knew at once that she had had some kind of a blow. The buoyancy seemed struck out of her. What had she heard? What could there be that was worse than she had suspected? How fortunate that he had come!

She looked up and saw him, and she didn't seem particularly surprised. She held out both hands to him. Without a word he took them, and then, after a hesitating moment, she turned and they walked slowly back in the direction she had come.

"Brenda," he asked, softly, "do you care for me?"

She looked up into his face and nodded. Then her eyes filled. "I did," she said. "I—I don't know now. I seem a different person." Her voice broke, and yet she laughed a little.

"Dearest," he hurried on, "don't you know that you can't be a different person to me? Don't you know that you are *you*? What do I care about anything else?"

"Are you sure of that?" she asked, in a queer little way.

"Oh, sweetheart—*sure* of it!" he scoffed. "And if you could know how I *love* the idea of what is behind you! Life that was never caught! A people of romance who wandered the earth and remained outside!"

Her face was strange. She looked a little as if she were going to cry. They turned off on a path that ran along under some willows.

"Don't you see?" he persisted. "How it's all a part of you? How it sets you apart? How it lights you up?"

For answer she sat down on a fallen tree and burst into tears.

"Brenda, *dearest*," he murmured, and tried to comfort her.

She lifted her face, and dabbed at her eyes with a handkerchief. "That's what I thought, too," she choked—"that it set me apart; that it lighted me up." She pulled at her handkerchief, and then after a moment grew quiet. Her eyes were as if fixed on something away across the prairie; she began speaking as if reading it off there. "I was about seven. We moved from here to Annisville. One day I was in the back kitchen and I heard my mother say to a woman who was making jelly with her in the kitchen: 'Well, now, I'll tell you—though I wouldn't want you to say anything about it—but Brenda isn't our child. She's adopted.' I went out into the back yard. I couldn't stay to hear the rest. I thought about it all the time. I wondered, 'If I'm not their child, whose child *am* I?' But I couldn't ask. Maybe you don't understand—I suppose you wouldn't."

His arm went about her, and he pressed her shoulder in token that he did understand.

"Even that made me different—that wondering. And then one day, a year or so later, a boy at school said, 'Hello, gypsy!' I said, 'I'm not a gypsy!' He said: 'You are, too! You're adopted. They got you from the gypsies.'" She paused. "Well, it changed me—that's all. I felt that I was different. I felt that I wasn't in my place—that I didn't belong. When I was little"—her lip trembled—"I was very lonely when I was little."

He tried to draw her a little nearer, longing to make her feel she was never going to be lonely again.

"But I came to like it," she went on, with more spirit. "I came to like the feeling that I didn't belong—that I was outside—by myself. It—it made me what I am."

"Thank Heaven!" he murmured.

"And then—you," she said, softly. "And I wasn't alone. And—I liked that, too."

"Sweetheart!" he murmured, in a rush of tenderness.

"And then, when you said that in class"—his arm tightened—"I got a feeling that I had to *know*. I remembered this woman—Mrs. Dott, a friend of ours here in this town. I've always had a queer feeling about her—a notion that she somehow connected me up with what I came from. So I wanted to get to her. I was afraid my mother wouldn't tell it all—and, anyhow, I didn't want it from my mother. Oh, I was sort of crazy, I suppose. I wanted to get as far back as I could. So I got up in the night and ran away." Her face tightened. "Well," she said, in a practical little voice, "I know now. I know all there is to know."

He was smoothing her shoulder, as if to assure her again that nothing she knew could make any difference.

"I was right about Mrs. Dott. I was with her first. My mother and father died of typhoid fever—the same week. She took me till she could find a home for me." She had picked up a branch from the fallen tree and was stirring the ground with it. "Now that I come to think of it," she said, meditatively, "that boy always was an awful liar." She threw away her stick, straightened, as if to get it over with. "I have nothing to do with any gypsies." She brought it out sharply. "Mrs. Dott was scandalized at the idea. My father mended boilers." A silence. "I suppose he mended other things, too"—drearily. "He had a little shop. They say there never lived a kinder or a better man."

Their eyes met, and for one instant fun threatened to run round their dismay as a tiny sprite of a blue flame will rim the decorously burning log. But Brenda hurried on:

"And my mother—my mysterious, romantic, *uncaught* mother!—she taught in Sunday school. They say they never had a more faithful teacher." It gave pause. "Of course they were legally married," Brenda pursued, bravely. "In church. By the Baptist minister." She jumped up. "And my name!—my strange name that I thought *proved* it—do you want to know how I came by that name? My mother named me after a *missionary* her church helped support! She hoped I'd grow up and be as *good* as that missionary." He was standing beside her. "So you see I'm not what you thought I was." She would not look at him.

His arms went round her. "Dearest," said Peyton Root, "you're *you*. Do you think *boilers* could unmake you now? Do you think all the Baptist ministers in the world could come between us?"

Their eyes met and laughed at them, and brought them together—that pervasive sharing of amusement which had done so much in finding them for each other.

But Brenda could not at once give it over to amusement. "Beautiful, uncaptured life!" was wrung from her.

He stooped and kissed her. Then he looked into her eyes. "Beautiful, uncaptured life!" said he—and not in bitterness.

Originally published in *Harper's Monthly Magazine* 133
(June 1916): 14–26

NOTES

1. Walter Pater (1839–1894) was a Victorian art historian and critic who was widely influential. His most well-known book, *Studies in the History of the Renaissance* (1873), sparked the fin-de-siècle aesthetic creed of "art for art's sake" with such famous statements as "To burn always with this hard, gemlike flame, to maintain this ecstasy, is success in life."
2. A toddy is a warm whiskey, water, and sugar drink, traditionally stirred by a toddy-stick. Peyton is telling his students here, in effect, that American

literature is all entertainment (toddy), and no backbone (stick), indicating his Anglophilic and continental preferences in literature. The uproar that ensues, with all the hints that Peyton is un-American, represents Glaspell's playful parody of an issue she took quite seriously in her play *Inheritors*: the suppression of free speech, particularly on college campuses, as a result of the Espionage Act of 1917 and the Sedition Act of 1918, which legalized government censorship of any printed or expressed opposition to American policy during World War I, as well as the "Red Scare" tactics used to whip up patriotic fervor and silence debate. Later Peyton applies his toddy-without-the-stick metaphor to girls, meaning that others seem spineless when compared to Brenda.

3. A "paragrapher" was a newspaper editorial writer.
4. A "gay young blade" meant a young man out to have a good time. Glaspell employs quite a bit of slang in this story, reflecting the youth of her characters.
5. Eastman Kodak introduced the Brownie box camera in 1900; it cost one dollar.

A Jury of Her Peers

WHEN MARTHA HALE OPENED the storm door and got a cut of the north wind, she ran back for her big woolen scarf. As she hurriedly wound that round her head her eye made a scandalized sweep of her kitchen. It was no ordinary thing that called her away—it was probably farther from ordinary than anything that had ever happened in Dickson County. But what her eye took in was that her kitchen was in no shape for leaving: her bread all ready for mixing, half the flour sifted and half unsifted.

She hated to see things half done; but she had been at that when the team from town stopped to get Mr. Hale, and then the sheriff came running in to say his wife wished Mrs. Hale would come too—adding, with a grin, that he guessed she was getting scary and wanted another woman along. So she had dropped everything right where it was.

"Martha!" now came her husband's impatient voice. "Don't keep folks waiting out here in the cold."

She again opened the storm door, and this time joined the three men and the one woman waiting for her in the big two-seated buggy.

After she had the robes tucked around her she took another look at the woman who sat beside her on the backseat. She had met Mrs. Peters the year before at the county fair, and the thing she remembered about her was that she didn't seem like a sheriff's wife. She was small and thin and didn't have a strong voice. Mrs. Gorman, sheriff's wife before Gorman went out and Peters came in, had a voice that somehow seemed to be backing up the law with every word. But if Mrs. Peters didn't look like a sheriff's wife, Peters made it up in looking like a sheriff. He was to a dot the kind of man who could get himself elected sheriff—a heavy man with a big voice, who was particularly genial with the law-abiding, as if to make it plain that he knew the difference between criminals and noncriminals. And right there it came into Mrs. Hale's mind, with a stab, that this man who was so pleasant and lively with all of them was going to the Wrights' now as a sheriff.

"The country's not very pleasant this time of year," Mrs. Peters at last ventured, as if she felt they ought to be talking as well as the men.

Mrs. Hale scarcely finished her reply, for they had gone up a little hill and could see the Wright place now, and seeing it did not make her feel like talking. It looked very lonesome this cold March morning. It had always been a lonesome-looking place. It was down in a hollow, and the poplar trees around it were lonesome-looking trees. The men were looking at it and talking about what had happened. The county attorney was bending to one side of the buggy, and kept looking steadily at the place as they drew up to it.

"I'm glad you came with me," Mrs. Peters said nervously, as the two women were about to follow the men in through the kitchen door.

Even after she had her foot on the doorstep, her hand on the knob, Martha Hale had a moment of feeling she could not cross that threshold. And the reason it seemed she couldn't cross it now was simply because she hadn't crossed it before. Time and time again it had been in her mind, "I ought to go over and see Minnie Foster"—she still thought of her as Minnie Foster, though for twenty years she had been Mrs. Wright. And then there was always something to do and Minnie Foster would go from her mind. But *now* she could come.

The men went over to the stove. The women stood close together by the door. Young Henderson, the county attorney, turned around and said, "Come up to the fire, ladies."

Mrs. Peters took a step forward, then stopped. "I'm not—cold," she said.

And so the two women stood by the door, at first not even so much as looking around the kitchen.

The men talked for a minute about what a good thing it was the sheriff had sent his deputy out that morning to make a fire for them, and then Sheriff Peters stepped back from the stove, unbuttoned his outer coat, and leaned his hands on the kitchen table in a way that seemed to mark the beginning of official business. "Now, Mr. Hale," he said in a sort of semiofficial voice, "before we move things about, you tell Mr. Henderson just what it was you saw when you came here yesterday morning."

The county attorney was looking around the kitchen.

"By the way," he said, "has anything been moved?" He turned to the sheriff. "Are things just as you left them yesterday?"

Peters looked from cupboard to sink; from that to a small worn rocker a little to one side of the kitchen table.

"It's just the same."

"Somebody should have been left here yesterday," said the county attorney.

"Oh—yesterday," returned the sheriff, with a little gesture as of yesterday having been more than he could bear to think of. "When I had to send Frank to Morris Center for that man who went crazy—let me tell you, I had my hands full *yesterday*. I knew you could get back from Omaha by today, George, and as long as I went over everything here myself—"

"Well, Mr. Hale," said the county attorney, in a way of letting what was past and gone go, "tell just what happened when you came here yesterday morning."

Mrs. Hale, still leaning against the door, had that sinking feeling of the mother whose child is about to speak a piece. Lewis often wandered along and got things mixed up in a story. She hoped he would tell this straight and plain, and not say unnecessary things that would just make things harder for Minnie Foster. He didn't begin at once, and she noticed that he looked queer—as if standing in that kitchen and having to tell what he had seen there yesterday morning made him almost sick.

"Yes, Mr. Hale?" the county attorney reminded.

"Harry and I had started to town with a load of potatoes," Mrs. Hale's husband began.

Harry was Mrs. Hale's oldest boy. He wasn't with them now, for the very good reason that those potatoes never got to town yesterday and he was taking them this morning, so he hadn't been home when the sheriff stopped to say he wanted Mr. Hale to come over to the Wright place and tell the county attorney his story there, where he could point it all out. With all Mrs. Hale's other emotions came the fear now that maybe Harry wasn't dressed warm enough—they hadn't any of them realized how that north wind did bite.

"We come along this road," Hale was going on, with a motion of his hand to the road over which they had just come, "and as we got in sight of the house I says to Harry, 'I'm goin' to see if I can't get John Wright to take a telephone.' You see," he explained to Henderson, "unless I can get somebody to go in with me they won't come out this branch road except for a price *I* can't pay. I'd spoke to Wright about it once before; but he put me off, saying folks talked too much anyway, and all he asked was peace and quiet—guess you know about how much he talked himself. But I thought maybe if I went to the house and talked about it before his wife, and said all the womenfolks liked the telephones, and that in this lonesome stretch of road it would be a good thing—well, I said to Harry that that was what I was going to say—though I said at the same time that I didn't know as what his wife wanted made much difference to John—"

Now, there he was!—saying things he didn't need to say. Mrs. Hale tried to catch her husband's eye, but fortunately the county attorney interrupted with:

"Let's talk about that a little later, Mr. Hale. I do want to talk about that, but I'm anxious now to get along to just what happened when you got here."

When he began this time, it was very deliberately and carefully:

"I didn't see or hear anything. I knocked at the door. And still it was all quiet inside. I knew they must be up—it was past eight o'clock. So I knocked again, louder, and I thought I heard somebody say, 'Come in.' I wasn't sure—I'm not sure yet. But I opened the door—this door," jerking a hand toward the door by which the two women stood, "and there, in that rocker"—pointing to it—"sat Mrs. Wright."

Everyone in the kitchen looked at the rocker. It came into Mrs. Hale's mind that that rocker didn't look in the least like Minnie Foster—the Minnie Foster of twenty years before. It was a dingy red, with wooden rungs up the back, and the middle rung was gone, and the chair sagged to one side.

"How did she—look?" the county attorney was inquiring.

"Well," said Hale, "she looked—queer."

"How do you mean—queer?"

As he asked it he took out a notebook and pencil. Mrs. Hale did not like the sight of that pencil. She kept her eye fixed on her husband, as

if to keep him from saying unnecessary things that would go into that
notebook and make trouble.

Hale did speak guardedly, as if the pencil had affected him too.

"Well, as if she didn't know what she was going to do next. And kind
of—done up."

"How did she seem to feel about your coming?"

"Why, I don't think she minded—one way or other. She didn't pay
much attention. I said, 'Ho' do, Mrs. Wright? It's cold, ain't it?' And she
said, 'Is it?'—and went on pleatin' at her apron.

"Well, I was surprised. She didn't ask me to come up to the stove, or
to sit down, but just set there, not even lookin' at me. And so I said: 'I
want to see John.'

"And then she—laughed. I guess you would call it a laugh.

"I thought of Harry and the team outside, so I said, a little sharp,
'Can I see John?' 'No,' says she—kind of dull like. 'Ain't he home?' says
I. Then she looked at me. 'Yes,' says she, 'he's home.' 'Then why can't
I see him?' I asked her, out of patience with her now. 'Cause he's dead,'
says she, just as quiet and dull—and fell to pleating her apron. 'Dead?'
says I, like you do when you can't take in what you've heard.

"She just nodded her head, not getting a bit excited, but rockin' back
and forth.

"'Why—where is he?' says I, not knowing *what* to say.

"She just pointed upstairs—like this"—pointing to the room above.

"I got up, with the idea of going up there myself. By this time I—didn't
know what to do. I walked from there to here; then I says: 'Why, what
did he die of?'

"'He died of a rope round his neck,' says she; and just went on pleatin'
at her apron."

Hale stopped speaking, and stood staring at the rocker, as if he were
still seeing the woman who had sat there the morning before. Nobody
spoke; it was as if everyone were seeing the woman who had sat there
the morning before.

"And what did you do then?" the county attorney at last broke the
silence.

"I went out and called Harry. I thought I might—need help. I got Harry

85

in, and we went upstairs." His voice fell almost to a whisper. "There he was—lying over the—"

"I think I'd rather have you go into that upstairs," the county attorney interrupted, "where you can point it all out. Just go on now with the rest of the story."

"Well, my first thought was to get that rope off. It looked—"

He stopped, his face twitching.

"But Harry, he went up to him, and he said, 'No, he's dead all right, and we'd better not touch anything.' So we went downstairs.

"She was still sitting that same way. 'Has anybody been notified?' I asked. 'No,' says she, unconcerned.

"'Who did this, Mrs. Wright?' said Harry. He said it businesslike, and she stopped pleating at her apron. 'I don't know,' she says. 'You don't *know*?' says Harry. 'Weren't you sleepin' in the bed with him?' 'Yes,' says she, 'but I was on the inside.' 'Somebody slipped a rope round his neck and strangled him, and you didn't wake up?' says Harry. 'I didn't wake up,' she said after him.

"We may have looked as if we didn't see how that could be, for after a minute she said, 'I sleep sound.'

"Harry was going to ask her more questions, but I said maybe that weren't our business; maybe we ought to let her tell her story first to the coroner or the sheriff. So Harry went fast as he could over to High Road—the Rivers' place, where there's a telephone."

"And what did she do when she knew you had gone for the coroner?" The attorney got his pencil in his hand all ready for writing.

"She moved from that chair to this one over here"—Hale pointed to a small chair in the corner—"and just sat there with her hands held together and looking down. I got a feeling that I ought to make some conversation, so I said I had come in to see if John wanted to put in a telephone; and at that she started to laugh, and then she stopped and looked at me—scared."

At the sound of a moving pencil the man who was telling the story looked up.

"I dunno—maybe it wasn't scared," he hastened; "I wouldn't like to say it was. Soon Harry got back, and then Dr. Lloyd came, and you, Mr. Peters, and so I guess that's all I know that you don't."

He said that last with relief, and moved a little, as if relaxing. Everyone moved a little. The county attorney walked toward the stair door.

"I guess we'll go upstairs first—then out to the barn and around there." He paused and looked around the kitchen.

"You're convinced there was nothing important here?" he asked the sheriff. "Nothing that would—point to any motive?"

The sheriff too looked all around, as if to reconvince himself.

"Nothing here but kitchen things," he said, with a little laugh for the insignificance of kitchen things.

The county attorney was looking at the cupboard—a peculiar, ungainly structure, half closet and half cupboard, the upper part of it being built in the wall, and the lower part just the old-fashioned kitchen cupboard. As if its queerness attracted him, he got a chair and opened the upper part and looked in. After a moment he drew his hand away sticky.

"Here's a nice mess," he said resentfully.

The two women had drawn nearer, and now the sheriff's wife spoke.

"Oh—her fruit," she said, looking to Mrs. Hale for sympathetic understanding. She turned back to the county attorney and explained: "She worried about that when it turned so cold last night. She said the fire would go out and her jars might burst."

Mrs. Peters' husband broke into a laugh.

"Well, can you beat the women! Held for murder, and worrying about her preserves!"

The young attorney set his lips.

"I guess before we're through with her she may have something more serious than preserves to worry about."

"Oh, well," said Mrs. Hale's husband, with good-natured superiority, "women are used to worrying over trifles."

The two women moved a little closer together. Neither of them spoke. The county attorney seemed suddenly to remember his manners—and think of his future.

"And yet," said he, with the gallantry of a young politician, "for all their worries, what would we do without the ladies?"

The women did not speak, did not unbend. He went to the sink and began washing his hands. He turned to wipe them on the roller towel—whirled it for a cleaner place.

"Dirty towels! Not much of a housekeeper, would you say, ladies?"
He kicked his foot against some dirty pans under the sink.

"There's a great deal of work to be done on a farm," said Mrs. Hale stiffly.

"To be sure. And yet"—with a little bow to her—"I know there are some Dickson County farmhouses that do not have such roller towels."
He gave it a pull to expose its full length again.

"Those towels get dirty awful quick. Men's hands aren't always as clean as they might be."

"Ah, loyal to your sex, I see," he laughed. He stopped and gave her a keen look. "But you and Mrs. Wright were neighbors. I suppose you were friends, too."

Martha Hale shook her head.

"I've seen little enough of her of late years. I've not been in this house—it's more than a year."

"And why was that? You didn't like her?"

"I liked her well enough," she replied with spirit. "Farmers' wives have their hands full, Mr. Henderson. And then—" She looked around the kitchen.

"Yes?" he encouraged.

"It never seemed a very cheerful place," said she, more to herself than to him.

"No," he agreed; "I don't think anyone would call it cheerful. I shouldn't say she had the homemaking instinct."

"Well, I don't know as Wright had, either," she muttered.

"You mean they didn't get on very well?" he was quick to ask.

"No; I don't mean anything," she answered, with decision. As she turned a little away from him, she added: "But I don't think a place would be any the cheerfuler for John Wright's bein' in it."

"I'd like to talk to you about that a little later, Mrs. Hale," he said. "I'm anxious to get the lay of things upstairs now."

He moved toward the stair door, followed by the two men.

"I suppose anything Mrs. Peters does'll be all right?" the sheriff inquired. "She was to take in some clothes for her, you know—and a few little things. We left in such a hurry yesterday."

The county attorney looked at the two women whom they were leaving alone there among the kitchen things.

"Yes—Mrs. Peters," he said, his glance resting on the woman who was not Mrs. Peters, the big farmer woman who stood behind the sheriff's wife. "Of course Mrs. Peters is one of us," he said, in a manner of entrusting responsibility. "And keep your eye out, Mrs. Peters, for anything that might be of use. No telling; you women might come upon a clue to the motive—and that's the thing we need."

Mr. Hale rubbed his face after the fashion of a showman getting ready for a pleasantry.

"But would the women know a clue if they did come upon it?" he said; and, having delivered himself of this, he followed the others through the stair door.

The women stood motionless and silent, listening to the footsteps, first upon the stairs, then in the room above them.

Then, as if releasing herself from something strange, Mrs. Hale began to arrange the dirty pans under the sink, which the county attorney's disdainful push of the foot had deranged.

"I'd hate to have men coming into my kitchen," she said testily— "snoopin' round and criticizing."

"Of course it's no more than their duty," said the sheriff's wife, in her manner of timid acquiescence.

"Duty's all right," replied Mrs. Hale bluffly; "but I guess that deputy sheriff that come out to make the fire might have got a little of this on." She gave the roller towel a pull. "Wish I'd thought of that sooner! Seems mean to talk about her for not having things slicked up, when she had to come away in such a hurry."

She looked around the kitchen. Certainly it was not "slicked up." Her eye was held by a bucket of sugar on a low shelf. The cover was off the wooden bucket, and beside it was a paper bag—half full.

Mrs. Hale moved toward it.

"She was putting this in there," she said to herself—slowly.

She thought of the flour in her kitchen at home—half sifted, half not sifted. She had been interrupted, and had left things half done. What had interrupted Minnie Foster? Why had that work been left half done?

She made a move as if to finish it,—unfinished things always bothered her,—and then she glanced around and saw that Mrs. Peters was watching her—and she didn't want Mrs. Peters to get that feeling she had got of work begun and then—for some reason—not finished.

"It's a shame about her fruit," she said, and walked toward the cupboard that the county attorney had opened, and got on the chair, murmuring: "I wonder if it's all gone."

It was a sorry enough looking sight, but "Here's one that's all right," she said at last. She held it toward the light. "This is cherries, too." She looked again. "I declare I believe that's the only one."

With a sigh, she got down from the chair, went to the sink, and wiped off the bottle.

"She'll feel awful bad, after all her hard work in the hot weather. I remember the afternoon I put up my cherries last summer."

She set the bottle on the table, and, with another sigh, started to sit down in the rocker. But she did not sit down. Something kept her from sitting down in that chair. She straightened—stepped back, and, half turned away, stood looking at it, seeing the woman who had sat there "pleatin' at her apron."

The thin voice of the sheriff's wife broke in upon her: "I must be getting those things from the front room closet." She opened the door into the other room, started in, stepped back. "You coming with me, Mrs. Hale?" she asked nervously. "You—you could help me get them."

They were soon back—the stark coldness of that shut-up room was not a thing to linger in.

"My!" said Mrs. Peters, dropping the things on the table and hurrying to the stove.

Mrs. Hale stood examining the clothes the woman who was being detained in town had said she wanted.

"Wright was close!" she exclaimed, holding up a shabby black skirt that bore the marks of much making over. "I think maybe that's why she kept so much to herself. I s'pose she felt she couldn't do her part; and then, you don't enjoy things when you feel shabby. She used to wear pretty clothes and be lively—when she was Minnie Foster, one of the town girls, singing in the choir. But that—oh, that was twenty years ago."

With a carefulness in which there was something tender, she folded the shabby clothes and piled them at one corner of the table. She looked up at Mrs. Peters, and there was something in the other woman's look that irritated her.

"She don't care," she said to herself. "Much difference it makes to her whether Minnie Foster had pretty clothes when she was a girl."

Then she looked again, and she wasn't so sure; in fact, she hadn't at any time been perfectly sure about Mrs. Peters. She had that shrinking manner, and yet her eyes looked as if they could see a long way into things.

"This all you was to take in?" asked Mrs. Hale.

"No," said the sheriff's wife; "she said she wanted an apron. Funny thing to want," she ventured in her nervous little way, "for there's not much to get you dirty in jail, goodness knows. But I suppose just to make her feel more natural. If you're used to wearing an apron— She said they were in the bottom drawer of this cupboard. Yes—here they are. And then her little shawl that always hung on the stair door."

She took the small gray shawl from behind the door leading upstairs, and stood a minute looking at it.

Suddenly Mrs. Hale took a quick step toward the other woman.

"Mrs. Peters!"

"Yes, Mrs. Hale?"

"Do you think she—did it?"

A frightened look blurred the other thing in Mrs. Peters' eyes.

"Oh, I don't know," she said, in a voice that seemed to shrink away from the subject.

"Well, I don't think she did," affirmed Mrs. Hale stoutly. "Asking for an apron, and her little shawl. Worryin' about her fruit."

"Mr. Peters says—" Footsteps were heard in the room above; she stopped, looked up, then went on in a lowered voice: "Mr. Peters says—it looks bad for her. Mr. Henderson is awful sarcastic in a speech, and he's going to make fun of her saying she didn't—wake up."

For a moment Mrs. Hale had no answer. Then, "Well, I guess John Wright didn't wake up—when they was slippin' that rope under his neck," she muttered.

"No, it's *strange*," breathed Mrs. Peters. "They think it was such a—funny way to kill a man."

She began to laugh; at sound of the laugh, abruptly stopped.

"That's just what Mr. Hale said," said Mrs. Hale, in a resolutely natural voice. "There was a gun in the house. He says that's what he can't understand."

"Mr. Henderson said, coming out, that what was needed for the case was a motive. Something to show anger—or sudden feeling."

"Well, I don't see any signs of anger around here," said Mrs. Hale. "I don't—"

She stopped. It was as if her mind tripped on something. Her eye was caught by a dish towel in the middle of the kitchen table. Slowly she moved toward the table. One half of it was wiped clean, the other half messy. Her eyes made a slow, almost unwilling turn to the bucket of sugar and the half empty bag beside it. Things begun—and not finished.

After a moment she stepped back, and said, in that manner of releasing herself:

"Wonder how they're finding things upstairs? I hope she had it a little more red up up there. You know,"—she paused, and feeling gathered,— "it seems kind of *sneaking*: locking her up in town and coming out here to get her own house to turn against her!"

"But, Mrs. Hale," said the sheriff's wife, "the law is the law."

"I s'pose 'tis," answered Mrs. Hale shortly.

She turned to the stove, saying something about that fire not being much to brag of. She worked with it a minute, and when she straightened up she said aggressively:

"The law is the law—and a bad stove is a bad stove. How'd you like to cook on this?"—pointing with the poker to the broken lining. She opened the oven door and started to express her opinion of the oven; but she was swept into her own thoughts, thinking of what it would mean, year after year, to have that stove to wrestle with. The thought of Minnie Foster trying to bake in that oven—and the thought of her never going over to see Minnie Foster—

She was startled by hearing Mrs. Peters say: "A person gets discouraged—and loses heart."

The sheriff's wife had looked from the stove to the sink—to the pail of water which had been carried in from outside. The two women stood there silent, above them the footsteps of the men who were looking for evidence against the woman who had worked in that kitchen. That look of seeing into things, of seeing through a thing to something else, was in the eyes of the sheriff's wife now. When Mrs. Hale next spoke to her, it was gently:

"Better loosen up your things, Mrs. Peters. We'll not feel them when we go out."

Mrs. Peters went to the back of the room to hang up the fur tippet she was wearing. A moment later she exclaimed, "Why, she was piecing a quilt," and held up a large sewing basket piled high with quilt pieces.

Mrs. Hale spread some of the blocks out on the table.

"It's log-cabin pattern," she said, putting several of them together. "Pretty, isn't it?"

They were so engaged with the quilt that they did not hear the footsteps on the stairs. Just as the stair door opened Mrs. Hale was saying:

"Do you suppose she was going to quilt it or just knot it?"

The sheriff threw up his hands.

"They wonder whether she was going to quilt it or just knot it!"

There was a laugh for the ways of women, a warming of hands over the stove, and then the county attorney said briskly:

"Well, let's go right out to the barn and get that cleared up."

"I don't see as there's anything so strange," Mrs. Hale said resentfully, after the outside door had closed on the three men—"our taking up our time with little things while we're waiting for them to get the evidence. I don't see as it's anything to laugh about."

"Of course they've got awful important things on their minds," said the sheriff's wife apologetically.

They returned to an inspection of the blocks for the quilt. Mrs. Hale was looking at the fine, even sewing, and preoccupied with thoughts of the woman who had done that sewing, when she heard the sheriff's wife say, in a queer tone:

"Why, look at this one."

She turned to take the block held out to her.

"The sewing," said Mrs. Peters, in a troubled way. "All the rest of them have been so nice and even—but—this one. Why, it looks as if she didn't know what she was about!"

Their eyes met—something flashed to life, passed between them; then, as if with an effort, they seemed to pull away from each other. A moment Mrs. Hale sat there, her hands folded over that sewing which was so unlike all the rest of the sewing. Then she had pulled a knot and drawn the threads.

"Oh, what are you doing, Mrs. Hale?" asked the sheriff's wife, startled.

"Just pulling out a stitch or two that's not sewed very good," said Mrs. Hale mildly.

"I don't think we ought to touch things," Mrs. Peters said, a little helplessly.

"I'll just finish up this end," answered Mrs. Hale, still in that mild, matter-of-fact fashion.

She threaded a needle and started to replace bad sewing with good. For a little while she sewed in silence. Then, in that thin, timid voice, she heard:

"Mrs. Hale!"

"Yes, Mrs. Peters?"

"What do you suppose she was so—nervous about?"

"Oh, I don't know," said Mrs. Hale, as if dismissing a thing not important enough to spend much time on. "I don't know as she was—nervous. I sew awful queer sometimes when I'm just tired."

She cut a thread, and out of the corner of her eye looked up at Mrs. Peters. The small, lean face of the sheriff's wife seemed to have tightened up. Her eyes had that look of peering into something. But next moment she moved, and said in her thin, indecisive way:

"Well, I must get these clothes wrapped. They may be through sooner than we think. I wonder where I could find a piece of paper—and string."

"In that cupboard, maybe," suggested Mrs. Hale, after a glance around.

One piece of the crazy sewing remained unripped. Mrs. Peters' back turned, Martha Hale now scrutinized that piece, compared it with the dainty, accurate sewing of the other blocks. The difference was startling. Holding this block made her feel queer, as if the distracted thoughts of the woman who had perhaps turned to it to try and quiet herself were communicating themselves to her.

Mrs. Peters' voice roused her.

"Here's a birdcage," she said. "Did she have a bird, Mrs. Hale?"

"Why, I don't know whether she did or not." She turned to look at the cage Mrs. Peters was holding up. "I've not been here in so long." She sighed. "There was a man round last year selling canaries cheap—but I don't know as she took one. Maybe she did. She used to sing real pretty herself."

Mrs. Peters looked around the kitchen.

"Seems kind of funny to think of a bird here." She half laughed—an attempt to put up a barrier. "But she must have had one—or why would she have a cage? I wonder what happened to it."

"I suppose maybe the cat got it," suggested Mrs. Hale, resuming her sewing.

"No; she didn't have a cat. She's got that feeling some people have about cats—being afraid of them. When they brought her to our house yesterday, my cat got in the room, and she was real upset and asked me to take it out."

"My sister Bessie was like that," laughed Mrs. Hale.

The sheriff's wife did not reply. The silence made Mrs. Hale turn round. Mrs. Peters was examining the birdcage.

"Look at this door," she said slowly. "It's broke. One hinge has been pulled apart."

Mrs. Hale came nearer.

"Looks as if someone must have been—rough with it."

Again their eyes met—startled, questioning, apprehensive. For a moment neither spoke nor stirred. Then Mrs. Hale, turning away, said brusquely: "If they're going to find any evidence, I wish they'd be about it. I don't like this place."

"But I'm awful glad you came with me, Mrs. Hale." Mrs. Peters put the birdcage on the table and sat down. "It would be lonesome for me—sitting here alone."

"Yes, it would, wouldn't it?" agreed Mrs. Hale, a certain determined naturalness in her voice. She had picked up the sewing, but now it dropped in her lap, and she murmured in a different voice: "But I tell you what I *do* wish, Mrs. Peters. I wish I had come over sometimes when she was here. I wish—I had."

"But of course you were awful busy, Mrs. Hale. Your house—and your children."

"I could've come," retorted Mrs. Hale shortly. "I stayed away because it weren't cheerful—and that's why I ought to have come. I"—she
looked around—"I've never liked this place. Maybe because it's down
in a hollow and you don't see the road. I don't know what it is, but it's a
lonesome place, and always was. I wish I had come over to see Minnie
Foster sometimes. I can see now—" She did not put it into words.

"Well, you mustn't reproach yourself," counseled Mrs. Peters. "Somehow, we just don't see how it is with other folks till—something comes
up."

"Not having children makes less work," mused Mrs. Hale, after a
silence, "but it makes a quiet house—and Wright out to work all day—
and no company when he did come in. Did you know John Wright,
Mrs. Peters?"

"Not to know him. I've seen him in town. They say he was a good
man."

"Yes—good," conceded John Wright's neighbor grimly. "He didn't
drink, and kept his word as well as most, I guess, and paid his debts. But
he was a hard man, Mrs. Peters. Just to pass the time of day with him—"
She stopped, shivered a little. "Like a raw wind that gets to the bone."
Her eye fell upon the cage on the table before her, and she added, almost
bitterly: "I should think she would've wanted a bird!"

Suddenly she leaned forward, looking intently at the cage. "But what
do you s'pose went wrong with it?"

"I don't know," returned Mrs. Peters; "unless it got sick and died."

But after she said it she reached over and swung the broken door.
Both women watched it as if somehow held by it.

"You didn't know—her?" Mrs. Hale asked, a gentler note in her
voice.

"Not till they brought her yesterday," said the sheriff's wife.

"She—come to think of it, she was kind of like a bird herself. Real sweet
and pretty, but kind of timid and—fluttery. How—she—did—change."

That held her for a long time. Finally, as if struck with a happy thought
and relieved to get back to everyday things, she exclaimed:

"Tell you what, Mrs. Peters, why don't you take the quilt in with you?
It might take up her mind."

"Why, I think that's a real nice idea, Mrs. Hale," agreed the sheriff's wife, as if she too were glad to come into the atmosphere of a simple kindness. "There couldn't possibly be any objection to that, could there? Now, just what will I take? I wonder if her patches are in here—and her things."

They turned to the sewing basket.

"Here's some red," said Mrs. Hale, bringing out a roll of cloth. Underneath that was a box. "Here, maybe her scissors are in here—and her things." She held it up. "What a pretty box! I'll warrant that was something she had a long time ago—when she was a girl."

She held it in her hand a moment; then, with a little sigh, opened it.

Instantly her hand went to her nose.

"Why—!"

Mrs. Peters drew nearer—then turned away.

"There's something wrapped up in this piece of silk," faltered Mrs. Hale.

"This isn't her scissors," said Mrs. Peters, in a shrinking voice.

Her hand not steady, Mrs. Hale raised the piece of silk. "Oh, Mrs. Peters!" she cried. "It's—"

Mrs. Peters bent closer.

"It's the bird," she whispered.

"But, Mrs. Peters!" cried Mrs. Hale. "*Look* at it! Its *neck*—look at its neck! It's all—other side *to*."

She held the box away from her.

The sheriff's wife again bent closer.

"Somebody wrung its neck," said she, in a voice that was slow and deep.

And then again the eyes of the two women met—this time clung together in a look of dawning comprehension, of growing horror. Mrs. Peters looked from the dead bird to the broken door of the cage. Again their eyes met. And just then there was a sound at the outside door.

Mrs. Hale slipped the box under the quilt pieces in the basket, and sank into the chair before it. Mrs. Peters stood holding to the table. The county attorney and the sheriff came in from outside.

"Well, ladies," said the county attorney, as one turning from serious things to little pleasantries, "have you decided whether she was going to quilt it or knot it?"

"We think," began the sheriff's wife in a flurried voice, "that she was going to—knot it."

He was too preoccupied to notice the change that came in her voice on that last.

"Well, that's very interesting, I'm sure," he said tolerantly. He caught sight of the birdcage. "Has the bird flown?"

"We think the cat got it," said Mrs. Hale in a voice curiously even.

He was walking up and down, as if thinking something out.

"Is there a cat?" he asked absently.

Mrs. Hale shot a look up at the sheriff's wife.

"Well, not *now*," said Mrs. Peters. "They're superstitious, you know; they leave."

She sank into her chair.

The county attorney did not heed her.

"No sign at all of anyone having come in from the outside," he said to Peters, in the manner of continuing an interrupted conversation. "Their own rope. Now let's go upstairs again and go over it, piece by piece. It would have to have been someone who knew just the—"

The stair door closed behind them and their voices were lost.

The two women sat motionless, not looking at each other, but as if peering into something and at the same time holding back. When they spoke now it was as if they were afraid of what they were saying, but as if they could not help saying it.

"She liked the bird," said Martha Hale, low and slowly. "She was going to bury it in that pretty box."

"When I was a girl," said Mrs. Peters, under her breath, "my kitten— there was a boy took a hatchet, and before my eyes—before I could get there—" She covered her face an instant. "If they hadn't held me back I would have"—she caught herself, looked upstairs where footsteps were heard, and finished weakly—"hurt him."

Then they sat without speaking or moving.

"I wonder how it would seem," Mrs. Hale at last began, as if feeling her way over strange ground—"never to have had any children around." Her eyes made a slow sweep of the kitchen, as if seeing what that kitchen had meant through all the years. "No, Wright wouldn't like the bird," she said after that—"a thing that sang. She used to sing. He killed that too." Her voice tightened.

Mrs. Peters moved uneasily.

"Of course we don't know who killed the bird."

"I knew John Wright," was Mrs. Hale's answer.

"It was an awful thing was done in this house that night, Mrs. Hale," said the sheriff's wife. "Killing a man while he slept—slipping a thing round his neck that choked the life out of him."

Mrs. Hale's hand went out to the birdcage.

"His neck. Choked the life out of him."

"We don't *know* who killed him," whispered Mrs. Peters wildly. "We don't *know*."

Mrs. Hale had not moved. "If there had been years and years of—nothing, then a bird to sing to you, it would be awful—still—after the bird was still."

It was as if something within her not herself had spoken, and it found in Mrs. Peters something she did not know as herself.

"I know what stillness is," she said, in a queer, monotonous voice. "When we homesteaded in Dakota, and my first baby died—after he was two years old—and me with no other then—"

Mrs. Hale stirred.

"How soon do you suppose they'll be through looking for the evidence?"

"I know what stillness is," repeated Mrs. Peters, in just that same way. Then she too pulled back. "The law has got to punish crime, Mrs. Hale," she said in her tight little way.

"I wish you'd seen Minnie Foster," was the answer, "when she wore a white dress with blue ribbons, and stood up there in the choir and sang."

The picture of that girl, the fact that she had lived neighbor to that girl for twenty years, and had let her die for lack of life, was suddenly more than she could bear.

"Oh, I *wish* I'd come over here once in a while!" she cried. "That was a crime! That was a crime! Who's going to punish that?"

"We mustn't take on," said Mrs. Peters, with a frightened look toward the stairs.

"I might 'a' *known* she needed help! I tell you, it's *queer*, Mrs. Peters. We live close together, and we live far apart. We all go through the same things—it's all just a different kind of the same thing! If it weren't—why do you and I *understand?* Why do we *know*—what we know this minute?"

She dashed her hand across her eyes. Then, seeing the jar of fruit on the table, she reached for it and choked out:

"If I was you I wouldn't *tell* her her fruit was gone! Tell her it *ain't.* Tell her it's all right—all of it. Here—take this in to prove it to her! She—she may never know whether it was broke or not."

She turned away.

Mrs. Peters reached out for the bottle of fruit as if she were glad to take it—as if touching a familiar thing, having something to do, could keep her from something else. She got up, looked about for something to wrap the fruit in, took a petticoat from the pile of clothes she had brought from the front room, and nervously started winding that round the bottle.

"My!" she began, in a high, false voice, "it's a good thing the men couldn't hear us! Getting all stirred up over a little thing like a—dead canary." She hurried over that. "As if that could have anything to do with—with— My, wouldn't they *laugh?*"

Footsteps were heard on the stairs.

"Maybe they would," muttered Mrs. Hale—"maybe they wouldn't."

"No, Peters," said the county attorney incisively; "it's all perfectly clear, except the reason for doing it. But you know juries when it comes to women. If there was some definite thing—something to show. Something to make a story about. A thing that would connect up with this clumsy way of doing it."

In a covert way Mrs. Hale looked at Mrs. Peters. Mrs. Peters was looking at her. Quickly they looked away from each other. The outer door opened and Mr. Hale came in.

"I've got the team round now," he said. "Pretty cold out there."

"I'm going to stay here awhile by myself," the county attorney suddenly announced. "You can send Frank out for me, can't you?" he asked the sheriff. "I want to go over everything. I'm not satisfied we can't do better."

Again, for one brief moment, the two women's eyes found one another. The sheriff came up to the table.

"Did you want to see what Mrs. Peters was going to take in?"

The county attorney picked up the apron. He laughed.

"Oh, I guess they're not very dangerous things the ladies have picked out."

Mrs. Hale's hand was on the sewing basket in which the box was concealed. She felt that she ought to take her hand off the basket. She did not seem able to. He picked up one of the quilt blocks which she had piled on to cover the box. Her eyes felt like fire. She had a feeling that if he took up the basket she would snatch it from him.

But he did not take it up. With another little laugh, he turned away, saying:

"No; Mrs. Peters doesn't need supervising. For that matter, a sheriff's wife is married to the law. Ever think of it that way, Mrs. Peters?"

Mrs. Peters was standing beside the table. Mrs. Hale shot a look up at her; but she could not see her face. Mrs. Peters had turned her face away. When she spoke, her voice was muffled.

"Not—just that way," she said.

"Married to the law!" chuckled Mrs. Peters' husband. He moved toward the door into the front room, and said to the county attorney:

"I just want you to come in here a minute, George. We ought to take a look at these windows."

"Oh—windows," said the county attorney scoffingly.

"We'll be right out, Mr. Hale," said the sheriff to the farmer, who was still waiting by the door.

Hale went to look after the horses. The sheriff followed the county attorney into the other room. Again—for one final moment—the two women were alone in that kitchen.

Martha Hale sprang up, her hands tight together, looking at that other woman, with whom it rested. At first she could not see her eyes, for the sheriff's wife had not turned back since she turned away at that suggestion of being married to the law. But now Mrs. Hale made her turn back. Her eyes made her turn back. Slowly, unwillingly, Mrs. Peters turned her head until her eyes met the eyes of the other woman. There was a moment when they held each other in a steady, burning look in which there was no evasion nor flinching. Then Martha Hale's eyes pointed the way to the basket in which was hidden the thing that would make certain the conviction of the other woman—that woman who was not there and yet who had been there with them all through that hour.

For a moment Mrs. Peters did not move. And then she did it. With a rush forward, she threw back the quilt pieces, got the box, tried to put it in her handbag. It was too big. Desperately she opened it, started to take the bird out. But there she broke—she could not touch the bird. She stood there helpless, foolish.

There was the sound of a knob turning in the inner door. Martha Hale snatched the box from the sheriff's wife, and got it in the pocket of her big coat just as the sheriff and the county attorney came back into the kitchen.

"Well, Henry," said the county attorney facetiously, "at least we found out that she was not going to quilt it. She was going to—what is it you call it, ladies?"

Mrs. Hale's hand was against the pocket of her coat.

"Knot it," was her low reply.

He did not see her eyes.[1]

Originally published by Associated Sunday Magazines, Inc., as a syndicated supplement in Sunday newspapers, here from the *Sunday Star Magazine, Washington Star*, March 4, 1917, 4–13

NOTES

1. When "A Jury of Her Peers" was included in *The Best Short Stories of 1917* (O'Brien, 256–82), the final sentence in the original published story was deleted, and the previous line slightly modified, so that the story ended with Mrs. Hale's statement: "We call it—knot it, Mr. Henderson." As changed, the final line of the story was the same as the final line of the one-act play *Trifles*, which Glaspell had written the year before she published "A Jury of Her Peers." The many anthologies that have included "A Jury of Her Peers" have reprinted the ending as it was later altered rather than as it is here, taken from its first appearance in the Sunday supplement published by Associated Sunday Magazines.

A Matter of Gesture

THERE ISN'T ONE OF MY REVOLUTIONARY friends who is not satisfied with his own conclusions about Harry Ruhl. Perhaps the reason my ideas about it haven't counted for more with them is that I haven't had anything as well-defined as conclusions. Indeed, I have scarcely had ideas—only gropings. I have given up trying to modify their feeling by mine, not only because of the difficulty in meeting the sure with the uncertain, but because it is perhaps kinder to Ruhl just to let it all go—and he went through enough, heaven knows. For almost two years he was forced to live face to face with himself, and with himself alone—and for a pretender that must be the ordeal that immeasurably passes strength. Only people who are real are spiritually equal to prison, it seems to me. All my other feeling about Ruhl—and it has been a pretty varied feeling —would be submerged in pity with the thought of his having to live alone with himself those days and nights, and with himself, as he came to be, stripped of his last tatter of romance.

But this story has to do with that stripping, so I mustn't get ahead of myself or the storytelling members of our group would not approve of me. I'm writing about Ruhl to see if I can't make my feeling clearer to myself than I ever succeeded in making it to anyone else. Though doubtless the impulse to try to set down the truth wouldn't have come if Bert Stephens had not produced a blaring story of Ruhl under the caption, "Remorse."

It was my brother Mark who disturbed our summer with Ruhl. I knew that Mark was up to something when he came and sat on the sands with me and the children that June morning. He had an intimate, melancholy manner that made me sniff trouble. Mark is never so tenderly sad as when about to sacrifice me to "the cause."

I was not in burnt-offering mood that morning, so I put on a hard shell of sprightliness and whenever that appealing note in Mark's voice as he spoke of the seagulls perching out there on the wire posts threatened me I thought of my ruined rugs and closed in again. Mark is a friend of revolution. Well, so am I—but they really were singularly beautiful rugs. You remember the unemployed demonstrations in New York two or three years ago? Mark was in the thick of that and the unemployed overran our house—and that in particularly slushy weather.[1] And when I complained about it, "Rugs!" cried Mark, "when they haven't *beds?*" I had come with a grievance and turned away with a feeling of unworth. Mark is himself so real and simple and passionate that he can do those things to me.

But that summer—the summer following the unemployed turmoil—I wanted a little surcease from the sorrow and strenuousness of others. We were at Cape's End, the place I love best in the world, the isolated little town by the sea where we live simply among a group of pleasant people—in the main writer and artist folk. The distressing things of the world seemed a long way off. Happy, lazy days stretched before us. I said something of the sort, whereupon Mark said that he had that morning had a letter from Harry Ruhl.

Hope sank in my heart. For at once I knew that Mark was going to propose Ruhl for the summer, and equally well did I know that I was going to agree to the intrusion.

It was just at the time that Ruhl was waiting to enter prison. Just that—waiting to enter prison. Free at the moment, out in the world, but waiting to enter prison in the fall—as one might be waiting to enter university. Can't you see how I resented the clutch there was in it?—the way Ruhl's situation forced Ruhl upon me? And what finished me was that Ruhl did not at all appear, in his letter to Mark, to be proposing himself or pointing out the pathos of his situation. He wrote in reply to a letter from Mark, saying that after all he would not be with the Hudsons at their Long Island cottage, as Mrs. Hudson was going to have a baby soon, and was not well, so that they all felt it would be too hard for her to have him there—with all his presence might keep before her. For the moment he was sharing a little apartment with Gorden Willcox, who had taken him in. Gorden was himself hard up, however, and might have to let the apartment go. But something else would turn up, he hoped. He was trying all the time to get work, but there had been too much written about his case. Nobody wanted to get mixed up with him. He closed with an appreciative word about all Mark had done for him, thanking him again for having made it possible to appeal the case.

I did not need Mark's reviewing of the Ruhl case to make me know I had to have Ruhl. But I listened to it, willing the thing should gain the proportions of inevitability, thus relieving me of the responsibility of my own surrender. Ruhl had swung into our ken at the time of a great mill-workers' strike in a nearby state. Mark and the rest of the so-called intellectuals of the labor movement were immersed in this strike.[2] And one night, after it had gone on for weeks and it seemed the workers were right up to the edge of defeat, this Harry Ruhl, almost a stranger, rose at a meeting and told the strikers that if they couldn't win by peaceful means they'd have to win any way they could. He "advocated violence," was arrested, tried, and sentenced to from two to seven years in the penitentiary. Not even Mark had any hope of his winning on this last appeal.

But Ruhl, out on bail which Mark had provided, was waiting through the summer. When, later in the day, my husband said that if I really didn't want the fellow around I should have had the firmness to say so, I wept with rage—rage that he couldn't *see* it. Harassed while he was yet free!—nothing to do with his precious little while of liberty—and me living in a rambling old house on the sea! Oh, well, Arthur is a sculptor, and absorbed in his work, so I mustn't revive my rage by dwelling on this. He's an artist—and sees what he cares to see.

Now it happened that I had never seen Ruhl, and while Mark had told me he did not suggest violence I was unprepared for the mild-looking young fellow who diffidently sat with us at luncheon that first day. The first strong feeling I had about Ruhl was one of indignation— when I looked at him, slim, boyish, shy, and thought of the judge who had sentenced him to the penitentiary for a possible seven years.

You can anticipate what happened. Mark had told me that I would not have to bother with Harry—he would look after him himself, but Mark was unable to relieve me of my own intense interest in Ruhl. I would try to check myself with the admonition that it was indelicate, that it was not nice feeling—this avid wondering what another person, and he under my roof, was feeling; but you see entertaining a man who was waiting to enter the penitentiary was scarcely an ordinary situation. And of course Ruhl himself did not know how my mind was misbehaving.

In fact, it early became apparent that Harry liked being with me better than with Mark and the little group of people then at Cape's End who were in one way or another identified with the movement, or perhaps I should say the feeling, to which Ruhl had sacrificed himself. Because of Mark our house was the center for those people—conspicuous among them the editor of a revolutionary monthly of satirical character[3]—and in their discussions there would usually be a moment when Ruhl would flame, as if that which in them was an intellectual interest, at best a strong social feeling, was in him a passion which took flame. They always fell back a little before him, and after his outburst Ruhl would usually get up and walk out of the room, leaving the impression of his feeling being too much for him. I can see him now as I have many times seen him after quitting the group on the porch or before the fire and alone walking rapidly along the beach, sometimes going quite from sight and not appearing again for several hours. Of course he never did that without leaving us wondering about it, speculating, interested in what his mood would be when he returned.

But as I was about to say, Ruhl spent much of his time with me and the children. He fell into the way of leaving what we called the storm center—the discussions of Mark and his friends, and coming down to the sands and there gathering shells and building houses with us. That was not difficult to understand; it was escape, of course. He had never been by the sea before; he learned to swim, to sail a boat. He had been thin and pale when he came; in the first month he filled out and browned. The way Ruhl threw himself into our play, his zest for it, somehow moved me more than anything else about him. Though there were always coming those times of breaking; he would be sailing and after an exhilarating hour would turn away as if suddenly stricken, motioning some of us to take the tiller—to be sailing the open sea and see one's self in a cell!

I tried in what I thought adroit and not unkind ways to get Ruhl to talking about himself, but as I afterwards put it, he had a strong instinct for keeping himself a mystery. I learned more than the others knew, but most of the things Ruhl told me came indirectly, not as confidences but in the off-guard conversation of people who play around together. He came from the Middle West, went to a little college out there no one had ever heard of—one of those obscure sectarian schools. I know them, for my husband comes from the Middle West and we spent two years in his hometown. And I don't think I could see Ruhl as well as I feel I do see him if there had not been one of those schools in that town. Bored to death, I took a notion. I would study Greek, and so for an hour each day I went to that tight, arid little school.

I think Ruhl was a little surprised by my interest when he laughingly told me one day that he had won the "state oratorical contest." He would have been more than a little surprised had he known of the times I thought of him in relation to that state oratorical contest. Ruhl was first a student and then, without having studied anywhere else—that I gleaned out of another conversation—a teacher at this school. He "got in bad" for saying Longfellow was not a great poet—the subject, you may remember, had agitated less inconspicuous institutions at a somewhat earlier time.[4] Ruhl was finally let out for his anti-Longfellow attitude, the trustees feeling that a blow had been struck at reverence.

There was a man in the town who had a general sympathy with dissenters—(this I got at still another time, and from another angle—it was remarkable the instinct Ruhl had against letting his life throw light upon him)—and this man got him a position with a relative of his in New York who published an encyclopedia—of a sort. Harry "made copy"—routine, tedious work. He went about to the various radical meetings the papers informed him of—was he not himself a rebel?—came to know a few people, got interested in the big strike. One night when speakers were needed at a meeting Ruhl volunteered, and astonished them all with what they called his passion. He began figuring in the papers as one of the strike leaders and lost his position with the makers of encyclopedias—thereby growing more important as strike leader, of course. There began the talk about holding Ruhl back—men of importance in the movement talked to him about not going too far; he was written up in one of their papers as "a revolutionist with passion." And then the strike situation grew more desperate, and one night Ruhl, in what Mark called a high passion for self-destruction, made the speech which led to his arrest.

There were times when he could make his face look like a poet's. But there—I shouldn't have said that at this time for it was only later I came to think of it so, and I'll be spoiling my story if I have no "surprise" at the end. Bert Stephens, who gets large prices for his stories, says there must always be a surprise.[5] It was Bert Stephens himself who gave Ruhl the second title—successor to "revolutionist with passion." One night Mark and Harry were disagreeing in an argument whereupon Bert, in his manner of knowing what the rest of us couldn't know, said quietly: "There's no use going on, Mark. You see you are a propagandist, while Ruhl is a poet."

Harry gave him a startled glance, then a disdainful little laugh and turned from us and stared moodily into the fire. When I looked at him a few moments later I saw that he had attained the poet look.

That last sounds so unfeeling that there seems nothing to do but give away my hand—tell why I am writing this story, what it is about. What interests me is not the startling and tragic story itself, but the inquiry into what Ruhl really was. Was he ever sincere?—was he ever real? These were questions often and bitterly put after he had, as one might say, betrayed the faith. The rest of them arrived at conclusions which satisfied them and so could put Ruhl out of their minds—trying to forget that he had ever been. But I think I saw a little further into it, and so I never was as sure as the others. Anyhow, what is sincerity? For my part I don't know how far anyone is sincere and how far he is taking the part of the person he wants to appear to be.

For the rest of the summer Ruhl played the part of the poet. But he had something to work with—there was something of the poet in him. What I don't know is how much was the poet in him and how much the desire to appear the poet. And I wonder, too, if playing the role of poet at all developed the poet. Those are interesting things to think about.

You will understand I don't mean that Harry wrote poetry. It was his quality, his attitude, his feeling. He would frequently say things disclosing that sensitiveness to beauty, to life, which we call the feeling of the poet. Then other things sounded as if thought out for the state oratorical contest, and still others left me wondering whether they were false or true—and I suspect they were something of both.

But here was the thing that began coming home to me too hard: that he should have to go back and pay the price for having been the revolutionist with passion after he had left that and become the poet. For he had left it. His outbursts grew less frequent, less convincing. I could see that he tried to avoid the situations that might expect them from him, could see that they were painful to him. The others thought it was because of what he was facing, and of course there was that in it, too—particularly as he was facing a penalty for a thing he no longer wanted to be. And among those complex things was a simpler and more appealing thing—a summer out of doors and the thought of prison in the fall.

There were times when I was so sorry for him I didn't care whether he was real or not. He grew afraid—his eyes were the eyes of one who is afraid; sometimes he would get up and run away from us as if driven, again he clung to us as if afraid to be left alone.

He took to leaving his door open at night. One night I heard him moving around and got up and his face just wrung my heart—fear was there, stark and distorting. And, God knows, real. And yet I'm certain there were times when he dramatized fear. I'm sure of it, and yet I'd rather not go into that—it seems too unkind to try to fix the line of reality there.

One fresh sunny September day Harry and I were down on the beach with the children. They—my little girl and boy and some of their playmates—were out on the flats digging for clams. We had brought out a volume of Yeats, and Harry had been reading to me, his voice lingering appreciatively on the magical words. He had just read the poem beginning, "Who dreamed that beauty passes like a dream?" and had fallen silent and lay there upon the sands, his back to me. I heard someone coming, and looking around I saw Mark. He had a telegram in his hand. I looked at the boy who had been reading "Who dreamed that beauty passes like a dream?" and even before I clearly saw Mark's face I knew, as we do know those things, that harm was coming to him.

It was a telegram sent to Mark by Ruhl's lawyer. The decision of the lower court was affirmed. The attorney said that Mark must bring Ruhl to town at once. The news was faintly palliated with talk of the progress of the movement for a pardon.

I shall remember always Mark's face as he told Harry. Ruhl himself simply looked sick—just totally incapacitated. I remember that we left the volume of poems lying out there on the sands. Somebody found it and brought it home later in the day—after Harry had gone.

They left on the afternoon train. There wasn't much eaten at luncheon that day—not by any of us. Ruhl got up and left the table before we had finished. He didn't bid us good-bye, and as I watched him walking down the road with Mark he looked so unable to go that I had an impulse to run after them and tell Mark he was to tell those people waiting for Harry that he was not able to come. And then I remembered who they were, what it meant, and that he would have to go whether able to or not. And there was one thing I can't bear to think of even yet. As they were about to go down one of the side streets, Ruhl turned and looked at the sea he was leaving behind.

It had developed that even outside labor circles there was a widespread feeling that Ruhl was being too severely dealt with; and they all think that a movement to let him off under certain conditions would have gone through had another strike not broken out just the week before. As it was, Harry entered the penitentiary five days after he read Yeats to me on the sands at Cape's End.

Mark looked as if he had been in prison himself when he came back. I never heard much about just what went on, for it was so hard for Mark to talk about it. He was with Harry as long as anyone could be with him. He said it was pretty bad, and that's all I could get out of him then; what he said afterwards was so full of bitterness that I don't feel I can give any clear picture of how Ruhl went through those days.

We had a beautiful fall. I sailed a great deal, and when the spray dashed around me and the wind beat upon my face I looked about me at the open sea and thought of my sailing companion of the summer. I did little speculating on Ruhl's sincerity those days; pity was too all-encompassing, and when there crept in the wondering how he got along with no one to pretend to, I wasn't considering it critically but only pitying him the deeper for his utter destitution.

In November came the blow—I'm thinking of Mark when I put it that way. We were still at Cape's End—I love the fall and early winter there, and Mark and a few of his friends had come up for the Thanksgiving holiday. It was I who opened the paper that day and in astonishment read out the heading, "Harry Ruhl Recants." An instant later they were all looking over my shoulder. Then they fell back and listened, speechless, to what I read.

I will say for them—I have many times charged them with hardness—that a more sickening recantation was never put upon paper. It was given out by Ruhl to the maker of encyclopedias in the form of a plea to the governor. He said he was sorry, said he had never really believed what he said, but had been unduly influenced by people who misrepresented to him and worked upon his sympathies. He said he could see now that agitation was wrong, that only through law-abiding methods could any good come. He affirmed his belief in all the virtues of the established order, spoke with pious horror of rebellion. Never have I known such complete and really loathsome crawling.

If you've never known Mark and his sort you may find it hard to get any idea of what this meant to them. If you don't get it, I don't believe I can say anything to bring it to you. Though they turned against Ruhl so bitterly as to rouse in me an instinct to stay by him I don't think I fail to understand their feeling, the blow it was to them. We sat before the fireplace until very late that night, and hard things were said against the man who had once sat there with us. You see, he hadn't really been one of them; he had come among them, played his spectacular part—then this. And it wasn't personal, their feeling of a wrong done was not the feeling of a wrong done them personally, but resentment and grief that what they looked upon as the most important thing in the world—what they called the fight of the workers for their own—should be repudiated by one conspicuously identified with it. And of course there was resentment because of what it would be taken to indicate of the caliber of the fighters. Naturally they felt that Ruhl had no business to go in with them if he couldn't see it through; in making that speech he had done what they never wanted him to do, had urged him not to do—and then the whole big thing was left to suffer for his spectacular moment. They said now that he never had been real, that he had done the whole thing just to show off—to bring himself to the front.

I couldn't sleep after I went upstairs that night, and so I threw on my big cape and went out on the porch that almost overhangs the sea. I had more than once heard Ruhl out on that porch nights when he could not sleep. And as the tide beat in I stood there and tried to satisfy myself of the truth about Ruhl.

My mind went back to that arid little school he came from. In quality he was not unlike that school. True, he had protested there, and yet I venture to say it was arid protest. Ruhl was not one who was refreshed from within. There was in him no quenchless spring, as in my brother Mark. This early protest, having to pay a price for it, made him see himself as much larger than he was. He had some imagination, but it chiefly turned upon himself as a romantic figure. He was simply not proportioned for large things. He did not have the structure for sustained feeling, as some of those friends of Mark's have.

And yet what I brought out of my attempt to see was a new and tremendous pity. Poor Ruhl—he was in a bad fix. There was something in him which the rest of him couldn't back up. It was not true that he did the whole thing just to show off. I am convinced that it was not as simple as that, for there were flashes of feeling in the arid places of his soul. And yet they were not of his fiber, and so what it came to was that they simply made him craven.

Yes, what I brought out of it was a new and tremendous pity. Only the strong of soul should have to be in prison; it came to seem to me that there was something utterly intolerable in keeping a weakling there—as unbearable to think of as the idea of driving a sick horse, as expecting a woman in labor to go about and get a meal. There is something not to be borne in that idea of exacting of living things that which is immeasurably beyond their strength. As I saw it then, Ruhl should be let out of prison simply because his spirit wasn't equal to the ordeal. The authorities would laugh at that as the most sentimental of bosh, but the more I think of it the surer I am that it is rock-bed truth.

I went in and read over the recantation. I knew Ruhl had utterly lost hold on himself or he never would have written it. For what was there left for him after this? How could he ever again play the part of the strong, the noble, the brave, the passionate? He had given up the revolutionist with passion, he had given up the poet. There was something utterly small in the thing. It hadn't a vestige of dignity. It was a whimper. If he had not gone to pieces he never would have done it that way. He would have sought for a high sorrowfulness, for something noble in recantation. He would, had he had any hold on himself, have tried to appear standing on new and higher ground—as one speaking with new vision he would have attempted to write had fear not wrecked him. And it seemed to me then that there was something to be said for pretense. Better let a man try to appear fine than cage him until he becomes the smallest and most whimpering thing it is in him to be. Oh, no—it isn't right. There are people too weak to be kept in prison. We haven't the right to reduce a fellow being to the state of mind that produced Ruhl's recantation.

And the cruel thing about it was that it disgusted the very people it was meant to move. Why, nobody wants to take a man in by such a door as *that*. Everybody hates a man who crawls—no matter what he's crawling away from. "If that's what you are, we don't want you, either," must have been the feeling, for there was no move from anyone to put through Ruhl's pardon.

In a distracted effort to get out he had surrendered all chance for appearing what he wished to appear—and then he was kept there for as long a time as he would have been kept anyhow. Desperation let him expose himself—by all odds the most desperate, the most humiliating thing Ruhl could do—and the exposure availed him nothing. He had to stay in prison, knowing that he had lost his chance—his chance to come out a hero, the chance to come out and make us feel he was one greater in soul for having been there. I used to try not to think of Ruhl—just as we try to put from us the picture of some torturing thing we have seen.

He got out just as he would have if he had not gone down on his knees and whimpered—no sooner, in no other way. In a little less than two years a new governor went in—a man whom our family knew well. It was Mark who went to him in Ruhl's behalf. Mark had said he would never do it. But when his chance came he did. He said that he had a certain feeling for his fellow creatures—for even those who happened to be worms. Of course what he was not able to rid himself of was a sense of responsibility. He knew it was his personality that had attracted Ruhl, that the desire to appear notable before him had led him to fling off caution in the way he did. So he got Ruhl out after a two-year imprisonment.

I thought of what that coming out would have been if only Ruhl had held his place. How they would have gathered around him—what a place they would have given him! It was too hard, too bitterly hard—to have gone through it all and to have come out of it with nothing. When Mark came back I asked him how Ruhl seemed. "He seems just what he is," he replied, "a crawling worm. You can see in his eyes that he is a sneak and a coward and a fake. We gave him a little money to tide him over till he can get work somewhere. We're through with him—and the best thing we can all do is simply to forget him."

But I couldn't; I couldn't forget him because I wasn't through with him. My mind wasn't through with him. My pity wasn't through with him. The thought of him being left to himself, stripped to the smallest thing he was, haunted me until one day I astounded Mark by suggesting we ask Ruhl to come and stay with us a while.

We had it out that night. Mark hotly gave all the reasons why we need not do anything of the kind—why the idea was preposterous. I gave my feeling—that we couldn't leave Ruhl like that, that after he had tried to be something before us we couldn't leave him reduced to sneak and coward and fake, that we had got to help him get something he could live up to. The passion with which Mark combated it made me know he felt there was something in it. He said that if Ruhl had a spark of decent feeling in him he wouldn't want to come to us. I admitted that unless he was pretty desperate he wouldn't do it and proposed that we ask him on the theory that if he was so badly off that he would come he was in too bad a way not to take in.

He came. He was there for four weeks. Then he left us. We did our best, but I can see the truth now—we gave him no place. We gave him a nice room looking out to sea, he had his place at the table, on the porch, on the beach, in the boat. But we gave him no place. We were kind to him; we did not take him in. The idea had been to let him become something again—something he could play up to. But we were not able to play the game. We never let him feel that we believed in his gesture.

His gesture—for that was what it was all through. He was one given to spiritual gesture. That speech was a gesture; himself as poet was a gesture; he tried to gesture now, but he was just all clogged up with resentment. Resentment was the thing Ruhl brought out of prison—blurring, infecund resentment. He was jaundiced with it—with resentment at having to go through what he did and then not being able to create the illusion of being greatened by it; resentment at having paid a tremendous price—and got nothing, at having lost a tremendous chance. And perhaps he would have brought out of it something significant, something real, but for that very resentment at not being able to appear to have done so. What he had done blocked him in every way—as pretender, as to what he really was, or might have become. I mean to say that prison might have really done something for Ruhl but for Ruhl's own chafing at having got in his own way. That absorbed him; it simply ate him up.

From any side you look at it it's a pretty sorry thing. The very thing that might have made him something real, as this complete loss, this reduction to himself, might have done, only made him less, because all it did was to seal him in with resentment. You had only to be with him to know that Ruhl had actually grown smaller through losing his chance to appear big. He would try to pretend now, but it was no good, and he knew it was no good. He gave no sense of large things. What he would have appear tragic brooding never seemed anything greater than nursing a grievance. His poor efforts to appear separated from us by a tremendous spiritual experience gave the sense of nothing more than sullenness. It was plain that he hated us for not being swayed by him. There was something fawning about him—prison had done that to him—and yet there was a bravado like contemptuousness, as if he would persuade himself that he cared little for people as incapable of "getting him" as we. Mark would try to talk to him, but it was so plainly an effort. Two of Mark's friends came—the editor I spoke of before and another labor leader who had been with us the summer before Ruhl went to prison. They were not unkind to Ruhl, but they did not treat him as an equal.

And I suppose I was like that, too, hard though I tried. I tried to lure him back to the poet, thinking there might be healing there, but somehow the whimpering note of that recantation was between me and the soul of beauty I tried to make him think he had. He felt it and resented it. I think he resented me the most of all. I wish I had done what I once had the impulse to do. I wanted to say, "Take a brace. What have you done, after all? You couldn't stand prison. You went to pieces. Well, you're out now; forget that; take from it what you really got from it—there must be something—and let the rest go. You broke—that's all—but now go on."

Some of us should have said that certainly, but the trouble was we couldn't have believed in it while we said it. It wasn't as simple as that. It wasn't what Ruhl did we despised him for. It was the light it threw on everything he had done. What it comes to is that we despised him for not being what he had tried to make us think he was. And of course that's unfair, for if we could put up with the small thing he really was we were wrong in hating him for not being something he wasn't. Oh, yes, I think there's a good deal to blame ourselves for.

And then one day we received an advance copy of a book written by a man we knew who had spent eight years in prison. It is a terrible and a wonderful book—a stark, truth-telling book, but the story of a spiritual triumph. So great was our emotion that we talked about it before Ruhl, and what must have humiliated him past all control was that we just forgot all about him, as if this were a thing with which he had nothing to do. Stung beyond endurance he jumped up and broke forth at us.

"What do *you* know about it?" he sneered.

We were startled, and just at first he held us and thrilled us. But it wasn't a gesture, it was a convulsion. He kept repeating, "You don't know anything about it!"—impotently, emptily, blubberingly repeating it until it grew so pitiable that I, unable to endure the humiliating exposure, got up and left the room. It was instinctive—instinctive kindness, but I think it was the thing that led to Ruhl's last gesture. He *had* to get us—had to get us some way. And more than that, he had to get himself—had to get himself some way. After the pitiful failure of his outburst he rushed from the house and he did not come back. The afternoon wore away and we began to wonder about him. I must say for ourselves that until we began to worry we did not speak of what had happened. For you see it was the sort of thing one doesn't speak of—not right away, anyhow; as one would not if a man tried to show his prowess in some way—lifting, jumping, and could not do it and finally stood there crying about it.

But when Ruhl was not there at dinnertime we began to talk about him. That evening we went walking in different directions, looking for him. I grew so nervous that I had to go back home. There is something too poignantly gruesome in looking for someone you are anxious about. After a little while of it you get afraid to look.

Bedtime came and Ruhl was not back. I said I couldn't go to bed. Mark tried to reason with me. Ruhl was just being spectacular again, he said; he'd wandered off on the dunes by himself and would come back sometime in the night. It would be absurd for us to sit up waiting for him. I spoke of how he must be feeling, but he simply refused to consider anything about Ruhl important. I said I would go to bed, but I didn't. I sat up listening to hear him returning. That is a fearful thing, too—sitting through hours growing ever later, waiting for the footstep of one you are becoming more and more concerned about. The night is so strange under circumstances like that. The world becomes unreal, yourself unreal, detached from common things.

At daybreak I woke Mark, and I was by that time in such a state that my feeling communicated itself to him. I told him that something must be done—an alarm given, a search made. He said he would go with me over to the lifesaving station on the other side of the cape, the "outside," we called it. The lifesavers patrolled the beach—they might have seen something of Ruhl.

Mark would try to say commonplace things as we walked across the dunes. But it is hard to be commonplace when crossing outside the dunes at dawn, on your way over to the outside sea, looking for a man who has disappeared. Once Mark said, with a sort of studied crossness, "Isn't Ruhl a damned fool?" and I knew by the effort it cost him to speak like that, that he was more alarmed than I had known. Another time he said, "How silly we are," and laughed—then cut the laugh abruptly short.

It was Mark and I who found Ruhl. We had crossed the dunes and were on the outside shore, going toward the lifesaving station. The tide was out and there was an expanse of bare wet sands before the steep shelving-off which I suppose makes the dangerous undertow which has given that outside shore its bad name. There had been a big surf the day before—when searching for Ruhl in the evening we had heard it clear across the cape. As if to show we were not afraid of those sands we spoke of the man who had been drowned over there the summer before, of whether the undertow was really as dangerous as it was said to be. Mark said he doubted it—that he'd always been meaning to come over and have a plunge in that surf himself, and as he was saying that I clutched his arm. The sun had come up, and out there on the sands, some distance ahead of us, I saw something. I pointed to it. We stood looking, saying nothing. Then we started that way. Once Mark said, "There's no use in your going out there and getting your feet wet," but I kept on, walking silently over the wet sands toward the thing I had seen stretched there in the sunlight.

It was Ruhl. We came within a little distance of him and then stood there still. His face was all purple and bloated, and yet as he lay stretched out in the merciless sunshine we got the feeling of something noble. It was Ruhl's last gesture, and there was, for the moment at least, something convincing about it. Mark went up to him to see if he was indeed past help, found that he was, yet nevertheless hurried to the station a little way down the beach. And I stood there and thought about Ruhl, of the price he had paid for this final gesture.

I suppose he *had* to do it. He couldn't stand it not to count. He had to do something—even this—to become, not what he was, but what he wanted to appear to be. After all, that wanting was the strongest thing in him. There was a certain spiritual dignity about the bloated dead man I looked at upon the sands that morning.

Of course I came to think of it less emotionally than I could then, and the reason I have written this out is the desire to make it clearer to myself. We all talked it over and the verdict of the majority was that Ruhl could not tolerate the thought of what he had done—that is the basis of Bert Stephen's story, "Remorse." Mark saw it better than that; he said that what Ruhl could not tolerate was the thought that he could not be reinstated—that it was because the quality of what he had done fixed him as impossible. He said that Ruhl had killed himself in a rage at his powerlessness; that he was one who could not live without pretending, and when he saw he could not appear noble, or even interesting, he destroyed himself in very frenzy, in an "I'll show them!" mood.

That's nearer it—but I don't think even Mark has the whole of it. I've tried to give my feeling to him, but I did it so gropingly that he thought it rather strained and sentimental. But I tell you I *got* something that morning as I stood there on the wet sands at sunrise looking at the poor purple swollen face of the man stretched before me. Ruhl's dissatisfaction with himself took on noble proportions in the presence of what it had cost him. Mark says he killed himself in a pettish rage, in a frantic disappointment of vanity; but beneath that there is something else, and I see it more and more clearly now for trying to formulate it. It's true that he was small and almost empty, but—he didn't want to be. I never thought I liked pretenders, but there's another way to look at it. And when a man has laid down his life to get himself believed in as finer and deeper and more beautiful than he was I shall try to think, not of what he was, but of the intensity of the need to appear something else. You can call it vanity and you can call it insincerity, but when a man dies to try and make his life look beautiful . . .

Originally published in *McClure's* 49
(August 1917): 36–38, 65–67

NOTES

1. As economic crisis gripped the country from 1913 to 1915, unemployment rates skyrocketed. By January 1915, as many as 18 percent of wage earners in New York City were out of work, and many of them were homeless and without money to buy food. Leaders of the more radical labor organizations, such as the Industrial Workers of the World (IWW), encouraged the unemployed to demonstrate in the streets in New York City and other metropolitan areas during these years, holding mass meetings and parades as a way to publicize their plight and protest the lack of government relief.

2. Glaspell may well be referring to the Lawrence Textile Strike, which occurred in early 1912 in Lawrence, Massachusetts. The woolen and cotton mills there employed mostly immigrants, who were forced to work at a grueling pace under dangerous conditions and who lived in congested and unsanitary tenements. When mill owners attempted to reduce wages, the IWW—one of the most radical labor organizations— sent representatives to Lawrence to plan and direct mass picket lines and protests and to provide food and relief for the strikers. The strike was nationally publicized, sparking national outrage against the mill owners and sympathy for the workers, and it ended only when the owners finally agreed to wage increases.

3. Probably an allusion to Max Eastman, editor of the *Masses* from 1912 to 1917. An illustrated socialist magazine published monthly in Greenwich Village, the *Masses* included reportage, editorials, literature, and art by leading radicals and artists of the time, such as Floyd Dell, John Reed, Inez Haynes Gillmore, John Sloan, and Sherwood Anderson, all of whom were well-known to Glaspell. The magazine reported on the major labor struggles of the day, including the Paterson Silk Strike of 1913 and the

Ludlow Massacre, supported the causes of the IWW, and argued for birth control and women's suffrage. Because it vigorously opposed American involvement in World War I and the draft, the *Masses* was shut down in 1917 under the Espionage Act. Glaspell wrote a one-act play about it, entitled *The People*, which was staged by the Provincetown Players in 1917 and featured an Eastman-like editor, Edward Wills, as its main character.

4. The Espionage Act of 1917 and the Sedition Act of 1918 enabled government censorship and prosecution of any printed or expressed opposition to American policy during World War I. Glaspell deplored these infringements on freedom of speech, particularly when faculty at universities were dismissed or forced into silence to keep their jobs, which is a major theme of her play *Inheritors*. Here she mocks this mandated patriotism on college campuses in a more lighthearted manner, suggesting that anyone who did not like the poetry of Longfellow was seen as un-American.

5. Glaspell's narrator is mocking Bert Stephens: by this time the "surprise" endings of O'Henry, which had inspired so many imitators in popular magazine fiction, were seen as dated and formulaic.

Poor Ed

Now HE WAS BEGINNING TO recognize old things. There was the island where they once went camping—then he must be within ten miles of Freeport. How many times he and Henry had sailed down this river! His eyes blurred, though as he cleared them he thought he would write an essay on "Going Back." He would make it a tribute to poor old Henry. Yes, he would be glad to do that. It would be something that would remain from Henry's life. And, who could say? It might be one of the best things he ever wrote. Success interpreting failure—and with gentle understanding.

He thought of Henry's life and his own. In his hand was a magazine in which he was referred to as "Edward Shackleton—the eminent critic." This appreciation said he was one of the forces molding public opinion. It did not seem to him to have the weakness of overstatement, for he had not made the mistake of less widely read essayists of getting too far ahead of his public to be able to influence it. He had not gone upon the rocks of detachment—the sale of his books could testify to that. Every time a movement showed its head he was there to analyze it, and in essays which were a real contribution to English literature—so his publishers said, and the more disciplined reviewers did not contradict them—he had given his conclusions and reflections to the American people. That was what he had done, while his brother Henry, two years older, reared in the same home and offered the same educational advantages, had remained an obscure farmer, living and dying in the house where he was born. How strange and interesting life was! What made those differences? Of course the answer was not far to seek; it was something in one's self that made them, a power that made for righteousness—and for success. The difference between him and Henry showed way back in the country school. He got high marks and Henry did not. And Henry never cared either about attainment or public opinion. He grinned over his report card in his lazy way and said, "What's the difference?" He wondered if Henry hadn't thought of the difference when he received each year, and sometimes oftener, the copy of his brother's new book—how glad he was now that he had always sent Henry his books; it must have meant something in his lonely life. Yes, Henry must have come to see that there was a difference. Poor Henry!

Peter Thompson, a neighbor of Henry's, was at the Freeport station for him with his horse and buggy. It amused Shackleton a little to find himself riding through the streets of Freeport in that farmer's buggy. He thought of the many people, readers of Edward Shackleton, who would be glad to have met him with their cars, claiming youthful acquaintance. But Henry's friends were apparently all among the country people. The Shackletons were people who had lived both in town and in the country—at their farm seven miles up the river. He himself, as a young man, had been part of social affairs in town—and Freeport, though a small city, was a rich one. But poor Henry had not been any more of a success socially than any other way. And after he was expelled from college, and came home and lived on the farm, he was referred to, when people were speaking of the Shackletons, as "the wild one" or "the bad one." In this essay, which would be a tribute to Henry, he would show that he wasn't really wild or bad, but just lacking in initiative, in energy, in purpose. And somehow life got twisted for Henry, and he was too indifferent to untwist it.

He engaged Peter Thompson in conversation. As a student of human nature he was interested in all types, and then he wanted to freshen his mind about Henry.

"Well, Mr. Thompson," he began, "how does the old place look?"

"'Bout the same," said Thompson.

"Henry, I suppose, has been improving it from time to time?"

Thompson, a small man with stiff red hair which gave the impression of being a weapon of defense, looked at him in a guarded way, as if to see how much he meant by improving.

"Henry never was one to fuss much," he said.

"That's true," reflected the brother, thinking of his essay.

"But he was a good enough farmer," went on Thompson. "He got things done—well, most things."

Apparently Henry had not changed.

"The trouble about Henry as a farmer," went on Henry's neighbor, "was that he had a way of doing what he wanted to do when he wanted to do it, and not always what he ought to do when it should be done."

"Very well put," said the eminent essayist.

"But I don't know as 'twas about as well," observed Thompson. He paused. "Anyhow, it's all the same now."

Edward was silent, entertaining his own reflections on death.

"The funniest thing of that kind I ever saw Henry do was when old Nickerson—place joins yours at the back, you may remember—was settin' his fence over about ten feet further 'an he had any business to set it. Well, I got wind of it, and was back there, and then I went running up to the place to tell Henry. 'Why the old skunk,' says he, and went on reading his book.

"'Aren't you comin' back to *stop* him?' said I.

"'Soon as I finish this book,' says Henry."

The essayist gasped. He thought of his own essay, now a famous one, on "My Books." Somehow he had a momentary quite unreasonable dissatisfaction with it.

"What was the book about?" he laughed.

"Well I looked over his shoulder to see. I wanted to know, too. Near as I could make out it was something about breaking rock in Egypt."

"Breaking rock in Egypt?" inquired Ed incredulously.

"And makin' it into monuments. In the past, that was."

So Henry was interested in the pyramids; more interested in the pyramids, it would seem, than in getting all the land that was coming to him. A nice little story for—but suddenly he realized that he himself was one of the inheritors of this land.

"Well, I hope when he finished his book he came down and settled the old fellow."

"He came down," said Peter, "and—had fun with him. I can see him now—coming over the hill in his slow way—Henry never moved very fast you know. 'Why Nick,' says he, 'why don't you take this hill, too? It's an awful nice hill. Don't you like it?'—and he kept on like that till the old thief did put it back part way—Henry never threatening him or anything, just having fun with him, and himself lyin' there in the sun on the hillside—I can see him just as plain. 'Say, Henry,' I says to him, bye and bye, 'he's still got some of what's yours.' 'Oh, what's the difference, Pete,' says he. Then he kind of grinned at me—remember how he used to grin?—slow, and says, 'I won't have it to plough.'"

That was Henry. A farmer who did not value his land!—too indifferent even to hold his own! Need one look further for the keynote of this life? Was not right here the secret of why Henry had failed in everything?

It was fifteen years since he had been back to the old place. He would not have been here now if the telegram about Henry's death had not reached him in Chicago, where he was giving his lecture on "A New Era in American Morals." He had yielded to an impulse to pay Henry the respect of coming home for his funeral, and now, as just at dusk they came up a hill and saw the old Shackleton place there on the next hill, he was glad that he had come. It gave him a new sense of his own life—to say nothing of Henry's.

Henry would be buried the next morning. This was his last night in the house where he had lived all his years. Through the evening his brother thought of those years, of what they must have meant to Henry. It was impossible to keep away from that contrast between his life and his brother's. The people around the house that night were, of course, Henry's friends; they were the people of the neighborhood, apparently the only friends Henry had. He tried to talk to them, but they were not articulate. And that was all Henry had known. Life was over for him and he had never lived. Poor, poor Henry!

He had the room that had been his when he was a boy. It was strange to be in it again, and think of all there was in between. It did not look as if it had been much used, probably Henry had little company. Suddenly he stood still and stared. Why, what a strange thing for Henry to do—for there, on a shelf, were his works, the uniform edition of the books which had come out through the years. So Henry had put them back in his old room—what a singular little piece of sentiment! He could see Henry, book by book, bringing them in here after he had read them.

He began looking them over; there they all were, the things Edward Shackleton had said about life. What a lot of effort and thinking they represented, what an indefatigable search to get ideas out of events— the ideas that would make essays. This was what he had done with his life—this row of books. It was not too much to say that he had been a teacher of the nation—constantly interpreting and admonishing, ever finding the significance of things which other people had not known were significant. As someone had said, he had been wise enough never to tell people to think what they wouldn't think. This had been in a not wholly sympathetic article—one of those articles written by a less successful man—but he had found pleasure in that idea of understanding people. "New Thought," "The New Relation Between Capital and Labor," "The Meaning of the Boy Scout Movement," "The Spiritual Significance of Conservation," "New Ideals in Marriage," "Free Verse and Restlessness"—what was there he had not fitted into its place?

He sat there a long time in the room of his boyhood with the work of his manhood, thinking of all he had written about life since he left that room. Henry must often have thought of it. Just what had Henry thought? Poor, poor old Henry!

He was looking through his latest book. He was reading the final chapter on "The Modern Woman and Responsibility," enjoying his own flowing style. He turned the last page; he read the last word. But below the last word were two other words, penciled in Henry's small writing. He held them close to make them out. They were: "Poor Ed."

He dropped the book. But quickly he picked it up again. He peered at the small dim words. Of course he had been mistaken. But he had not been mistaken. It was Henry's queer writing, and the words unmistakably were: "Poor Ed."

He gasped; he choked; he blinked. Poor *Ed?* But it was poor *Henry!* Why, the thing was incomprehensible! "Poor *Ed?*" What did it *mean?* To think Henry should be so ignorant—! And what could he possibly have *meant?*

He'd like to go and ask him! He'd just like to call upon him to explain this! But he couldn't very well call upon him to explain, for Henry was lying dead in the room below, and the dead don't explain. And here was what Henry had left—Henry's sole comment on his seventeen books! "Poor Ed." Not even an exclamation point after it! A *period.* Just calmly disposing of him like that!

Oh, well, of course Henry would be pretty sore. What had *Henry* ever done? Nothing. Precisely nothing. Failure did not often look kindly upon

success. Poor Henry! Poor *Henry!* He thought "Poor Henry" a great
many times, as if with "Poor Henry" to put down "Poor Ed."

But poor Henry could not put down poor Ed. As he looked at the long
row of his books, the work of his life, and considered that for Henry
they ended with "Poor Ed," he grew angry in a way he had never been
angry in his life. It was that kind of anger which has got to do something, and the maddening thing was that there was no way of getting at
Henry. He was furious at Henry for blocking him like this. He tried to
find satisfaction in reviewing the fact of his brother's life. Poor Henry!
There was nothing you could think about him that didn't fittingly end
with that comment. Take college. What had Henry been at college except
a total failure? The very first month he was there he got in bad by one of
his stupid remarks. It was a church college their parents had sent them
to, and a big revival was in process. Most of the students who didn't
belong to the church were joining it then. Of course he himself had soon
passed on to more sophisticated forms of religious experience—but this
was what was being done at the time. "Brother," the revivalist had one
night said to Henry, "won't you come and be saved?" "From what?"
Henry inquired, thereby giving at once the impression that he was stupid
and obstinate. And then in civics class, "What *do* you know about this
subject?" the teacher had demanded. "Nothing," Henry had answered.
"Well, when will you know something about it?" the teacher pursued.
"Never," replied Henry. "You may leave this class never to return!" cried
the professor. "Oh, thank you," said Henry—and went out and sprawled
in the sun. Oh, Henry was in a fine position to say "Poor Ed!" A nice
record *he* had made at school! While "Poor Ed," the very first year, had
won the oratorical contest and been elected to the college paper. And he
himself—"Poor Ed!"—had instantly become a part of the best social life
there was in college, while Henry had finally been expelled for going to
a prize fight and then afterwards to a saloon with a low crowd he had
picked up in the town!

And look at the difference after they came home from college. He had
at once taken his place among the best people of Freeport; the Atwoods
he had known—and their sort—while Henry had stayed up at the farm,
and his only associates were the country louts who hung around the village store and saloon. And Henry's marriage! If *he* had made a marriage

like that he wouldn't call anybody else "poor." Henry had married a vulgar girl whose father kept the saloon. He could shudder yet—and was at great pains to shudder—in the memory of how humiliated they had all been at the marriage of a Shackleton to this common person. And the next year she left with a man who was going West to look for gold. He remembered a preposterous picture he had of Henry when he went up to see him after he heard he had been deserted by his wife—he had thought it only brotherly to go, much as he had disapproved of the marriage—he had always been good to Henry! As he came up to the door there was Henry trotting the young child of this disastrous wedlock up and down on his knee, and singing this outrageous little song—he had been so shocked that he had never forgotten it:

> "Your mummy's gone a–travelin',
> Travelin'–a–travelin'.
> Your mummy's gone a–travelin'
> Into the bounding West!"

That was all marriage had meant to Henry!—while he, "Poor Ed!"— had said some of the most beautiful things about it that had ever been uttered in America!

But it would be quite too absurd to permit himself to be upset by Henry's sorry little way of trying to evade the difference between the Shackleton boys. Apparently Henry was not big enough to face the fact that his brother had become a man of importance. He himself must be bigger than Henry; he must understand and not hold malice. After all, the thing was pretty much of a joke—that *Henry* should write "Poor Ed." Poor old Henry!—not much wonder he had become a little sour. Such were Edward's insistent reflections as he settled himself with his own books, to let them make an end of "Poor Ed."

He opened at his essay on "Happiness." The point of the essay was that happiness is necessary to the well-rounded life, that there must be some happiness, but that all should not be happiness. It was an inquiry into just what things happiness must be mixed with in order to be most energizing. But an annoying thing was happening. He could not get into his essay because of the loud, slow ticking of the clock in the hall

outside his door. The clock was beating off—"Poor—Ed—Poor—Ed"
and when he painstakingly completed his essay on "Happiness" he had
an irritating picture of Henry sprawling in the sun on the campus after
he had gratefully said "Oh, thank you," when told he needn't return to
civics class. . . .

That clock would drive him mad! He went out to see if he could stop
it, but he couldn't get at the thing that stopped it. It grew more and more
malicious. It said, "Poor Ed" until he wanted to smash it!—and he felt
so insufferably helpless, as if the clock, like Henry, was something that
could madden him and give him no comeback. As he stood there, full of
impotent rage, his eyes filled with a rush of hot tears. Suddenly he picked
up his lamp and went down to the room where Henry lay in his coffin.

He stood there looking at his dead brother. He would have given
anything in the world to be able to ask him what he meant by "Poor
Ed" and to get the truth in reply. He *had* to get it, and he looked and
looked at Henry as if by looking he would get it. Henry wasn't going to
get out of it like this! He needn't think he could say a thing of that sort
and not tell why he'd said it!

How calm Henry was. How very quiet and at rest. This was death;
all death was calm and rest. His hands had gripped the coffin in that
almost insane moment when he was going to force from Henry what
Henry had thought about him, but now they fell away—his was such a
small and helpless rage before this large calm.

And suddenly he knew that Henry had always had this large calm,
and for an instant there was something he almost saw—he almost saw
himself as a small thing fussing around in the place where Henry dwelt
largely and serenely. He tried to think of the words about the "eminent
critic" in the magazine he had upstairs. But words about the eminent
critic couldn't pierce this calm.

Henry had been a failure. Anyone would say so. What else *could* they
say? But now Henry was dead, and the brother who stood beside him,
in life and perplexed, was appalled by a feeling that Henry had not
frittered away his life. He had not troubled about doing things because
other people were doing them, or because good would be said of him
if he did them. That must have been a happy hour Henry had reading
about the pyramids. He would not let it be spoiled because someone was

trying to take his land away from him. He would have let the land go rather than give up the hour. Now he lay in his coffin, and not leaving behind a few feet of land that should have been his, didn't seem to mark him with failure, but having had the hour he wanted gave him a strange, large, quiet kind of success.

It was a kind of success with which the eminent critic had no personal touch, and after a moment he had to get away from it, and so he left the room where his untroubled brother lay, and went out in the kitchen where Peter Thompson was "sitting up."

Thompson was making coffee, and asked Ed to join him. The coffee steadied him, and the shabby kitchen and uneducated man did something toward restoring his normal appreciation of himself. "Henry must have been very lonely here," he said, in a pitying but inquiring voice.

"Henry never was one that seemed lonely," said Thompson quietly.

After drinking some coffee in an offensive way, Henry's neighbor volunteered: "Henry'll certainly be missed down to Dyer's."

"Where's Dyer's?" asked Ed.

"Why Dyer's is the saloon down here at the corner," said Thompson.

This practically completed the restoration. Henry would be missed at the corner saloon! Edward thought of the things that would appear in the papers—news stories and editorials—if he himself were to die. And yet—again he only saw it through the glass of self-esteem darkly—just where would he be "missed"—speaking the word as Henry's friend had spoken it?

"Henry drank a good deal?" he inquired hastily.

"No," said Thompson, "Joe Dyer never made much of it off of Henry— that is, not off of what Henry drank himself. He liked his beer when the weather was hot, and something warming on a cold night, but what he was there for was to sit around with the boys and talk."

What a life! His only companionship the loungers in a country saloon!

"Henry wasn't much of a talker when I knew him," said Henry's brother.

Thompson ran his hand through his stiff red hair. "Not a big talker," he finally admitted, "and yet I'd call him a talker."

Ed looked at him inquiringly. "Because," Thompson pursued, "he might say the least that was said of an evening, and yet what he said'd be all you'd remember."

The eminent critic was silent. "Did Henry ever say anything about me?" he suddenly burst out.

"Why, yes; he used to kind of—well, brag about you sometimes."

"He did?" eagerly inquired Ed.

"That is—well, I guess you'd call it bragging."

"What did he say?"

"I've heard him say, 'My brother is the eminent critic.'"

He looked at Thompson suspiciously. "Well, what did he mean by that?" he asked sharply.

"Why, I don't know," said Thompson. "Henry wasn't one to explain what he meant."

"And was that all he ever said about me?" demanded Ed, with rising voice.

"No," said Thompson. "No; he said other things."

He waited, wanting to curse the man for his stupid slowness. He was forced to ask it. "What things?"

"Well," said Thompson, "I remember once when we was arguin' Henry said—'It's too bad my brother isn't here. He'd tell us.'"

Again a pause which Thompson seemed willing to let become eternal. "And—what were you arguing about at the time?" inquired Ed, carefully casual.

"Why, I think," said Thompson, "that was the time we had the argument about space—what it did about stopping."

Edward got up and went to the kitchen door and stood there looking out. His face was burning. He didn't see how he could possibly write any essay about Henry! To do that he shouldn't have come home.

"Poor Henry," he said, turning back, "it makes me feel very sad to think of him."

"Does it?" said Thompson so dryly that Ed flamed: "What did Henry ever have from life? Nothing—just nothing at all. Think of his marriage, for instance. What a failure! Henry died knowing nothing whatever about love."

He had turned back to close the door and Thompson's laugh made him spin round. "What are you laughing at?" he demanded.

"Well, if you'd live round here," said Thompson, "you'd laugh too."

"Laugh at what?"

"At what you just said."

"Which that I just said?" pressed the eminent critic, pertinently if not purely.

"Henry knowing nothing about love."

"But—but Henry didn't marry again."

"No—he didn't marry again." One of those stupid pauses! "Emil Johnson had married her first."

"You mean Henry was involved in a scandal?" sharply asked the other Shackleton.

Thompson looked a little surprised. "We never called it such," he said simply.

"She didn't live with her husband," he went on, as if trying to figure out why they hadn't called it such. "She couldn't, not unless she lived in an insane asylum—and I guess they didn't want her there. And then she was Rose Mason." He screwed up an eye contemplatively. "Don't seem to come natural to call what some folks does scandal." Suddenly he chuckled. "Wonder what Henry would 'a done, if someone had come along and told him it was scandal." He chuckled again as if this idea had many entertaining ramifications.

"Well, here on this hill lived Henry," he went on in a musing way, "and over on the next one she lived. My place is in the valley down between. So—kinda tickled me—Henry knowing nothing about love." He had his knife out and took a stick from the woodbox and went to whittling, his back to Ed. "Then I was there the night she died. Henry and I walked from there together—just as it was gettin' light. When we got to where I turn off"—he took his stick and examined it, as if his real interest was in the knot round which he whittled. "When we got to where I turn off," he picked it up, "we stood a minute by the creek, and—if you'd seen Henry's face then—huh!—guess you wouldn't say it so sure—nothing from life."

He found a new approach to the knot. "Henry was pretty lonesome this last year—just a year ago Rose died. But his face—huh!—it never lost the whole of what it had there by the creek—at sunup that morning." The whittling became violent.

Edward again opened the door and stood looking out. Some night bird—a whippoorwill, a quail—was calling "P-o-o-r Ed"–"P-o-o-r Ed." It did not infuriate him. He stepped out and stood looking over at the hill where the woman his brother loved had lived. He was thinking about Henry. Something big and simple and undismayed about his brother made the eminent critic almost real. Things that weren't worth anything never touched Henry at all—as civics didn't, or his marriage. And not being shut in with things that didn't matter he was open to the things that counted. He stood there in the yard where he and Henry had been boys together and he wished he might have known his brother. Henry could have helped him. He wondered why it was no one had helped him, or why no one had ever really cared for him. He supposed it was because he was always trying to impress people. He had never become anything because he was always trying to seem something. Wisdom didn't grow in the hearts of men who were thinking about appearing learned. He thought of all the things he had written about life. They had held him away from it. His years had been one nervous quest for saying a thing before someone else should say it. And people had taken this for something valuable. People were like that. No, not all of them. Henry hadn't taken it for something valuable. He wondered if he could, after all, write about Henry—failure interpreting success. . . .

Next morning, as he walked from his brother's grave, a woman stepped up to speak to him, a woman quite unlike the other people around him.

"Mr. Shackleton?" she inquired, in the subdued voice right for the situation. "I *do* hope I'm not intruding. I was Helen Atwood. I married Bob Owens. Don't tell me you've forgotten us, for it's our proudest boast that we knew you."

He assured her he had not forgotten her. And indeed he hadn't—he wouldn't. She was of Freeport's "leading family."

"If I *am* intruding, do say so. But now that you are here, we can't bear not to see you. I wish I could tell you"—her voice grew sweetly serious—"what your work has meant to us. I wonder," she went on more brightly, "if you won't give us a chance to try to tell you? Mayn't I take you home for a little stay with us?"

He was grateful for the comfort of her car after the poor springs of the carriage which had taken him to the cemetery. She was discreetly quietly, respecting possible grief, or at least mindful of the fitness of things. They stopped at the Shackleton place for his bag. He was glad to be leaving—tired and dispirited after the night there. On the way to Freeport she talked gently and with some eloquence of what his books had meant to her, how they had always made her know what to think. "Yes?" he would only say at first, and "I am glad," having an instinct for keeping away from his books, as we keep away from a place that has been sore. But her words, like her car, were soothing. It occurred to him that a strange situation creates overwrought ideas. And night—night in the country, and with death there—it was peculiarly depressing; distorting, in fact. Think of the people he had reached through his books!—people whom he had guided as Helen Atwood said he had guided her.

And then, with tact, she was speaking of his brother, commenting on the retired life he led, upon the differences in families. "I hadn't seen him for years until last spring, when my sister took a place up the river. It seems she met Mr. Shackleton on the road one day and asked him where she could get some fertilizer for her garden, and so the next afternoon—I happened to be there at the time—he very kindly drove over with a load of manure."

The eminent critic sighed. Drove over with a load of manure!

But this load of manure was fertilizing. The essay he had first had in mind began to sprout and thrive. Yes, he would write about Henry—generously and with insight he would picture a man who had failed and yet had won from failure a certain sort of success. Perhaps—who could say?—it was more satisfying than real success, with its myriad responsibilities, its ceaseless demands. He was the better for having touched Henry's quiet life; the memory of it would sometimes flow restfully into his own busy days. And there would remain no memory of the disappointing thing—Henry's perhaps inevitable jealousy of the brother who was counting in the world of affairs and thought. No, all of that had died with Henry. He saw the Freeport streets through misty eyes. Poor dear old Henry!

Originally published in *Liberator* 1 (March 1918): 24–29

Beloved Husband

For twoscore years and ten Amos Owens really had something to worry about. In the first part of the first score he had to worry about his pants, for his mother made them out of his father's pants. He had to worry about not having the guns and bats and boats that make for popularity among one's fellows. He even had to worry about getting his schoolbooks—not that he really wanted them, but his mother's tone in speaking of his not being able to have them led him to associate this possibility with catastrophe too great to look in the face. And then from the time he was ten years old he began to worry about getting up early enough—at ten he got a route and began delivering morning papers. Perhaps if in those years which might have been tenderer he had just once looked the worst that could happen straight in the eye, and with bold reasonableness inquired, "Well, what if it does happen?"—if just one morning a little boy of ten had done that, maybe the life of a man would have been different. Maybe. But his mother's voice shaped his years. She couldn't say, "What a beautiful sunny morning!" without giving you a sense of impending doom. And when she said, "Amos, you get to bed and right to sleep, or you'll not be able to wake up when I call you," he couldn't anymore have taken a good look at the possibility of not being able to wake up than he could have struck a match and looked at the monstrous figure which must be there when a door creaked in the night.

And then, from the first, he saw things from the early-morning angle. There is that about the world when people are not up to make it seem something is bound to happen to them when they do get up. The cats were too queer in the dawn. Many houses with pulled-down shades *do* something to you. When he got to the office and crowded in with all the other fellows the world was itself again—a place of loud voices and much edging of you out of line, but there was a certain three blocks— whistling didn't help and running made it worse.

His early-morning life did not stop with the papers. He got a job in the fish market and it was his business to meet the four-o'clock train and get the stuff right on ice. If he missed that train— He never finished that sentence—more's the pity.

He began working in the fish market at sixteen and he bought it at thirty-two. From the time he was twenty-eight he was afraid old Doe would die, or give up the business, before he had enough saved to buy it. Amos's savings account ran a race with old Doe's kidneys, and there is something hounding about an opponent you can't measure. In the second year Mr. Doe had an acute attack and was taken to the hospital—that was what made Amos an investor. To get money faster he lent the savings which were bringing him four percent to a man who wanted to build a house and would pay eight percent. He never would have risked this if he could have had an accurate report on the kidneys. Having risked it was anguishing as he walked through still, gray streets; securities became as thin and unreal as that light which fills in between night and day. Of course he was going to lose his money. Money became to him a thing you are practically certain to lose. He did not lose it, and he found out how to make it, but that light which is never seen in night or day became the light in which he saw things.

When he bought the fish market he thought how nice it was going to be to sleep mornings. For years, as he walked past those drawn shades, he had envied the people warm and unaware in their beds. But when you have done an unpleasant thing for twenty-two years it isn't so easy to leave off doing it. Of course he continued to wake at half past three, and as that was the hour when things had long seemed all wrong, of course they continued to seem so. He could hear the whistle of the four-o'clock train, and he was sure Fred Long had not been there to meet it. It got so he couldn't bear to lie abed and listen for that whistle. After a month of knowing Fred would not be there—a month in which Fred never once failed to be there—he told him he'd meet the train himself.

His wife told him he was crazy; when he acquired the fish market he acquired as wife Josie Smith, bookkeeper in the grocery store next door. "You don't have to do it," she told him again and again. And he couldn't explain to her, not being able to explain it to himself, that he did have to.

There was a great deal he was never able to explain to Josie—or to himself. There were things in him that fought with other things, and his makeup brought him pain. With all his terror about his pennies he had that quite special romantic sense which points some men to money. He was a 'fraid-cat and a gambler, and all through his life the gambler tortured the 'fraid-cat. He borrowed money up to the hilt, and made money on the borrowed money. His capital was never big enough for his business. This consigned him to years most men will understand better than most women. Josie was one of the women who didn't understand it at all. She had a tidy little bookkeeping mind which would have things balance no matter what the balance might be. Those were dreadful days in the Owens household when he had to pull out of his pocket a note for Josie to sign. Josie thought it all quite simple. They could get along very well if it weren't for that terrible interest. She never could see that they moved from a flat on Third Street to a home on River Heights out of what the borrowed money made. She wanted what it made, but her mind—and her judgments—never got past what it cost.

And as he carried away Josie's signature he always carried with it a nervous chill. It was true he was bearing a fearful burden of interest. Suppose the bank came down on him—as she said it would—as something in him felt sure it must. He suffered, but he went on. He had to suffer, and he had to go on. He was like that.

And then one day he made his pile. He was one of three men who financed a young inventor. The 'fraid-cat had been more tortured by this than by anything he had done—and the gambler more intrigued. It was a new sort of motor engine, and there was a fortune in it. The man who every morning met the four-o'clock train was the richest man in town.

But he went right on meeting it. When Josie complained about its looking queer, he said there was nothing else to do at that hour in the morning. She spoke of sleep. What was the good of sleep if you couldn't sleep? They bought an imposing house called the Manor—an edifice erected by a man with a romantic sense which had played him false, and at twenty minutes of four every morning this heavy mahogany door opened and there slunk out of it the master of the house, the richest man in town, Amos Owens on his old hard way to get his fish.

As he went out he sometimes met his son coming in—Walter was less inept than his father in taking his place among the wealthy. One morning, in the lower hall, he met his daughter, just home from a fancy-dress Christmas ball. Edna put out her arm, not unkindly, and cried, "Father!" at the thought of his going out in the storm. Her arm was bare and some gold thing was wound round and round it. All the way to the train it bothered him. It must have cost a great deal. Why need she have her arm bound like that? While absorbed in figuring out what the adornment must have cost he slipped on the ice and broke his ankle.

That night Josie and Walter and Edna gathered round his bed and read him the evening papers. They all had the story of how Amos Owens, on his way to the four-o'clock train from which he had long taken his fish, had slipped on the ice. Josie and Edna cried—and not over his broken ankle. Walter said it would set them back—they weren't well enough established to be "quaint." They argued with him, telling him he was Freeport's leading citizen and urging him not to injure them by being queer. And because his foot hurt so much he wanted them to go away, he finally promised to give up the fish business.

So Freeport's leading citizen tried to lie abed mornings. But the trouble was, all through his years he had felt so relieved at finding himself awake. Always there had moved just under sleep that awful idea that he might not be able to wake up. So he not only continued to wake, but continued to feel he had averted catastrophe, and on that feeling he always got right up. Now he tried to stay in bed, even though he was awake. He fought a good fight, but he couldn't win it. He would get up and prowl round the house, trying not to be heard, for he disliked discussion of his ways. He would see things about the house that distressed him—and he didn't have the fish to turn to. Though one morning, after finding three empty champagne bottles in the billiard room, he did go down and watch a tall Swede take fish off the four-o'clock train. He followed him as far as the market, watched him go in, stood there a little, then started up the hill toward the Manor—a slight, stooped figure going through silent streets as if pursued.

Josie and Walter and Edna would have done better to have let him alone. The Manor was a lonely place at daybreak. Things that seemed wrong grew monstrously wrong because there was nothing to do but think about them—and no one to speak to of what he thought. He would find good food thrown away, and, unable to bear such things, he would go out and walk up and down the street. He would look about for someone to talk to. Waking up before other people do may seem an incident—but it leaves one alone in the world. More and more he came to have a need of talking at that hour, as if companionship might take the place of the fish and let him out from things that stalked him before it was really day—old worries which new conditions were so queerly unable to touch. Not having other people's habits cuts you off from the sympathies of the human race. Everyone disliked and despised him for his queer ways. Neighbors who were light sleepers would hear him on his beat and mutter, "Old Owens, out worrying about his money; pity the old fool can't stay in bed at this hour!"—and none of them felt sorry for him, for did he not have more money than he knew what to do with? None of them saw any pity in this broken connection between his money and his feeling about money.

One morning, in a room off Josie's bedroom, he found a dress which had come home and not been unpacked. He lifted the paper and looked at it. It was stuffed out as if there were a form within. It seemed unbearably useless, as if it were just made—and *bought*—to go over paper stuffing. He tiptoed into Josie's room and opened the door and looked at the dresses. Rows and rows of them—and now she had bought another! Josie lay there asleep, turned from him. He wanted to talk to her. He sat in a chair before the closet door, hoping she would wake. It must be said for him that he never thought of waking her—sleep was to him too escaping a thing to bring anyone from it. But he couldn't sit there any longer in the stillness, so quietly he slipped out, not looking at the stuffed-out dress in the outer room. He looked in at Edna's door, at Walter's—maybe one of them was awake. He wanted terribly to speak to someone. But they weren't, and he went very softly, not to rouse them. Walter, too, had made a purchase. It was in an open drawer. He stood looking at it awhile; then, to stop looking, hurried out of the house and walked a long way off—soft and fast, as if getting away from something. After a while he found himself on that street which, as a little boy, he had taken from home to the office where he got his papers. The houses were as still and strange as they used to be. Again those three blocks *did* something to him. He made a quick turn toward home, and Josie. He would talk to her; maybe he could tell her about things. He must try.

She stirred as he came in this time, said, "Oh, *Amos!*" as she saw him in overcoat and hat. Sleepily she rubbed her eyes, then exclaimed, "I think it's just too bad for you to act like this!"

He did not answer, but stood there quiet and helpless. She cried: "If you're determined not to enjoy things yourself, I don't see why you want to spoil them for me and the children!" Then she turned her back and pulled the covers up around her as if to say she'd thank him to go away and let her sleep in peace—as a sensible person should.

So he went away. He tiptoed into Walter's room and looked again at that purchase Walter had made. He stood looking at it until he heard one of the servants on the stairs. Then he could move. Things were never so bad when someone else was up.

All through the next week he would get right out of the house, trying not to see anything, trying especially not to go in Walter's room. He would find people to speak to—policemen, early teamsters, men collecting garbage. He would go up to them in that timidly ingratiating way of one pathetically afraid he will not be well received, wistfully trying to cover with a casual tone the importance to him of being received. He would say, "Well, *this* is a fine morning," or, "There's nothing like being up early," and they would answer, "That's right," and when he went on, "The nut." There was one policeman who really talked to him, and he could talk more to this policeman than he had ever talked to anyone. He told him how he always had got up early and now he couldn't quit it. He could laugh with him about it. He even told how he used to feel as a little boy going through the still streets, and while he didn't say he still felt that way, telling about it helped the way he felt now. He would walk for blocks with this policeman and talk to him about the fish business. He was a big, hearty policeman, with a warm voice—a voice not at all like the dawn.

All this while he had not lost his touch with his affairs, or his power to deal with them. He went on making money. He was not looked upon as a fool, despite the fact that some said he was "touched." It was only before it was really day, when things were still and thin and very lonely, when they *waited*, that old fears cut him loose from present security and left him alone and afraid in a world not quite right. This was a week of special good fortune for him; the return on a southwestern investment sent him ahead almost fifty thousand dollars, but this increased fortune had absolutely no reach into the anguish of finding half an uncarved chicken in the garbage can.

And in the morning after the half a chicken sent him out into the streets, something else sent him there. Going through the upper hall, he looked into the sitting room off Josie's bedroom and there he saw *another new dress*. It sat in an easy chair as a person might sit—stuffed out with tissue paper—*another* dress! In a circle which did not bring him very near he walked round it. It was a strange and to him a terrible color—that thin, weird gray in which a world not quite right waits for day. Slowly his circles came a little closer. Josie had *bought* this thing—this useless thing—she would have to *pay* for it. One arm of the dress hung limply and the other bulged grotesquely. He had to get away! As if someone were after him, he ran soft-footed into Walter's room and took what he had tried not to know was there. Softly he closed the big front door, as so many times he had closed it while others slept.

He went a little way in the fast, still way he had all his life gone through sleeping streets. He was looking for someone. He wanted that policeman whose voice was like taking you in out of the cold. But he couldn't find him. Frantic and bewildered, he walked round blocks like a lost child. He forgot about the policeman and just *went*—he didn't care where, he didn't know. If he stopped . . . Anyway, he went on. Dimly he knew there were people about him now, and then he heard a sound that had sounded through most of his years—the pounding rush of an incoming train.

He was meeting it—the four-o'clock train. He walked to the front, where they took off the fish. He saw the familiar crate come through the big door of the baggage car. It was put on a truck. He stepped up to it. But no—it wasn't his anymore. He couldn't take it. He looked around. Who *was* going to take it? He waited. And then he knew that it was happening!—the thing he had feared all his life would happen. The four-o'clock train was in and there was no one to meet it and take the fish.

He waited. It was a rainy morning, and warm. The stuff must be got right to fresh ice! He ran to one end of the station, to the other. He would run back and stand there by the crate—on one foot, on the other, trying not to cry, powerless and watching the thing happen he had shaped his life to keep from happening. He waited as long as he could. And when he couldn't bear it another second he pulled out Walter's revolver and shot himself.

Yet it is a benign world. Things are so arranged that our deaths precede our funerals. Few of us would like our funerals, and the thought of Amos Owens enduring his is something not to be dwelt upon—as torture to an animal is not to be dwelt upon. The Owens family tried to make up for the "queerness" of his death by the munificence of his funeral. His death might be quaint—but he had such a funeral as Freeport's leading citizen should have. Indeed, never did any leading citizen have such a funeral before. The old man lay on a couch of violets—something quite new in Freeport funerals. Josie commanded the florist to be right at hand and replace withering violets with fresh ones. Violets never withered faster. It is pleasant to think—indeed necessary to believe—that death is unaware. To feel fresh violets being stuck around him while old ones were really quite fresh enough—even the neighbors who had heard him at daybreak would not wish him *that*. The words "Beloved Husband," which in orchids formed the back of the couch, cost just seven times as much as the dress that drove him to Walter's room for the revolver. But not even the four-o'clock train disturbed him on his couch of violets. At last "Beloved Husband" slept through dawn.

Originally published in *Harper's Monthly Magazine* 136
(April 1918): 675–79

The Busy Duck

If Mora Arthur hadn't been so pretty of course we never would have stood for all her talk about the needs of her mind. She had deep dark-blue eyes which I think might honestly be called violet, and a woman with violet eyes has a great many privileges. She had soft curly hair. I liked to watch the dip it made round her ear. I would be thinking of this when tired of listening to her plan for furthering the working of her mind. It made it possible for me to listen a long time—and I presume Hastings and all the others had their little compensations. Anyway it doesn't much matter what you say if you have a vibrant colorful voice for saying it. And she had such an intensity about the starved life of her mind that you felt it must end with "I love you!" It didn't seem the kind of intensity that could be getting anywhere else.

She had come from a terrible home. She would tell us about it with a fury that made you feel she was beating her hands together. So passionate were the pictures she drew of this pinched childhood that I would have the feeling I must instantly get up and knock somebody down. It was the way her mouth quivered while her eyes blazed. Then, when I was away from flashing eye and grieving mouth and would turn over just what it was she had said, I would come to feel that perhaps, after all, such cases could be more calmly dealt with.

Her parents were rich and unintellectual—a terse and unemotional statement of the facts.

"To *think* of it!" Mora would cry. "When I think of those wasted years I could *tear something apart!*"

Dear me! We would all get terribly wrought up about it, quite unmindful of the fact that most of our own years were wasted ones.

"And so," she would finish, plaintively, "you see what I have to make up for."

The trouble was, she made up for it so unceasingly. You couldn't venture upon an idea without getting Mora's determined eye and knowing that she was now making up for some fraction of her wasted years. Then you would have to halt your idea to think about her need of it—not a condition in which your mind can function happily.

Functioning was a word of Mora's. "My mind doesn't *function*," she would say in such angry distress that you would feel for your mind to go on doing what her mind couldn't do was not the part of kindness or good manners. Whenever a really interesting idea was put forth it left Mora indignant to think she had never heard this idea before. The night she met Hastings—a man of ideas—I walked home with her and she walked so fast I could scarcely keep up. She was absolutely outraged to think of how much had been withheld from her.

At her door I made a suggestion. "Don't you think," I said, "that it might be better now to think more about the idea itself and less about the fact that you never heard it before?"

She gave me the strangest look, getting *this*, and hard. Anything she got she got so hard that you almost hated to see her do it. "Why, *yes!*" she cried breathlessly, and laughed in her charming way. "Why—what a fool I am!"

"You're like a horse," I said "taken to a beautiful pasture, and so indignant to think of never having been taken to this pasture before that he can do nothing but run round snorting with indignation."

"And never eating a thing!" cried Mora, in that way of hers which gave you the feeling she was clapping her hands. Seeing more in it. "Yes," she said, very earnestly. Then indignantly, "Now I never would have thought that!" And then, seeing she was doing precisely what she had been admonished not to do, she laughed at herself as she said good night.

She was really a charming child; she was younger than the rest of us, and her eagerness and her fury had much the quality of a child's. Of course, looks or no looks, we never would have put up with her if there hadn't been that freshness and charm in the avidity. And no denying that we were a good deal flattered at her being so bowled over by our knowledge and originality.

She came into our group through Edna Moore, who writes a good deal about what women ought to be and aren't. One night when I asked Edna to come to our place the next Sunday evening, to meet a fellow from South America who was lecturing at the university (no use trying any longer to conceal that I am a teacher), she asked:

"Oh, could I bring poor starved little Mora Arthur? I'm trying to get her into a different atmosphere—poor dear."

As I impolitely hesitated, not unfamiliar with the kind of woman Edna was trying to get in a different atmosphere, she added, "She won't do a bit of harm."

Now if there is anything you don't want at your party it is a girl who won't do a bit of harm. What Edna had said about the different atmosphere made me think this starved Mora Arthur was someone she had picked up on the East Side, and I hadn't meant it to be that kind of a party. If you know people from South America you will understand. So when Edna came in that evening with this young woman who knew so much more about coming in than Edna did, I was delighted to think there had been an exchange of prisoners, so to speak. And when she introduced me to Miss Arthur, of whom she had spoken, I wanted to say to Edna:

"Think you're clever, don't you?"

But before I had a chance to ask Edna what she was up to I rather came to see what she meant. There was something in the exquisite Miss Arthur's attention as humble and as eager as I should have expected from the young woman I had been anticipating. I wish to say that those of us who are university people are the sort of university people who are always being suspected by universities, so an evening with us is not necessarily as dull as you may imagine.[1] And many of my friends are people who maintain that universities and ideas have nothing in common—a position which I myself am inclined to think extreme. Anyway, that night people were talking interestingly, and suddenly I noticed that Miss Arthur's face had flushed as if she were excited about something. When she bade me good night she said sternly:

"You have talked about things here tonight which I never knew existed!" and she who had entered like a young ladies' finishing school marched away, leaving her host in doubt as to her opinion of his hospitality. The more I thought about it the surer I was she had left in high dudgeon. I tried to recall what we had talked about that need send a young lady away offended. Of course Menger had gibed at marriage; but even in society isn't that one of the ways of passing an evening? And had the young lady never been taken to the theater? It must have been the biological section of the conversation, when Door had such a good time explaining why certain Africans are what they are. But that was too dry to offend anyone. Finally I hit upon it. It was the facetious allusions to our unsuspected depravity as recently revealed through the study of our unconscious minds.[2] Well—next time she could stay away!

But when I saw Edna Moore she exclaimed, "My dear, it's *pitiful* the time Mora Arthur had at your house the other night!"

"I don't see that there was anything to get so huffy about," said I, huffily.

"*Huffy?* Why, she's at your feet!"

I should say, rather, she was at our throats demanding we give up all we had.

"My mind *needs* this" she would say, and with such simple fervor that it wasn't as absurd as it must sound.

After all, there aren't many people who can be naive about their minds. She was one human being who did actually treat ideas as realities. She would go anywhere to get them—take up with anyone. The trouble was, she treated them as the only realities. All the other things which enter into our estimates of people simply didn't exist for her. She cared nothing about their morals or their clothes—not conscious of those extraneous things. She went about with me because she liked my mind and my friends. She told me so, not saying whether she liked me or not.

I lead what you might call a double life. At least there is a side of my life which is at loose ends, and at these loose ends are loose friends—people not tied to anything, people with a philosophy which sets them apart from a social order, men and women who not only carry their theories into personal relationships, but who have personal relationships as tests for theories. Some of them are tiresome frauds and some of them are the most brilliant people I know. One night I took Mora to a cafe where they hold forth, and after that I was compelled to go so often to this place that I would wonder how soon I was due to lose my position in the university. Mora simply ate them up—lapped them up, I want to say, for she always gave me the feeling of lapping up ideas.

146

And then she met Hastings. He's the biggest person of that queer crowd. Well, he's the biggest person I know. At least, now that I try to think of a bigger one and mull over the list of my distinguished friends, I don't find anyone I can say matches Hastings. He sees things in new combinations which startle you out of old ones. He would be an important writer if only he would write. But he'd rather entertain himself thinking new things than bother himself writing down the ones already thought. He says that's what makes writers so tiresome and unprofitable—they are always writing about a stale thing. And all they care about in a thing, according to Hastings, is what they can write from it. Exploiters of life—feeling, vision, the whole terror and splendor of life—something to write about. So it is not possible for writers to be pure souls. Hastings has no money, and he makes his living translating various impure souls who lived and wrote in Europe. This is to him a subordinate thing, not threatening his purity. He also does a little frankly subordinate writing—a sort of journalist of ideas. But the thing he cares about in himself—and has a right to care about—he doesn't try to capitalize, or even capture. Laziness probably has something to do with it—impure souls really have to work. But those of us who know him get a lot from him—busily lapping. He's splendidly prodigal, not having the slightest instinct for keeping ideas to himself in order to do something with them. What he cares about is his own satisfaction in seeing a thing. If you happen to be around while he's seeing it you're perfectly welcome to anything you can get out of it.

If Mora hadn't met Hastings, I think she would have married me. Did I want to marry Mora? I don't think I should have had much to say about it. Had she decided she could get more through me than from anyone else, she should have made up her mind to marry me, and her violet eyes would have put it through. But of course I'm nothing compared to Hastings. What she gets through me I got through somebody else. I just happened to get it before she did. Hastings creates. She perceived the difference quickly enough.

One night, this after she had met Hastings two or three times, she stopped right in the middle of the street and cried:

"Why, it seems terrible to spend a moment away from him!"

Now you know most girls would never say *that*.

I suppose she came to see that the only way to save herself the pain of spending a moment away from him was to marry him. This wasn't simple. Hastings was forty-five and had never married. He wasn't at all for marriage. If there was anything he didn't want it was someone who thought it terrible to spend a moment away from him.

I don't think Mora would have got him if he hadn't at this time got a cough. The thing surely would have amused Mora's friends—those friends of her ill-spent youth—except that they would have been too outraged to be amused. Here was a beautiful well-brought-up girl of twenty-five, a girl with money and what they would call position, *trying* to marry a man almost twice her age, a penniless writer who had low associates, a ne'er-do-well who sat around and talked! And I am unable to conceive what they would have said (I fancy they would have been speechless) could they have known that the only reason she finally got him was that he contracted a cough which made it possible for her to persuade him he needed to be taken care of!

Mora's father and mother were dead, which I think quite as well for them. Various aunts and cousins, who didn't understand a thirst for ideas, made an ineffectual fuss about "the life she was leading." A brother was what Mora called really troublesome at times, but to Mora these things simply weren't considerations. She didn't reject them—she didn't have to! They just didn't exist for her. The brother had this same singleness of purpose, only what he wanted was money—which, of course, makes him a great deal easier to understand.

So Mora turned her violet eyes upon Hastings, and there came a day when she said to me, "I'm taking John out of town."

"Taking John out of town?" said I, dazed.

She nodded. "Think of a mind like that being threatened! Why, just *think*," she expanded, in one of her bursts of fury, "what we should all lose if anything happened to him!"

I sat and stared. She struck me then as the most cold-blooded creature I had ever known.

"Do you mean that you're going to marry Hastings, Mora?" I asked.

"Oh yes," she said, indifferently.

"Does Hastings want to be married?" I asked, brutally.

She smiled. "He wants to be taken care of."

"But, Mora," I demanded, "are you in love with him?"

"I'm in love with his thinking," she said.

"And you think that's enough?" I scoffed.

"For me, yes." She paused. "Because it's all I care about."

Upon my soul, I believe it was! The next day I thought all the things anyone naturally would think, and that evening I went to see Mora. But her brother was there, saying, in his fashion what I had been prepared to say in mine.

"But what does he *do?*" he of course demanded.

"He talks," said Mora.

Her brother got up and moved from one chair to another, from that to the sofa, then stood up and whirled round.

"And you are going to marry a man because he *talks?*" he at last found it possible to say.

"What better reason for marrying a man?" asked Mora, quite honestly.

Then the brother talked. And no one would marry him for the way he talked then.

And then Mora talked. "Horace," said she, "you married for money. I want something else and I am marrying for that thing. I congratulated you because you got what you wanted, though it isn't at all what I want. You can't do as much for me because you aren't as practical as I am. So what is there for you to do but do nothing?"

Followed a few terse words about her life and her money being in her own hands. This being true, Horace took leave.

So did I, Horace having shown me how ridiculous you make yourself when you expend energy uselessly. But I was more practical than Horace; I made a little speech befitting the occasion.

"Mora," I said, "I hope with all my heart that your intellectual development will be very happy."

"Thank you," said the betrothed one, happily.

Mora didn't take John so far out of town as to make it impossible for us to go to see him. The first time I went I saw Mora bearing milk to John, who was in the hammock. It would not seem there should be anything disgusting in the sight. A wife carrying a glass of milk to an ailing husband—a beautiful young wife at that—why should an uncared-for bachelor not see this as a happy domestic picture? But I had a moment of wanting to go back to town.

"Feeding him up," thought I, sourly, "so he'll talk. Give him a glass of milk—he may give you an idea."

Quite so. Hastings was glad to see me in the mood for talking, and Mora sat by, getting visibly excited about her increasing wealth. It grew cooler and Mora went to the house for a rug. I was irritated by the way she came hurrying back with it—afraid she would miss something! And yet, she did go for it; so much subordination was her grasping little ego equal to. But, I considered a moment later, if she didn't get the rug John might take a cold and cut off the supply of ideas for at least a week!

I suppose I'm unfair to her; in fact, I know I am—selecting these things from all the other things is a method as absurd as her own. Anyone not understanding Mora would have seen her as a charmingly interested woman, quite humble before her husband's astonishing mind. But I did understand her, and I was so stirred up by what I understood that I set out to write an essay on Culture, the point of which was that you didn't get it by trying to get it. I saw that this was not a new idea, though Mora made it seem new. I gave up the essay and thought about Mora, wondering why I was now so down on her. Of course there was the fact that she had selected the crumbs from Hastings' table rather than from my own, but I should have been genuinely distressed had she not met Hastings and made up her mind to marry me. And after seeing her with her husband I was more than ever thankful I wasn't the husband. It would get quite dreadful to have your thoughts hung upon like that. I should think it might in time reduce one to something like imbecility—just as a protection. Fortunately there was little danger of its doing that to Hastings. He was too absorbed in the world of his constant remaking to be aware of a lapping little mind on the outskirts. So far, at least, he hadn't become enough aware of her to mind her. This unawareness was Mora's salvation, as well as his own—saving her from being pushed to farther outskirts. I wondered if she would ever guess how little she mattered. And yet would she mind? It was Hastings' counting for her that she cared about. A queer sort of egoist she was. She wasn't vain; she didn't want to show off. She wanted to *have*. I once knew a woman who wanted to have spoons. I never knew why she wanted to have them. She didn't show them, she didn't do anything with them, and, so far as I could see, they didn't do anything to her. But the idea of there being a sort of spoon she didn't have was torture to her. Well, at least no one could say Mora didn't value the mind, and it seems odd a university man should be so upset by this trait.

As I had been all keyed up for writing something and the essay on Culture refused to be reborn, I wrote verses about a duck:

> A duck, when first he saw the sea,
> Cried, "This must all belong to me!"
> To move it to his duck-yard pan,
> He took a beakful and began.

> He was too busy far to swim,
> So light a thought unworthy him;
> From dawn till dark he waddled fast,
> Because the sea was wet and vast.

> His legs grew thin, his mind *distrait*,
> His mother cried, "What *is* it, pray?"
> "Oh, mother, do not bother me;
> I'm busy bringing home the sea."

This put me in so good a humor as to give me more kindly feelings toward Mora. Thinking of her as a perturbed duck made me enjoy going to see her. When about to be irritated by a too fervent manner I would murmur:

> From dawn till dark he waddled fast,
> Because the sea was wet and vast,

and straightway I would have the most amiable feelings in the world. Perhaps my method would not have the endorsement of our best social usages, and still anything that gives you more kindly feelings must have something to be said for it. Each visit would result in a new verse, as:

Deeper grew the path he wore
Between the duck yard and the shore;
His beak it was a little thin
To fit the sea quite neatly in.

This might have become one of the longest poems in history had Hastings not grown so much worse as to make it necessary that Mora take him to the Southwest.[3] I couldn't write of her as a pop-eyed duck when her husband's life was in question; some usages of my own saw to that, peculiar though her marriage had been. I missed the fussy duck; he had been such a companionable little absurdity. Now my speculations about Mora took on a more serious character. You have to call it pretty hard luck. She was to give him a glass of milk, he give her an idea; now the balance shifts so that her giving the glass of milk is the enormously important thing. Many things may seem more important than living, but nothing remains important before the possibility of not going on living—quite in line with our general absurdity. In Mora's eyes was the light of a fervent determination—the determination to get John well. I must say it was a light with which I was not unfamiliar; I had seen it in Mora's eyes many times when she was trying to wrench an idea from my possession. This does not mean that the determination to get John well was less than it should be, but merely that it was impossible for her to be more determined now than she had been before, there being, after all, a limit to determination. She made no complaint; she was far too zealous for complaint; and I saw them off with the feeling that John would get well—he would simply have to, that being part of Mora's program.

After they had been down there awhile I had a letter from him which worried me about Hastings and set me on a lot of new speculations about Mora. For Hastings wasn't in that letter. The distinctive, the unique thing just wasn't there. I never realized before what sickness can do to us. And Mora? How about it? I must confess I even went so far as to wonder whether Mora would stick. A monstrous wondering, I know, but monstrous, too, was her singleness of purpose. A sick husband might become one of the things which simply did not exist for her.

Later came a letter from Mora—very short, asking me to attend to something for her in New York, and beyond that saying only this:

"John hasn't begun getting better. He is very sick."

Most anything in feeling might be behind those terse sentences. I tried to see behind them.

Then another letter about a business matter, and only this which was personal:

"I think John is now beginning to get better."

I was exasperated by this brevity. Again I tried to figure out the most likely reason for it. Trouble was, you could figure it several ways, and if you knew Mora, you might not interpret it in the way most creditable to human nature.

One evening I met some interesting new people, one man, in particular, who could startle you out of stale thinking a little as Hastings used to. I came away all keyed up, and on the way home it occurred to me, "What a wonderful time Mora would have had tonight!" It brought up the old picture of the earnest duck, and I wondered what the indefatigable duck was doing now that there was so little to be indefatigable about. I got to thinking of Hastings, and it ended with my sitting down and writing them a report of the evening. I myself was much delighted with the letter. It was alive.

Mora's reply bore witness that she was still Mora. She sent me a check and commanded I come to New Mexico at once! It was precisely Mora not to have any of the usual feelings, and not to have any idea of my having them—about the check, I mean. She said my mind was just what she and John needed. As she needed my mind, it was to her a perfectly normal matter, she having money and I not having it, that she buy the ticket which could take my mind to New Mexico. She said, in conclusion:

"Let nothing stand in the way of your coming. John needs you—and so do I."

I enjoyed the "so do I." It was so like old times.

Well, I went. It was vacation time—and why must one always go to Maine? Certainly, anything I could do for Hastings I should regard as time happily spent, and I had a curiosity to see what had really happened to Mora.

At first I couldn't tell whether anything had really happened to her. She seemed older, she was quieter; she was like one who has been much alone, and alone with worry. And yet I told myself she had not changed fundamentally, that these were but matters of circumstance and only brushed the surface. What backed me up in this was the resolute light which had not died in her eyes; it was a deeper, a more intense light, but this was because she had been long biding her time. That first day I had the feeling that she was watching me, appraising. I would see her watching in her eager way when Hastings and I were talking, as if to see whether I was, after all, bringing as much as she had expected me to bring. Oh no, Mora had not changed!

The change in Hastings was the arresting thing. He was as one who has come back a long way, and he gave me a feeling that it was perhaps only a shadow of him which had come back. Through those first few days he was so much more like an invalid than he was like Hastings. He was pathetically glad to see me, and yet he seemed to be holding off from me. I wondered if it could be that the unique thing, that quality of his mind which was like a beam of sunlight darting through a veiled day—like an *escaped* thing—had itself been caught in gray. I could not bear to think this, but in those first days no playing thing shot light and color into our talk.

Oddly enough—or should I say neatly enough?—it was a talk about death which brought Hastings to life. I was telling him of a theory one of the men at the university was working on, and suddenly we had it, that dancing beam which could play through another man's thinking, lighting flaws, lighting beauty. Immediately the whole Hastings changed—exhilarated, confident, happy. Mora was there, but I was too delighted with the playing beam to give thought to her, beyond the amused thought that the busy duck was on the job, leaning forward with shining eyes, not going to let a thing escape! Then I forgot all about her—too interested.

I don't know how long we talked, but finally I saw that Hastings was tired, and then I noticed that Mora was not there. I was surprised that I hadn't known she was gone, but astounded at her doing such a thing! Mora *leaving?* when there were ideas to be had?

I went away, that Hastings might rest. They were living at the outskirts of a little town, in strange desert country which I didn't know whether I liked or not. I walked along, still all aglow with the pleasure of my talk with Hastings. Ahead was a clump of those bushy things which grow in the desert, and as I made a turn, to go up the mound and sit there—I came upon Mora. Turned from me, she was lying there flat on the ground. I saw that she was crying.

I was too amazed to know what to do; but some sand slid down and Mora raised up and saw me.

She herself did not seem at all embarrassed by her red eyes. She smiled a little, then cried afresh.

"Why—Mora! Why—what did you go away for?" I asked, in the foolish way we try to make conversation with the weeping. "John was talking so wonderfully."

"That's why," she gulped.

I couldn't get my bearings, so I stayed still.

"I'd—waited too long," said Mora, crying under her breath. "I'd—been too afraid."

Well, that was possible, I suppose, given her preposterous intensity in having to have what she wanted.

"It's nice to have him himself again," I said, to fill in.

"*Nice?*" Mora stared at me, then laughed—a laugh which rather offended me, as if I were a person who could have no comprehension of how nice it was.

Then she jumped up. "I must go home. Did John seem tired?" She hurried along so fast it was hard to keep up with her.

As I thought of it I became increasingly puzzled. It wasn't what she had done, erratic though that was; it was her eyes—a light in them which no amount of zeal in intellectual affairs could quite account for. And still, I assured myself, would not the intense duck become emotional if taken back to the sea after long away from it?

Next day something struck me that struck hard. Mora came in the room with a glass of milk for John. It brought back that other time when I saw her with the glass of milk and said to myself, "Give him a glass of milk, he may give you an idea." But as she gave him this it struck me, hard, that she gave it as if expecting nothing in return.

Absurd! How could you tell a thing like that? Every time I thought upsetting things I scoffed at them. Mora was one person I understood. On my understanding of Mora I would build my church!

But my church seemed built upon one of those balanced boulders which startle you anew every time you look at them. John and Mora and I had a long talk that night, and after I went to my room it occurred to me we had been three people talking, not two people exchanging ideas and a third clutching at them as they passed. Another notion! It was merely that Mora was a little out of practice in snatching.

But two days later the really outrageous thing happened. Mora and I were out on the porch; we had been talking for an hour or more. Suddenly I jumped up and cried, in hurt astonishment:

"But, Mora, you're a *restful* person!"

She was momentarily surprised at the violence of the attack, then smiled understandingly.

"But—but look here," I thundered on, "what's become of your *mind?*"

She smiled again; then her eyes went grave. She was looking over the desert, looking far, not thinking of me. Then she turned her grave eyes to me and said, simply, "I thought John was going to die."

Her eyes—no, I can't describe them. There's a certain *dumb* look that leaves *you* dumb.

"So I didn't care about anything else," she finally said. "And after that," she smiled, her face beautifully lighting, "oh, I knew I *had* the important thing, so—I could just take other things a little easier."

Again she seemed to have forgotten me, and it was quite as well I should be forgotten! A balanced boulder had tumbled on my brain.

"But," I finally began, "you cared about John for what John could give you. You were to give him a glass of milk," I went on, with growing indignation, "and he was to give you an idea."

Mora laughed. "And I got so interested in giving him the glass of milk—" She broke off, considered, then said, with something of her old eagerness, but not that thin, flurried eagerness: "Yes—how queer. You want something. You will do anything to get what you want—but what you do shapes you to a thing that wants something else. Why—what a mean trick!" But Mora laughed, as if it were a trick at which she could afford to laugh.

I did not laugh. I could *not* afford to. Things were all muddled up and I was indignantly trying to straighten them out. I went back and interpreted in the light I now had, and each time this present light illumined a past thing I would feel newly betrayed. That dumb look in Mora's eyes told why Mora's letters had been so brief. There are things we can't talk about. Mora hadn't sent me the check to come to New Mexico because she herself thirsted for new ideas. I had been peremptorily summoned because I might be just what was needed to bring John back to himself. She hadn't watched me like a hawk to see whether my ideas were going to be worth their salt for *her*. I was just another kind of glass of milk she could give John! And when she finally saw John himself again she goes running away from what he has to offer to sob out her joy in merely seeing him himself!

Well, it served her quite right. Her means to an end proved a trap that had sprung, and in that trap serenely sat Mora, happily *serving*. She was so grasping that she had been willing to give in order to grasp, and then giving made her into something which was not grasping. One of life's very neatest little tricks!

My indignation thus settled down into comfortable and not unfriendly gloating; but I wasn't even left in peace with *that*. In the six weeks I was down there the wind was slowly taken out of the sails of my certitudes. I couldn't even complacently think of Mora's sweet womanliness as just punishment for her avidity, for each day it came home to me anew that, now that she had stopped lapping, she had begun getting. Her dreadful little lapping had dammed the tide. Now things had a chance to flow in. One day it came to me as quite preposterous that Mora actually *thought*. Fancy Mora taking time to think, and never worrying for fear that she would miss something while taking this time off!

"Well, I must say, Mora," I said to her, crossly, the last day I was there, "I never thought to see you become an interesting woman."

"Do you think I am?" she asked, wistfully. "I want to be—because I want to interest John."

Mora wanting to be something in order to *give* something! On what rock *could* one build a church? Perhaps the temple of truth would have to be a houseboat, and float.

This made me think of the wet, vast sea and the earnest duck, and so that last night I wrote out all the verses about the busy duck to leave as a farewell present for Mora. This might not seem a gracious return for hospitality, but I knew Mora would enjoy the picture of herself bearing the sea to her duck-yard pan.

But the poem seemed unfinished, and that wistful note in Mora's voice made me want to write some new verses, leaving with her the picture of the hero triumphant. So thus the poem closes:

> And then one day he stopped to swim,
> It quite refreshed and changéd him.
> "It is not good to move the sea;
> I'll leave it where it is," said he.

> So now he rides upon the waves,
> And knows that ducks should not be slaves;
> He contemplates the boundless sea,
> And thinks, "This all belongs to me!"

Originally published in *Harper's Monthly Magazine* 137
(November 1918): 828–36

NOTES

1. Glaspell strongly opposed the "Red Scare" tactics used during this period to suppress criticism of American involvement in World War I, particularly when it led to the arrest or firing of university faculty. The dismissal of Henry W. L. Dana and James M. Cattell from Columbia University in 1917 may have been the inspiration for this theme in her play *Inheritors*, although the persecution of academics for "disloyalty" or for being "un-American" spread to campuses throughout the country. Here the narrator implies that the "sort of university people" he associates with are leftists who "are always being suspected" of sedition by university administrations.
2. This paragraph refers to notable topics of the day: "free love," a theory that men and women should pursue sexual relationships outside of marriage, which was popular amongst Greenwich Village intellectuals and artists and parodied in plays at the Provincetown Players' theater; social Darwinism, which provided a pseudoscientific rationale for racism; and Freudianism.

Glaspell commented dryly in 1915 that one "could not go out to buy a bun without hearing of someone's complex" (qtd. in Barbara Ozieblo, *Susan Glaspell: A Critical Biography* [Chapel Hill: University of North Carolina Press, 2000], 67). She also collaborated with George Cram Cook on a spoof of the Freudian craze, *Suppressed Desires*, which was one of the first plays produced by the Provincetown Players.

3. When Glaspell published this story in 1918, her readers would have assumed that Hastings, with his cough and worsening condition, had contracted tuberculosis, a contagious disease affecting the lungs that was then one of the leading causes of death in the United States and was claiming up to one thousand lives a week in Europe. Despite the lack of scientific evidence, thousands of patients were encouraged by their doctors to avoid cold winters and migrate to warmer climates in hopes of a cure, just as Mora and John traveled to New Mexico. While some improved with rest, most of those suffering from tuberculosis eventually died after a long and painful illness. Tuberculosis continued as a major health threat until an effective vaccine was finally discovered in the early 1940s.

Pollen

"IRA WILL DO IT IN HIS OWN WAY," Mrs. Mead used to say, and people believed her. They believed her because they knew Ira. "You have to let Ira alone," was another of the sayings of Ira's mother. And people did let him alone—again, because they knew Ira.

He had a way of not looking straight at you; not a sneaky way, but merely that, through some choice of his own, he didn't come into direct communication with you. When you spoke you had a feeling that what you had said hadn't come into direct communication with what he was thinking. Probably a man doesn't have to be communicated with if he does not want to be, and as most of the people Ira knew were farmers, with a lean to the taciturn, and a feeling that it would be better if other folks minded their own business more than they did, Ira was not as much disliked as it would seem he would be—or as indeed he would have been in another walk of life. He was, in fact, not a little respected for being so well able to get along without other people. "If you don't say anything to him, he won't say anything to you," was their way of summing up Ira Mead, and he was not infrequently summed up as a reflection on some other person who would say something to you when you had said nothing to him.

He always seemed too preoccupied with what he was doing to pay much attention to what you were doing. Even as a little boy, he was a good deal like that. When the boys dammed the creek that ran through the Mead orchard, Ira, after a little, would go upstream and become much occupied with a dam of his own—a different sort of dam. He didn't tell you his plans—either about catching a chicken or doing an example. "You don't know what's in his mind," his mother said, and never really tried to find out—it being more impressive to regard him as unfathomable. Everyone, more or less, picked this up from her. Even Ira more or less picked it up.

When you are apart from others, what you do has to be superior to the works of others, else—why are you apart from them? Ira, going his own way, early acquired a proficiency in certain things. He could do amazing things by throwing his knife—so he threw his knife a great deal. He wasn't good at leapfrog, so when leapfrog was being leaped he would be deep in some consideration of his own—to which he did not give voice. He was good in arithmetic and very poor at compositions. So he did arithmetic as though he had some respect for it, and as to essays gave the impression, not so much that he failed in them as that he withdrew himself from them.

When he grew older, and all the other boys had girls, he did not have a girl. You are not likely to have a girl if you have that way of saying nothing to her unless she says something to you. At least in that Birch Schoolhouse part of the county you weren't likely to, for they were a bashful lot of girls, mostly patterning themselves after John Paxton's girls, who, as was said of the eldest when she died, were modest and retiring. It was to one of these Paxton girls Ira almost said something even though she had said nothing. This was at the county fair, and he was going to ask Bertha Paxton to ride home with him. While he was still thinking about it, and about ready to do it, up came Joe Dietz and said, "Want to ride home behind my old nag?"—Joe's old nag being a three-year-old that could *go*. Bertha pretended to be afraid, and said to Ira, "Where can I get my life insured?" which would have been Ira's chance to say, "Come with me; you don't need any insurance." But this, alas! was all too true—and, Joe having the better horse, Ira became deeply absorbed in the activities of a certain machine—as one who had no concern with horses. And while he was still intently watching the machine, Bertha and Joe set out to find the charging "old nag."

Bertha married Joe Dietz, and they bought the old Allen place to the north of the Meads'. Joe Dietz wasn't much of a farmer. It was about this time that Ira Mead became more of a farmer than he had been. He took to spraying his trees and trying rotation of crops and doing things to the soil that had never been done to Mead soil before. In just a few years there was a great difference in the look of the Mead place and the look of the Dietz place.

Old Mr. Mead died, Ira's sister married, his brother said he was going to get into a business the Lord didn't have so much to do with (alluding to droughts and insect pests), and this he proceeded to do by moving to town and getting himself a job at the courthouse. So there remained on the farm Ira and his mother. Ira was the pride of her life—and the thing she was proudest of was that you couldn't reach him. Sometimes the Balches, whose place joined the Meads' at the south, would come and ask Ira to parties—they were a great family for parties. "Well, I'll *tell* him," Mrs. Mead would say, and then to Ira: "Fred Balch was here, sayin' everybody was to come to their place Saturday night. I told him I'd *tell* you." On Saturday night Ira would have his books out, all taken up with some new thing you were to do to the soil, and when his mother would say, "Folks are goin' by to the Balches'," he would be too deep in his own occupations to give thought to her, or the Balches. And so she would say, with a gratified sigh, "I knew you wouldn't go."

When you don't have anything to do with the people around you there grows in your mind the idea that there is something the matter with those people. "It'll just bring them down on us," was the way Ira and his mother disposed of every suggestion that entailed taking any matter up with the Balches. They even gave up the new fence because it might "bring them down on us." More than likely, what the Balches would have come down with would have been an invitation to supper, but the Meads had this growing distrust of all things outside themselves.

So every bit of Ira went into the farm. The Balches, who didn't care whether school kept or not, just so they had a good time, had a farm that was good enough if you didn't know what a farm might be. To the north of him, Joe Dietz had a place that was running downhill, because Joe, as they said, didn't have it in his bones to be a farmer. One day Ira saw Bertha Dietz standing by her south line, looking from her potato field over to his.

"Those are fine potatoes of yours, Ira," she called, in a friendly way.

"Well—they're comin' along," granted Ira.

"Ours don't seem to be doing much this year."

For this Ira had no comment. He was not one to talk about a neighbor's potatoes—even to telling the neighbor what he knew about draining the soil. It was five years now since Bertha Paxton had married Joe Dietz, and today she stood at the fence and saw that Ira's potatoes were better than Joe's. Ira wasn't one to look an idea in the face any straighter than he looked a person. He didn't consider that for five years he had worked for some such satisfaction as this, and so didn't have to consider just how satisfying the moment was. Bertha's little boy came running out after her. On his way back to the barn Ira jerked the horses' mouths in a way not his wont. Thank Heaven *he* didn't have any children to run screaming around the place!

To make his own thing perfect seemed a way of showing he needed nothing from without. Not that he and his program ever came face-to-face with each other. But more and more he let other folks alone, and he did his work better than the others did theirs. The thing he came to care most about was the corn. Corn was a thing to make a special appeal to a man who wanted to make his own thing perfect. It thanked you for what you did for it. It recorded your proficiency. He gave it the best soil there could be for it—rich, pulverized. He learned just when to put it out, just how deep to cultivate. He found out by trying what it would do in rows and what it would do in hills. As he planted it, sometimes without knowing he was going to say them, he would repeat lines his father used to say, one of those verses which were the old way of handing down teaching about planting:

> Four seeds I drop in every hill;
> One for the worm to harm,
> One for the frost to kill,
> And two for the barn.

His father had learned it, when a little boy, from his father; and when that other little boy—his father's father—came to this middle western country he found the maize which the Indians were cultivating. In planting his corn Ira would sometimes find himself thinking back to the Indians. As he did things over and over the movements made for themselves a sort of rhythm, and it was as if this rhythm swung him into all that was back of him. He was less awkward at such times; he seemed less a figure outside all other things. They had never been able to interest Ira Mead in politics, and certainly he wasn't one to sit around and talk about his country, but sometimes as he listened to his whispering field of corn he would think with a queer satisfaction that corn was American. It was here before we were; it was of the very soil of America—something bequeathed us which we carried along. He would think of all that corn did—things that could go on because of it. And then he would wonder, with a superiority in which there was a queer tinge of affection, what those Indians who had perhaps tended maize in this very field would say if they could see one of his ears of corn. Perhaps it was because he would like to have them see his corn that he sometimes had a feeling they were *there*. Such thoughts once in a while broke into his mind, things that said something to him even though he had said nothing to them. To the south of him, at the Balches', where there was so often a lively crowd of young folks, where they played the piano and danced, where girls and fellows wandered around when it was moonlight—and when it wasn't—they laughed about Ira Mead, and one gay, bold girl wondered what he'd do if she'd up and kiss him! If anybody had hinted that he had his own substratum of romance—a romance of the race, a growth passion that seeped up under the walls which shut him in, they would have looked blank and said, "*Ira Mead?*" For more and more he touched that circle of life which was the Balches' at an angle which seemed to be sending him off by himself. There was Mary Balch, gay like the rest—and then something beside gay. She had a way of saying his name—no one had ever said his name like that before. Everyone else said it all in one breath— which seemed to make it the name of a person who naturally would be by himself. But Mary Balch said it almost as if it were in a song. "Why, hello, I–ra!" she'd say, sliding down from the I to the ra in a way—well, in a way that didn't get right out of your mind. And it was because he didn't get it right out of his mind that he became the more preoccupied with the things he was doing by himself—just as he used to be all taken up with some other thing when leapfrog was going on. He excelled in social graces as little as he had excelled in hurdling other boys' backs, and there was this thing in him which kept him from appearing to want to do what he couldn't do well.

To the north of him, at the Dietzes', they'd say, when the children were bad, "Maybe you'd like us to give you to Mr. Mead?" and the children howled loudly and were good. Mr. Mead appeared all a child would not ask in a father. He did not talk to them; he did not look at them. If they said anything to him, he did not hear them. And when children speak and it is as if they hadn't spoken—yes, *indeed* they'd rather be good. They were afraid of him. He was always around alone, and he was always looking the other way.

All Dietzes would have opened wide their eyes at the idea that Ira Mead had that sense of what has been and what may be in which is rooted the instinct of fatherhood. "Some *joke!*" Dietzes would reply. "Why, all he cares about's *corn!*"

It did go to corn. He found he could create new varieties of corn. By carefully selecting the seed he could produce corn that was unlike the other corn. This was more exciting than there might seem any reason for its being. To study his seed—compare, reject; choosing that which was best, or those kernels of new life which had in common interesting differences from the old life; then to give soil the care that would give seed every chance, to watch over it when it began to grow, guarding it from all that could hurt its health, giving it those things which would let it realize its possibilities to the utmost—to do this was something more than doing his work well—though it was also the incontrovertible testimony that he did do his work well. The corn proved Ira Mead's supremacy over Balches and Dietzes and all the other people around there. After he had been experimenting with corn for a couple of years he exhibited it at the state fair, where it made no little commotion, and was pronounced a new variety of corn, and called Mead corn.[1]

The night after he got the letter giving an award to Mead corn he didn't seem to want to sit inside with his mother, and thought of things to do that took him out. He went down to the barn, to make sure that he had closed the door. He stood before a full corn bin—corn bigger and better than any corn around. He wandered down into the field, where his late corn still grew. This was a starry night—still, except for a slight breeze that set the corn to talking. He stood still and listened to it. Why was it that it seemed to run such a long way back, and to take in so many things? He walked along between the corn until he had come to the place where his corn stopped and the Balches' corn began. And where his corn stopped and Balch corn began, big corn stopped and runty corn began.

As he stood there remarking the difference he heard a laugh—not close at hand, but up by the Balches' house—a girl's laugh borne on the south-west wind that carried from Balches' to him. It came again, Mary Balch's laugh—like that little way she had in saying his name, a soft sliding from one thing to another thing. Then came a man's laugh.

The man at the dividing line sharply turned toward home. He was thankful he didn't have to have anything to do with slack folks like Balches. He should think they'd be ashamed of such corn! His rancor at them mounted, and on the way back the whispering corn did not seem to be taking in so many things. . . . He didn't need neighbors—and he was glad he didn't, being such neighbors as they were! On the way back he had not that open, affectionate way of regarding his corn. It was a sort of sideways, a calculated, gloating way; the love for the thing he had created narrowed into the shrewd determination to make this thing do something more for *him*. Before he went in the house he looked over toward the Dietzes'. It would be a long day before Joe Dietz created a new variety of corn! Created a new variety? Why, he didn't know what to do with varieties that had been created for him! They said the Dietz place was mortgaged. No mortgage on *his* farm. He went to bed that night shut in with the resolve to make this corn *do* something for him. He'd bring it along and show what a man could do when he minded his own business and didn't fritter his time and his mind away on—on this and that—on nothing.

A few days later he met Fred Balch on the road. "Like to get some seed from you if I can," he called. "Think I'll try a little Mead corn myself."

The originator of Mead corn seemed to be considering things which this thing only remotely touched. "Guess it's all spoke for this year," he said, and drove on.

Suppose he *had* let him have some—he went over it to himself, more directly in touch with the thought than his manner had indicated. What would he make of it? What did he *know* about growing corn? And so with arguments he guarded jealously this chance to have a thing that was better than the thing around him, fought with himself for this way of showing everyone—of showing himself—he needed nothing from without.

Ira Mead was now thirty years old. He seemed older than that. He himself was like an ear of corn that has fertilized itself too long and needs the golden dust from other corn to bring new life. The next year he threw all his energies into bringing Mead corn up to an even higher standard than it had had when he showed it to the world. So he watched over it carefully, and there were things that worried him—things he seemed powerless to do anything about. The bulk of his ground he had of course planted for crop—there would be thirty-nine acres of Mead corn to sell in the fall. But there was an acre he kept for experiment—to see what Mead corn would go on doing, a plot for adventures in cross-fertilization. But the trouble was, the adventures were not all of his ordering. Corn was not at all like Ira Mead. It associated with other corn. You could fairly *see* it doing it. He stood one afternoon and watched the golden dust go through the air on a day of sunshine and wind—pollen from his standardized Mead corn blowing over and fertilizing his experiment corn, whose cross-fertilization he himself wanted to direct. There it came—procreate golden dust, the male flower that was in the tassel blowing over to the female flower hidden in the ear. From the depth of a bitter isolation Ira Mead hated this golden dust. Hated it and hated it impotently. For what could he do about it? Winds blew and carried seed. Winds blew and brought the life that changed other life. "Damn sociable stuff!" he said, with anger that a little astonished him.

Of course, certain things he could do. Next year he would give his corn for experiment a place farther away from other corn. He selected a place up near the house where this corn would have no neighbors. But there were other things that worried him all through this year of careful watching of his corn. There was not that year a perfect crop of Mead corn. Part of it was inferior. That part of it which was inferior was the part which grew nearest the Balches' corn.

He tried not to know this. It was too *thwarting* a thing for a man like Ira Mead to recognize if there was any way of keeping from recognizing it. He'd say, "Now I wonder what's the matter with this soil?" and under his plans for the further enrichment of the soil he'd bury what it foiled his life to know.

It was from the other side of the fence, speaking both literally and not so literally, that the truth came as if blown by wind. One day, in husking time, he was at work over near the Dietzes'. The Dietzes were in their field. And he heard a pleased, excited voice call:

"Why, Joe! Just look at this ear of corn! Down at this end the corn's *fine.*"

Truth came as if borne by wind. He stood quite still, as if knowing now there was nothing he could do, and into his sterile mind it came—it came! As if it were the golden dust that brought new life, it came. It was Bertha Dietz who cried, "Down at this end the corn's fine!"—Bertha Paxton, who had married Joe Dietz. He had wanted to make his thing perfect that he might have what she couldn't have. And now, because he had it, she had it, too. And he couldn't *help* this. As the wind goes on blowing, it came—it came! The Balches were south of him, and a little to the west. The prevailing wind was southwest. Pollen from the Balches' corn blew over and hurt his corn. The Dietzes were north of him, and this end of the field, to the east. Pollen from the Mead corn went over and enriched the Dietz corn. And he couldn't *help* this.

He stood there within his corn—corn which was changed by the corn around it, corn which impressed itself upon the corn around it. And suddenly, not knowing he was going to do it, he had twisted a stalk of corn until it snapped. Without knowing it was coming, there was suddenly that anger which makes men kill. He wanted to be let *alone.* He wanted to keep to him*self.* Hadn't a man a *right* to do that? He dug his boot into the ground where corn was rooted, wanting to *hurt*—hurt the corn, the earth, those things that wouldn't let him be what he wanted to be! His closed-in years fought for what closed-in years had made him as only a trapped thing will fight.

But the wind moved the corn and the corn responded—swayed, spoke. The torn stalk he clenched dropped from his hand. When you fight things larger than you you only know that you are small. Because they *were* so much larger than he, he could let himself go with them—only a fool will fight the winds that blow. He thought. For the first time in his whole life, without trying to limit his thinking, he thought. The corn . . . men . . . nations. . . . And he couldn't *help* this. It was that released him as wind releases life for other life.

That evening he put some seed corn in a basket. He took up his hat.

"Why, where you goin'?" asked his mother.

"To the Balches'."

"To the *Balches'*?"

"To the Balches'."

"But—what you goin' to the Balches' for?"

"To take them seed and tell them what I know about raising corn."

The old woman looked at her son—he who never said anything to you unless you said something to him.

"Why—what you goin' to do *that* for?" she asked, weakly.

"Because I can't have good corn while their corn's poor."

It was not, after all, easy to go to the Balches'. His whole life made it hard for him to go, and tried to turn him back. But what he had last said to his mother was saying itself to him, "I can't have good corn while their corn's poor." He found himself stepping to the swing of it, and that somehow kept him from turning back. He moved to this now as he used to move to the old verses his father had taught him about planting. A new rhythm. . . . His own creation.

It took him right up to the door. He knocked. The door opened and took him into a circle of light. And, after her first astonished moment, Mary Balch was saying, in her voice like sunshine and wind:

"Why, *hel*–lo, I–ra!"

Originally published in *Harper's Monthly Magazine* 138
(March 1919): 446–51

NOTE

1. Glaspell was fascinated with the theories of evolution, natural selection, and genetics of Darwin, Mendel, and Ernst Haeckel, which inform many of her works from her earliest novel, *The Glory of the Conquered* (1909), to one of her latest, *Norma Ashe* (1942), as well as both of her full-length plays, *Inheritors* and *The Verge*. While she celebrated humanity's ability to evolve and create, which she often described as a leap forward, breaking through limitations and boundaries, she also often portrayed the dark side of such Nietzschean striving for superhuman creative power.

Government Goat

Joe Doane couldn't get to sleep. On one side of him a family was crying because their man was dead, and on the other side a man was celebrating because he was alive.

When he couldn't any longer stand the wails of the Cadaras, Joe moved from his bedroom to the lounge in the sitting room. But the lounge in the sitting room, beside making his neck go in a way no neck wants to go, brought him too close to Ignace Silva's rejoicings in not having been in one of the dories that turned over when the schooner *Lillie-Bennie* was caught in the squall last Tuesday afternoon and unable to gather all her men back from the dories before the sea gathered them. Joe Cadara was in a boat that hadn't made it—hence the wails to the left of the Doanes, for Joe Cadara left a wife and four children and they had plenty of friends who could cry, too. But Ignace Silva—more's the pity, for at two o'clock in the morning you *like* to wish the person who is keeping you awake was dead—got back to the vessel. So tonight his friends were there with bottles, for when a man *might* be dead certainly the least you can do is to take notice of him by getting him drunk.

People weren't sleeping in Cape's End that night.[1] Those who were neither mourning nor rejoicing were being kept awake by mourners or rejoicers. All the vile, diluted whiskey that could be bought on the quiet was in use for the deadening or the heightening of emotion.[2] Joe Doane found himself wishing *he* had a drink. He'd like to stop thinking about dead fishermen—and hearing live ones. Everybody had been all strung up for two days ever since word came from Boston that the *Lillie-Bennie* was one of the boats "caught."

They didn't know until the *Lillie-Bennie* came in that afternoon just how many of her men she was bringing back with her. They were all out on Long Wharf to watch her come in and to see who would come ashore—and who wouldn't. Women were there, and lots of children. Some of these sets of a woman and children went away with a man, holding on to him and laughing, or perhaps looking foolish to think they had ever supposed he could be dead. Others went away as they had come—maybe very still, maybe crying. There were old men who came away carrying things that had belonged to sons who weren't coming ashore. It was all a good deal like a movie—only it didn't rest you.

So he *needed* sleep, he petulantly told things as he rubbed the back of his neck, wondered why lounges were made like that, and turned over. But instead of sleeping, he thought about Joe Cadara. They were friendly thoughts he had about Joe Cadara; much more friendly than the thoughts he was having about Ignace Silva. For one thing, Joe wasn't making any noise. Even when he was alive, Joe had made little noise. He always had his job on a vessel; he'd come up the Front street in his oilskins, turn in at his little red house, come out after a while and hoe in his garden or patch his woodshed, sit out on the wharf and listen to what Ignace Silva and other loud-mouthed Portuguese had to say—back to his little red house. He—well, he was a good deal like the sea. It came in, it went out. On Joe Cadara's last trip in, Joe Doane met him just as he was starting out. "Well, Joe," says Joe Doane, "off again?" "Off again," said Joe Cadara, and that was about all there seemed to be to it. He could see him going down the street—short, stocky, slow, *dumb*. By dumb he meant—oh, dumb like the sea was dumb—just going on doing it. And now—

All of a sudden he couldn't *stand* Ignace Silva. "*Hell!*" roared Joe Doane from the window, "don't you know a man's *dead?*" In an instant the only thing you could hear was the sea. In–Out—

Then he went back to his bedroom. "I'm not sleeping either," said his wife—the way people are quick to make it plain they're as bad off as the next one.

At first it seemed to be still at the Cadaras. The children had gone to sleep—so had the friends. Only one sound now where there had been many before. And that seemed to come out of the sea. You got it after a wave broke—as it was dying out. In that little letup between an in, an out, you knew that Mrs. Cadara had not gone to sleep, you knew that Mrs. Cadara was crying because Joe Cadara was dead in the sea.

So Joe Doane and his wife Mary lay there and listened to Annie Cadara crying for her husband, Joe Cadara.

Finally Mrs. Doane raised on her pillow and sighed. "Well, I suppose she wonders what she'll do now—those four children."

He could see Joe Cadara's back going down the Front street—broad, slow, *dumb*. "And I suppose," he said, as if speaking for something that had perhaps never spoken for itself, "that she feels bad because she'll never see him again."

"Why, of course she does," said his wife impatiently, as if he had contradicted something she had said.

But after usurping his thought she went right back to her own. "I don't see how she will get along. I suppose we'll have to help them some."

Joe Doane lay there still. He couldn't help anybody much—more was the pity. He had his own three children—and you could be a Doane without having money to help with—though some people didn't get that through their heads. Things used to be different with the Doanes. When the tide's in and you awake at three in the morning it all gets a good deal like the sea—at least with Joe Doane it did now. His grandfather, Ebenezer Doane, the whaling captain—In—Out—Silas Doane—A fleet of vessels off the Grand Banks—In—Out—All the Doanes. They had helped make the Cape, but—In—Out— Suddenly Joe laughed.

"What are you *laughing* at?" demanded his wife.

"I was just laughing," said Joe, "to think what those *old* Doanes would say if they could see us."

"Well, it's not anything to laugh at," said Mrs. Doane.

"Why, I think it is," good-humoredly insisted her husband, "it's such a *joke* on them."

"If it's a joke," said Mrs. Doane firmly, "it's not on *them*."

He wasn't sure just *who* the joke was on. He lay thinking about it. At three in the morning, when you can't sleep and the tide's in, you might get it mixed—who the joke was on.

But, no, the joke *was* on them, that they'd had their long slow deep *In—Out*—their whaling and their fleets, and that what came after was *him*—a tinkerer with other men's boats, a ship's carpenter who'd even work on *houses*. "Get Joe Doane to do it for you." And glad enough was Joe Doane to do it. And a Portagee livin' to either side of him!

He laughed. "You've got a funny idea of what's a *joke*," his wife said indignantly.

That seemed to be so. Things he saw as jokes weren't jokes to anybody else. Maybe that was why he sometimes seemed to be all by himself. He was beginning to get lost in an *In—Out*. Faintly he could hear Mrs. Cadara crying—Joe Cadara was in the sea, and faintly he heard his wife saying, "I suppose Agnes Cadara could wear Myrtie's shoes, only—the way things are, seems Myrtie's got to wear out her *own* shoes."

Next day when he came home at noon—he was at work then helping Ed Davis put a new coat on Still's store—he found his two boys—the boys were younger than Myrtie—pressed against the picket fence that separated Doanes from Cadaras.

"What those kids up to?" he asked his wife, while he washed up for dinner.

"Oh, they just want to see," she answered, speaking into the oven.

"See *what?*" he demanded; but this Mrs. Doane regarded as either too obvious or too difficult to answer, so he went to the door and called, "Joe! Edgar!"

"What you kids rubberin' at?" he demanded.

Young Joe dug with his toe. "The Cadaras have got a lot of company," said he.

"They're *crying!*" triumphantly announced the younger and more truthful Edgar.

"Well, suppose they are? They got a right to cry in their own house, ain't they? Let the Cadaras be. Find some fun at home."

The boys didn't seem to think this funny, nor did Mrs. Doane, but the father was chuckling to himself as they sat down to their baked flounder.

But to let the Cadaras be and find some fun at home became harder and harder to do. The *Lillie-Bennie* had lost her men in early summer and the town was as full of summer folk as the harbor was of whiting. There had never been a great deal for summer folk to do in Cape's End, and so the Disaster was no disaster to the summer's entertainment. In other words, summer folk called upon the Cadaras. The young Doanes spent much of their time against the picket fence; sometimes young

Cadaras would come out and graciously enlighten them. "A woman she brought my mother a black dress." Or, "A lady and two little boys came in automobile and brought me kiddie-car and white pants." One day Joe Doane came home from work and found his youngest child crying because Tony Cadara wouldn't lend him the kiddie-car. This was a reversal of things; heretofore Cadaras had cried for the belongings of the Doanes. Joe laughed about it, and told Edgar to cheer up, and maybe he'd have a kiddie-car himself some day—and meanwhile he had a pa.

Agnes Cadara and Myrtie Doane were about of an age. They were in the same class in high school. One day when Joe Doane was pulling in his dory after being out doing some repairs on the *Lillie-Bennie* he saw a beautiful young lady standing on the Cadaras' bulkhead. Her back was to him, but you were sure she was beautiful. She had the look of someone from away, but not like the usual run of summer folk. Myrtie was standing looking over at this distinguished person.

"Who's that?" Joe asked of her.

"Why," said Myrtie, in an awed whisper, "it's Agnes Cadara—in her *mourning*."

Until she turned around, he wouldn't believe it. "Well," said he to Myrtie, "it's a pity more women haven't got something to mourn about."

"Yes," breathed Myrtie, "isn't she *wonderful?*"

Agnes's mourning had been given her by young Mrs. MacCrea who lived up on the hill and was herself just finishing mourning. It seemed Mrs. MacCrea and Agnes were built a good deal alike—though you never would have suspected it before Agnes began to mourn. Mrs. MacCrea was from New York, and these clothes had been made by a woman Mrs. MacCrea called by her first name. Well, maybe she was a woman you'd call by her first name, but she certainly did have a way of making you look as if you weren't native to the place you were born in. Before Agnes Cadara had anything to mourn about she was simply "one of those good-looking Portuguese girls." There were too many of them in Cape's End to get excited about any of them. One day he heard some women on the beach talking about how these clothes had "found" Agnes—as if she had been lost.

Mrs. MacCrea showed Agnes how to do her hair in a way that went with her clothes. One noon when Joe got home early because it rained and he couldn't paint, when he went upstairs he saw Myrtie trying to do this to *her* hair. Well, it just couldn't be *done* to Myrtie's hair. Myrtie didn't have hair you could do what you pleased with. She was all red in the face with trying, and being upset because she couldn't do it. He had to laugh—and that didn't help things a bit. So he said:

"Never mind, Myrtie, we can't all go into mourning."

"Well, I don't care," said Myrtie, sniffling, "it's not fair."

He had to laugh again and as she didn't see what there was to laugh at, he had to try to console again. "Never mind, Myrt," said he, "you've got *one* thing Agnes Cadara's not got."

"I'd like to know what," said Myrtie, jerking at her hair.

He waited; funny she didn't think of it herself. "Why—a father," said he.

"Oh," said Myrtie—the way you do when you don't know *what* to say. And then, "*Well,*—"

Again he waited—then laughed; waited again, then turned away.

Somebody gave Mrs. Cadara a fireless cooker.[3] Mrs. Doane had no fireless cooker. So she had to stand all day over her hot stove—and this she spoke of often. "My supper's in the fireless cooker," Mrs. Cadara would say, and stay out in the cool yard, weeding her flowerbed. "It certainly would be nice to have one of those fireless cookers," Mrs. Doane would say, as she put a meal on the table and wiped her brow with her apron.

"Well, why don't you kill your husband?" Joe Doane would retort. "Now, if only you didn't have a *husband*—you could have a fireless cooker."

Jovially he would put the question, "Which would you rather have, a husband or a fireless cooker?" He would argue it out—and he would sometimes get them all to laughing, only the argument was never a very long one. One day it occurred to him that the debates were short because the others didn't hold up their end. He was talking for the fireless cooker—if it was going to be a real debate, they ought to speak up for the husband. But there seemed to be so much less to be said for a husband than there was for a fireless cooker. This struck him as really quite funny, but it seemed it was a joke he had to enjoy by himself. Sometimes when he came home pretty tired—for you could get as tired at odd jobs as at jobs that weren't odd—and heard all about what the Cadaras were that night to eat out of their fireless cooker, he would wish that someone else would do the joking. It was kind of tiresome doing it all by yourself—and kind of lonesome.

One morning he woke up feeling particularly rested and lively. He was going out to work on the *Lillie-Bennie*, and he always felt in better spirits when he was working on a boat.

It was a cool, fresh, sunny morning. He began a song—he had a way of making up songs. It was, "I'd rather be alive than dead." He didn't think of any more lines, so while he was getting into his clothes he kept singing this one, to a tune which became more and more stirring. He went over to the window by the looking glass. From this window you looked over to the Cadaras. And then he saw that from the Cadaras a new arrival looked at him.

He stared. Then loud and long he laughed. He threw up the window and called, "Hello, there!"

The new arrival made no reply, unless a slight droop of the head could be called a reply.

"Well, you cap the climax!" called Joe Doane.

Young Doanes had discovered the addition to the Cadara family and came running out of the house.

"Pa!" Edgar called up to him, "the Cadaras have got a *Goat!*"

"Well, do you know," said his father, "I kind of *suspected* that was a goat."

Young Cadaras came out of the house to let young Doanes know just what their privileges were to be with the goat—and what they weren't. They could walk around and look at her; they were not to lead her by her rope.

"There's no hope now," said Joe, darkly shaking his head. "No man in his senses would buck up against a *goat.*"

The little Doanes wouldn't come in and eat their breakfast. They'd rather stay out and walk round the goat.

"I think it's too bad," their mother sighed, "the kiddie-car and the ball-suit and the sailboat were *enough* for the children to bear—without this goat. It seems our children haven't got *any* of the things the Cadaras have got."

177

"Except—" said Joe, and waited for someone to fill it in. But no one did, so he filled it in with a laugh—a rather short laugh.

"Look out they don't put you in the fireless cooker!" he called to the goat as he went off to work.

But he wasn't joking when he came home at noon. He turned in at the front gate and the goat blocked his passage. The Cadaras had been willing to let the goat call upon the Doanes and graze while calling. "Get out of my way!" called Joe Doane in a surly way not like Joe Doane.

"Pa!" said young Joe in an awed whisper, "it's a *government* goat."

"What do I care if it is?" retorted his father. "*Damn* the government goat!"

Everyone fell back, as when blasphemy—as when treason—have been uttered. These Portuguese kids looking at *him* like that—as if *they* were part of the government and he outside. He was so mad that he bawled at Tony Cadara, "To *hell* with your government goat!"

From her side of the fence, Mrs. Cadara called, "Tony, you bring the goat right home," as one who calls her child—and her goat—away from evil.

"And keep her there!" finished Joe Doane.

The Doanes ate their meal in stricken silence. Finally Doane burst out, "What's the matter with you all? Such a fuss about the orderin' off of a *goat*."

"It's a *government* goat," lisped Edgar.

"It's a *government* goat," repeated his wife in a tense voice.

"What do you mean—government goat? There's no such animal."

But it seemed there was. The Cadaras had, not only the goat, but a book about the goat. The book was from the government. The government had raised the goat and had singled the Cadaras out as a family upon whom a government goat should be conferred. The Cadaras held her in trust for the government. Meanwhile they drank her milk.

"Tony Cadara said, if I'd dig clams for him this afternoon he'd let me help milk her tonight," said young Joe.

This was too much. "Ain't you kids got no *spine*? Kowtowing to them Portuguese because a few folks that's sorry for them have made them presents. They're *ginnies*. You're Doanes."

"I want a goat!" wailed Edgar. His father got up from the table.

"The children are all right," said his wife, in her patient voice that made you impatient. "It's natural for them to want a few of the things they see other children having."

He'd get *away!* As he went through the shed he saw his line and picked it up. He'd go out on the breakwater—maybe he'd get some fish, at least have some peace.

The breakwater wasn't very far down the beach from his house. He used to go out there every once in a while. Every once in a while he had a feeling he had to get by himself. It was half a mile long and of big rocks that had big gaps. You had to do some climbing—you could imagine you were in the mountains—and that made you feel far off and different. Only when the tide came in, the sea filled the gaps—then you had to "watch your step."

He went way out and turned his back on the town and fished. He wasn't to finish the work on the *Lillie-Bennie.* They said that morning they thought they'd have to send down the Cape for an "expert." So *he* would probably go to work at the new cold storage—working with a lot of Portagee laborers. He wondered why things were this way with him. They seemed to have just happened so. When you should have had some money it didn't come natural to do the things of people who have no money. The money went out of the "Bank" fishing about three years before his father sold his vessels. During those last three years Captain Silas Doane had spent all the money he had to keep things going, refusing to believe that the way of handling fish had changed and that the fishing between Cape's End and the Grand Banks would no longer be what it had been. When he sold he kept one vessel, and the next winter she went ashore right across there on the northeast arm of the cape. Joe Doane was aboard her that night. Myrtie was a baby then. It was of little Myrtie he thought when it seemed the vessel would pound herself to pieces before they could get off. *He* couldn't be lost! He had to live and work so his little girl could have everything she wanted— After that the Doanes were without a vessel—and Doanes without a vessel were fish out of sea. They had never been folks to work on another man's boat. He supposed he had never started any big new thing because it had always seemed he was just filling in between trips. A good many years had slipped by and he was still just putting in time. And it began to look as if there wasn't going to be another trip.

Suddenly he had to laugh. Some *joke* on Joe Cadara! He could see him going down the Front street—broad, slow, *dumb*. Why, Joe Cadara thought his family *needed* him. He thought they got along because he made those trips. But had Joe Cadara ever been able to give his wife a fireless cooker? Had the government presented a goat to the Cadaras when Joe was there? Joe Doane sat out on the breakwater and laughed at the joke on Joe Cadara. When Agnes Cadara was a little girl she would run to meet her father when he came in from a trip. Joe Doane used to like to see the dash she made. But Agnes was just tickled to death with her mourning!

He sat there a long time—sat there until he didn't know whether it was a joke or not. But he got two haddock and more whiting than he wanted to carry home. So he felt better. A man sometimes needed to get off by himself.

As he was turning in at home he saw Ignace Silva about to start out on a trip with Captain Gorspie. Silva thought he *had* to go. But Silva had been saved—and had *his* wife a fireless cooker? Suddenly Joe Doane called.

"Hey! Silva! You're the government goat!"

The way Doane laughed made Silva know this was a joke; not having a joke of his own he just turned this one around and sent it back. "Government goat yourself!"

"Shouldn't wonder," returned Joe jovially.

He had every Doane laughing at supper that night. "Bear up! Bear up! True, you've got a father instead of a goat—but we've all got our cross! We all have our cross to bear!"

"Say!" said he after supper, "every woman, every kid, puts on a hat, and up we go to see if Ed Smith might *happen* to have a soda."

As they were starting out, he peered over at the Cadaras in mock surprise. "Why, what's the matter with that *goat?* That goat don't seem to be takin' the Cadaras out for a soda."

Next day he started to make a kiddie-car for Edgar. He promised Joe he'd make him a sailboat. But it was uphill work. The Cape's End summer folk gave a "Streets of Baghdad" and the "disaster families" got the proceeds.[4] Then when the summer folk began to go away it was quite natural to give what they didn't want to take with them to a family that had had a disaster. The Doanes had had no disaster; anyway, the Doanes weren't the kind of people you'd think of giving things to. True, Mr. Doane would sometimes come and put on your screen doors for you, but it was as if a neighbor had come in to lend a hand. A man who lives beside the sea and works on the land is not a picturesque figure. Then, in addition to being alive, Joe Doane wasn't Portuguese. So the Cadaras got the underwear and the bats and preserves that weren't to be taken back to town. No one father—certainly not a father without a steady job—could hope to compete with all that wouldn't go into trunks.

Anyway, he couldn't possibly make a goat. No wit or no kindness which emanated from him could do for his boys what that goat did for the Cadaras. Joe Doane came to throw an awful hate on the government goat. Portagees were only Portagees—yet *they* had the government goat. Why, there had been Doanes on that Cape for more than a hundred years. There had been times when everybody round there *worked* for the Doanes, but now the closest his boys could come to the government was beddin' down the Cadaras' government goat! Twenty-five years ago Cadaras had huddled in a hut on the godforsaken Azores! If they knew there was a United States government, all they knew was that there *was* one. And now it was these Cadara kids were putting on airs to *him* about the government. He knew there was a joke behind all this, behind his getting so wrought up about it, but he would sit and watch that goat eat leaves in the vacant lot across from the Cadaras until the goat wasn't just a goat. It was the turn things had taken. One day as he was sitting watching Tony Cadara milking his goat—wistful boys standing by—Ignace Silva, just in from a trip, called out, "Government goat yourself!" and laughed at he knew not what.

By God!—'twas true! A Doane without a vessel. A native who had let himself be crowded out by ignorant upstarts from a filthy dot in the sea! A man who hadn't got his bearings in the turn things had taken. Of a family who had built up a place for other folks to grow fat in. *Sure* he was the government goat. By just being alive he kept his family from all the fancy things they might have if he was dead. Could you be more of a *goat* than that?

Agnes Cadara and Myrtie came up the street together. He had a feeling that Myrtie was *set up* because she was walking along with Agnes Cadara. Time had been when Agnes Cadara had hung around in order to go with Myrtie! Suddenly he thought of how his wife had said maybe Agnes Cadara could wear Myrtie's shoes. He looked at Agnes Cadara's feet—at Myrtie's. Why, Myrtie looked like a kid from an orphan asylum walking along with the daughter of the big man of the town!

He got up and started toward town. He wouldn't stand it! He'd show 'em! He'd buy Myrtie— Why, he'd buy Myrtie—! He put his hand in his pocket. Change from a dollar. The rest of the week's pay had gone to Lou Hibbard for groceries. Well, he could hang it up at Wilkinson's. He'd buy Myrtie—!

He came to a millinery store. There was a lot of black ribbon strewn around in the window. He stood and looked at it. Then he laughed. Just the thing!

"Cheer up, Myrt," said he, when he got back home and presented it to her. "You can mourn a *little*. For that matter, you've got a *little* to mourn about."

Myrtie took it doubtfully—then wound it round her throat. She *liked* it, and this made her father laugh. He laughed a long time—it was as if he didn't want to be left without the sound of his laughing.

"There's nothing so silly as to laugh when there's nothing to laugh at," his wife said finally.

"Oh, I don't know about that," said Joe Doane.

"And while it's very nice to make the children presents, in our circumstances it would be better to give them useful presents."

"But what's so useful as mourning?" demanded Doane. "Think of all Myrtie has got to mourn *about*. Poor, poor Myrtie—she's *got* a father!"

You can say a thing until you think it's so. You can say a thing until you make other people think it's so. He joked about standing between them and a fireless cooker until he could see them *thinking* about it. All the time he hated his old job at the cold storage. A Doane had no business to be ashore *freezing* fish. It was the business of a Doane to go out to sea and come home with a full vessel.

One day he broke through that old notion that Doanes didn't work on other men's boats and half in a joke proposed to Captain Cook that he fire a ginnie or two and give him a berth on the *Elizabeth*. And Bill Cook was *rattled*. Finally he laughed and said, "Why, Joe, you ought to be on your own vessel"—which was a way of saying he didn't want him on *his*. Why didn't he? Did they think because he hadn't made a trip for so long that he wasn't good for one? Did they think a Doane couldn't take orders? Well, there weren't many boats he *would* go on. Most of them in the harbor now were owned by Portuguese. He guessed it wouldn't come natural to him to take orders from a Portagee—not at sea. He was taking orders from one now at the cold storage—but as the cold storage wasn't where he belonged it didn't make so much difference who he took orders from.

At the close of that day Bill Cook told him he ought to be on his own vessel, Joe Doane sat at the top of those steps which led from his house down to the sea and his thoughts were like the sails coming round the point—slowly, in a procession, and from a long way off. His father's boats used to come round that point this same way. He was lonesome tonight. He felt half like an old man and half like a little boy.

Mrs. Cadara was standing over on the platform to the front of her house. She too was looking at the sails to the far side of the breakwater—sails coming home. He wondered if she was thinking about Joe Cadara—wishing he was on one of those boats. *Did* she ever think about Joe Cadara? Did she ever wish he would come home? He'd like to ask her. He'd like to know. When you went away and didn't come back home, was all they thought about how they'd get along? And if they were getting along all right, was it true they'd just as soon be without you?

He got up. He had a sudden crazy feeling he wanted to *fight* for Joe Cadara. He wanted to go over there and say to that fireless-cooker woman, "Trip after trip he made, in the cold and in the storm. He kept you warm and safe here at home. It was for you he went; it was to you he came back. *And you'll miss him yet*. Think this is going to keep up? Think you're going to interest those rich folks as much next year as you did this? Five years from now you'll be on your knees with a *brush* to keep those kids warm and fed."

He'd like to get the truth out of her! Somehow things wouldn't seem so *rotten* if he could know that she sometimes lay in her bed at night and cried for Joe Cadara.

It was quiet tonight; all the Cadara children and all the Doanes were out looking for the government goat. The government goat was increasing her range. She seemed to know that, being a government goat, she was protected from harm. If a government goat comes in your yard, you are a little slow to fire a tin can at her—not knowing just how treasonous this may be. Nobody in Cape's End knew the exact status of a government goat, and each one hesitated to ask for the very good reason that the person asked might know and you would then be exposed as one who knew less than someone else. So the government goat went about where she pleased, and tonight she had pleased to go far. It left the neighborhood quiet—the government goat having many guardians.

Joe Doane felt like saying something to Mrs. Cadara. Not the rough, wild thing he had wanted to say a moment before, but just say something to her. He and she were the only people around—children all away and his wife upstairs with a headache. He felt lonesome and he thought she looked that way—standing there against the sea in light that was getting dim. She and Joe Cadara used to sit out on that bulkhead. She moved toward him, as if she were lonesome and wanted to speak. On his side of the fence, he moved a little nearer her. She said,

"My, I hope the goat's not lost!"

He said nothing.

"That goat, she's so tame," went on Joe Cadara's wife with pride and affection, "she'll follow anybody around like a dog."

Joe Doane got up and went in the house.

It got so he didn't talk much to anybody. He sometimes had jokes, for he'd laugh, but they were jokes he had all to himself and his laughing would come as a surprise and make others turn and stare at him. It made him seem off by himself, even when they were all sitting round the table. He laughed at things that weren't things to laugh at, as when Myrtie said, "Agnes Cadara had a letter from Mrs. MacCrea and a *mourning* handkerchief." And after he'd laughed at a thing like that which nobody else saw as a thing to laugh at, he'd sit and stare out at the water. "Do be *cheerful*," his wife would say. He'd laugh at that.

But one day he burst out and said things. It was a Sunday afternoon and the Cadaras were all going to the cemetery. Every Sunday afternoon they went and took flowers to the stone that said, "Lost at Sea." Agnes would call, "Come, Tony! We dress now for the cemetery," in a way that made the Doane children feel that they had nothing at all to do. They filed out at the gate dressed in the best the summer folk had left them and it seemed as if there were a fair, or a circus, and all the Doanes had to stay at home.

This afternoon he didn't know they were going until he saw Myrtie at the window. He wondered what she could be looking at as if she wanted it so much. When he saw, he had to laugh.

"Why, Myrt," said he, "*you* can go to the cemetery if you want to. There are lots of Doanes there. Go on and pay them a visit.

"I'm sure they'd be real glad to see you," he went on, as she stood there doubtfully. "I doubt if anybody has visited them for a long time. You could visit your great-grandfather, Ebenezer Doane. Whales were so afraid of that man that they'd send word around from sea to sea that he was coming. And Lucy Doane is there—Ebenezer's wife. Lucy Doane was a woman who took what she wanted. Maybe the whales were afraid of Ebenezer—but Lucy wasn't. There was a dispute between her and her brother about a quilt of their mother's, and in the dead of night she went into his house and took it off him while he slept. Spunk up! Be like the *old* Doanes! *Go* to the cemetery and wander around from grave to grave while the Cadaras are standin' by their one stone! My father—he'd be glad to see you. Why, if he was alive now—if Captain Silas Doane was here, he'd let the Cadaras know whether they could walk on the sidewalk or whether they were to go in the street!"

Myrtie was interested, but after a moment she turned away. "You only go for near relatives," she sighed.

He stood staring at the place where she had been. He laughed; stopped the laugh; stood there staring. "You only go for *near* relatives." Slowly he turned and walked out of the house. The government goat, left home alone, came up to him as if she thought she'd take a walk too.

"Go to hell!" said Joe Doane, and his voice showed that inside he was crying.

Head down, he walked along the beach as far as the breakwater. He

185

started out on it, not thinking of what he was doing. So the only thing he could do for Myrtie was give her a reason for going to the cemetery. She *wanted* him in the cemetery—so she'd have some place to go on Sunday afternoons! She could wear black then—*all* black, not just a ribbon round her neck. Suddenly he stood still. Would she *have* any black to wear? He had thought of a joke before which all other jokes he had ever thought of were small and sick. Suppose he were to take himself out of the way and then they didn't *get* the things they thought they'd have in place of him? He walked on fast—fast and crafty, picking his way among the smaller stones in between the giant stones in a fast, sure way he never could have picked had he been thinking of where he went. He went along like a cat who is going to get a mouse. And in him grew this giant joke. Who'd *give* them the fireless cooker? Would it come into anybody's head to give young Joe Doane a sailboat just because his father was dead? They'd rather have a goat than a father. But suppose they were to lose the father and *get* no goat? Myrtie'd be a mourner without any mourning. She'd be *ashamed* to go to the cemetery.

He laughed so that he found himself down, sitting down on one of the smaller rocks between the giant rocks, on the side away from town, looking out to sea.

He forgot his joke and knew that he wanted to return to the sea. Doanes belonged at sea. Ashore things struck you funny—then, after they'd once got to you, hurt. He thought about how he used to come round this point when Myrtie was a baby. As he passed this very spot and saw the town lying there in the sun he'd think about her, and how he'd see her now, and how she'd kick and crow. But now Myrtie wanted to go and visit him—*in the cemetery*. Oh, it was a joke all right. But he guessed he was tired of jokes. Except the one *great* joke—joke that seemed to slap the whole of life right smack in the face.

The tide was coming in. In—Out—Doanes and Doanes. In—Out—Him too. In—Out—He was getting wet. He'd have to move up higher. But— *why move?* Perhaps this was as near as he could come to getting back to sea. Caught in the breakwater. That was about it—wasn't it? Rocks were queer things. You could wedge yourself in where you couldn't get yourself out. He hardly had to move. If he'd picked a place he couldn't have picked a better one. Wedge himself in—tide almost in now—too hard to get out—pounded to pieces, like the last vessel Doanes had owned. Near as he could come to getting back to sea. Near as he deserved to come—him freezing fish with ginnies. And there'd *be* no fireless cooker!

He twisted his shoulders to wedge in where it wouldn't be easy to wedge out. Face turned up, he saw something move on the great flat rock above the jagged rocks. He pulled himself up a little; he rose; he swung up to the big rock above him. On one flat-topped boulder stood Joe Doane. On the other flat-topped boulder stood the government goat.

"Go to hell!" said Joe Doane, and he was sobbing. "Go to *hell!*"

The government goat nodded her head a little in a way that wagged her beard and shook her bag.

"Go home! Drown yourself! Let me be! Go 'way!" It was fast, and choked, and he was shaking.

The goat would do none of these things. He sat down, his back to the government goat, and tried to forget that she was there. But there are moments when a goat is not easy to forget. He was willing there should be *some* joke to his death—like caught in the breakwater, but he wasn't going to die before a *goat.* After all, he'd amounted to a little more than *that.* He'd look around to see if perhaps she had started home. But she was always standing right there looking at him.

Finally he jumped up in a fury. "What'd you come for? What do you *want* of me? How do you expect to get home?" Between each question he'd wait for an answer. None came.

He picked up a small rock and threw it at the government goat. She jumped, slipped, and would have fallen from the boulder if he hadn't caught at her hind legs. Having saved her, he yelled: "You needn't expect *me* to save you. Don't expect anything from *me!*"

He'd have new gusts of fury at her. "What you out here for? Think you was a *mountain* goat? Don't you know the tide's comin' in? Think you can get back easy as you got *out?*"

He kicked at her hind legs to make her move on. She stood and looked at the water which covered the in-between rocks on which she had picked her way out. "Course," said Joe Doane. "Tide's in—you fool! You damned *goat!*" With the strength of a man who is full of fury he picked her up and threw her to the next boulder. "Hope you kill yourself!" was his heartening word.

187

But the government goat did not kill herself. She only looked around for further help.

To get away from her, he had to get her ashore. He guided and lifted, planted fore legs and shoved at hind legs, all the time telling her he hoped she'd kill herself. Once he stood still and looked all around and thought. After that he gave the government goat a shove that sent her in water above her knees. Then he had to get in too and help her to a higher rock.

It was after he had thus saved the government goat from the sea out of which the government goat had cheated him that he looked ahead to see there were watchers on the shore. Cadaras had returned from the cemetery. Cadaras and Doanes were watching him bring home the government goat.

From time to time he'd look up at them. There seemed to be no little agitation among this group. They'd hold on to each other and jump up and down like watchers whose men are being brought in from a wreck. There was one place where again he had to lift the government goat. After this he heard shouts and looked ashore to see his boys dancing up and down like little Indians.

Finally they had made it. The watchers on the shore came running out to meet them.

"Oh, Mr. Doane!" cried Mrs. Cadara, hands outstretched, "I am *thankful* to you! You saved my goat! I *have* no man myself to save my goat. I *have* no man. I *have* no man!"

Mrs. Cadara covered her face with her hands, swayed back and forth, and sobbed because her man was dead.

Young Cadaras gathered around her. They seemed of a sudden to know they had no father, and to realize that this was a thing to be deplored. Agnes even wet her mourning handkerchief.

Myrtie came up and took his arm. "Oh, Father," said she, "I was so 'fraid you'd hurt yourself!"

He looked down into his little girl's face. He realized that just a little while before he had expected never to look into her face again. He looked at the government goat, standing a little apart, benevolently regarding this humankind. Suddenly Joe Doane began to laugh. He laughed— laughed—and laughed. And it *was* a laugh.

"When I saw you lift that goat!" said his wife, in the voice of a woman who may not have a fireless cooker, but—!

Young Joe Doane, too long browbeaten not to hold the moment of his advantage, began dancing round Tony Cadara with the taunting yell, "You ain't *got* no pa to save your goat!" And Edgar lispingly chimed in, "Ain't *got* no pa to save your goat!"

"Here!" cried their father, "Stop devilin' them kids about what they can't help. Come! Hats on! Every Doane, every Cadara, goes up to see if Ed Smith might *happen* to have a soda."

But young Joe had suffered too long to be quickly silent. "You ain't *got* no pa to get you soda!" persisted he.

"Joe!" commanded his father, "Stop pesterin' them kids or I'll *lick* you!"

And Joe, drunk with the joy of having what the Cadaras had not, shrieked, "You ain't *got* no pa to lick you! You ain't *got* no pa to lick you!"

Originally published in *Pictorial Review* (April 1919)

NOTES

1. Cape's End is Glaspell's fictional pseudonym for Provincetown, Cape Cod, Massachusetts, where she and her husband, George Cram Cook, spent summers, along with other artists and writers, and bought their home in 1914 at 564 Commercial Street, where Glaspell lived for most of her life after Cook's death in 1924.

2. In the United States, the sale, manufacture, and transportation of alcohol for consumption were illegal during the period of Prohibition, which started in January 1920 and lasted for the next thirteen years. Although the national law wasn't yet in effect when Glaspell published this story in 1919, the law had already been passed by Congress, and the Eighteenth Amendment to the Constitution (mandating prohibition) had been ratified by most states, including Massachusetts. Even before 1920, local prohibition laws were enforced by many state and county governments, and most licensed saloons moved to larger cities and towns. In rural areas, alcoholic beverages were often home-brewed or obtained illegally.

3. "Fireless cookers were very popular in the early 1900s to save labor and

fuel, rather like our crock pots. . . . In electric fireless cookers 'the current is applied just long enough to bring the food to a proper temperature . . . then the current automatically shuts off, but the dinner continues to cook without expense.' In a 1925 letter: 'We prepared our dinner in the morning before breakfast, stowed it away in the electric fireless cooker and at night we set the table and served it.'" See Patricia Bixler Reber, "Fireless Cookers" http://www.hearthcook.com/aaFirelesscooker.html.

4. The practice of holding street fairs to raise money for charitable purposes originated in England in the early nineteenth century and later became popular in the United States. Often these charity bazaars displayed "oriental" influences and featured decorated stands selling handicrafts and imported novelties, most famously recorded in James Joyce's story "Araby." Since profits were to be donated to specific causes, the fairs could be promoted as entertainment with a benevolent purpose.

The Nervous Pig

IF YOU WERE WRITING A BOOK on the comparative civilizations of ancient and modern India, how would you like to have a young woman come bounding up to your window to tell you that the neighbor's pig had eight little pigs?

Horace Caldwell was displeased by the information; not so much by the information as by the method and time of acquiring it. He suspended his pen over the half-written word "indigent" (he had taken great pleasure in writing it, as it was so precisely the word) and looked at the head of Vivian Truce, which vibrated there above the window box as though it were a flower above the flowers. He did not want to think of the comparative beauties of Vivian's face and nasturtiums; he wanted to think of the comparative attitudes toward women of ancient and modern Hindus. That was the trouble with Vivian. She took you from the thing you wanted to be thinking.

"*Eight!*" she squealed.

"Eight?" he repeated, helplessly, for the wind played lightly with her hair and through the nasturtium leaves—she made the Hindus remote. *That* was the trouble with her. She made things remote.

"*Eight,*" she said again, and her hands came up and fluttered with the leaves—fluttering Sanskrit back into obscurity!

"Eight," he announced after her, as if to let her know he was quite aware of the number of pigs the neighbor's pig had had. She continued to stand there, letting the breeze try this and that with her hair. "Well," he added, severely pushing back his own hair, as if in rebuke to all hair, "isn't that all right?"

Her nose went down into a nasturtium; and while her nose smelled the flower her eyes regarded him. "Why, yes," she finally assured him, "it's *quite* all right." She again regarded him—laughed as if there were something to laugh *at*—was gone.

Mr. Caldwell did not enjoy finishing the word "indigent." The neighbor's pig had eight little pigs. Naturally, she would have eight little pigs—or thereabouts. Why need this stand between him and an old and beautiful civilization? He kept looking at the window box. Nasturtiums were not much, after all.

And then he heard Vivian within the house, telling his sister what she had told him—a little less exuberantly, excitement having lost its flush in the first telling. Still, there was enough left; Vivian could lose a good deal of exuberance and still have enough left. "Gertrude," she was saying, "what do you *think?* Mr. Moon's pig has eight *little* pigs!"

"No! Not *really?*" rejoined Gertrude—why in the world did they act as though it were something so *extraordinary?*

Though with Gertrude nothing was extraordinary for long. "Vivian," he heard her say, "I'm thinking of having this room done over. Do you think a lavender—" Then they moved into the room, thank Heaven, and he no longer heard them.

Poor Vivian—no one was properly excited. The neighbor's pig might have eighty little pigs, and if Gertrude was thinking of turning a green bedspread lavender, eighty little pigs would be nothing to her. All the wonders of the world would never take Gertrude out of that house. At least Vivian wasn't *that* way.

But thinking of the way Vivian wasn't made him think of the way Vivian was. He moved impatiently and ran his hand back through his hair with indignation. So far no word had followed "indigent." And the word that finally came did not follow "indigent." It was written at the side. It was "volatile." He waited a little while and then he wrote down "emotional." This made him feel better, as if to assure himself his interest in Vivian was a purely scientific one, and, having pigeonholed her, he could now keep her out of the way. He would get the book he wanted from the library, then settle *down*. But as he passed through the hall:

"Horace," called Gertrude, as one who imparts a pleasant bit of news, "Mr. Moon's pig has eight little pigs."

"I *know* it," snapped Horace. He heard a laugh—Vivian's!

He went back and wrote some very severe things about the women who had once lived in India. Women never *had* been—what they should be! But by evening it pleased him to be satiric. When his brother-in-law, getting home from the city, drove up to the door, Horace rose from his place on the veranda and called, excitedly: "Ben! *Ben!* What do you *think?* Mr. Moon's pig has eight *little* pigs!"

Ben appeared rather astonished at such a greeting from this source, but, being a businessman, he was prepared to adjust himself to anything. "Eight little pigs?" he replied. "Well, it's always nice to see things moving on!" Then he spoke of the price of pork.

But the news they gave Ben that night was as nothing to the news they had for him the next night.

In the afternoon Horace went with Vivian to see the little pigs. That is, they started for a walk, and Vivian proposed they stop and visit the pigs. She said the little pigs were just too darling.

"Just too darling" was for Horace a new attitude toward pigs, but he smiled tolerantly upon Vivian, who in her bright sweater and gay woolly skirt was enough to make even a student of India smile. Mr. Caldwell was feeling in the best of spirits. He had had a good morning's work and he quite approved of giving himself this pleasure of a tramp over the hills with Vivian. It was a part of his program to take walks. One worked the better for them.

But when they got to the back of Mr. Moon's house they found something going on which was not part of anyone's program—one of those mad things which knock programs over.

Mr. Moon was running round and round the pigsty with a pitchfork. He jabbed the air wildly with the pitchfork; he jabbed it also with wild words, "Gol-darn fool!" and words yet wilder.

"Why, Mr. *Moon!*" cried Vivian, running up, "what are you doing to the pigs?"

"What am *I* doin' to the pigs?" retorted the outraged Moon. "What's *she* doin' to the pigs!" And he stabbed his pitchfork toward the mother pig as if to run her through. "*Ask* her!" he went on in fury. "Ask her *where's her eighth little pig!*"

"Well," asked Vivian, "where is it?"

"In her belly," replied Mr. Moon, terse if not elegant.

Vivian's mind seemed unequal to grasping the extraordinary sequence of events required to bring the eighth little pig to the place where Mr. Moon said it was. To tell the truth, this was likewise true of Mr. Caldwell's mind, so when Vivian gasped, "She *ate* it?" it came to him with a shock that *that* was what had happened.

"She ate it," asserted Mr. Moon. "Ate the pig she bore! That's the kind of a sow *she* is."

"I didn't know they ate them," said Mr. Caldwell, speaking of it as a phenomenon.

"And so they don't," said the raiser of pigs, with less scientific detachment, "not them that has *sense*. But *her*. *That* pig." He waved his pitchfork around her—violent and ineffectual.

All this while the seven uneaten pigs were squealing. When seven little pigs squeal at once there is a large volume of discordant sound.

"Shut up!" cried Mr. Moon, turning the pitchfork on the air above the little pigs. "You want to be *in*side? Keep your mouths shut—or go back to the belly you came from!"

Vivian stepped back, shocked, but Horace was pleased by the phrase. It had violence; there was blood in it; it was of the earth—somehow of the race. "Back to the belly you came from!" He didn't know whether it was bitter or largely soothing.

But Vivian was thinking of the pig. "But, Mr. Moon," she asked, "*why* did she eat her own little pig?"

"Ask *her*," replied Mr. Moon. As Vivian did not do this, "She's nervous," he said for the pig.

The pig stirred—so did the pitchfork. "I think that pitchfork makes her nervous," ventured Vivian.

"That pitchfork is here to make her *quit* such foolishness," and he was as menacing as if addressing all females with nerves.

One little pig began squealing anew; six other little pigs took it up.

"Listen to them!" he cried, transferring his wrath and his pitchfork. "Wouldn't they make *you* nervous?" and here with swift unreasonableness his ire shifted to Vivian. "Squealin' for food from the minute they strike the air!"

"Strike the air" also had scope—and gave Horace things to ponder.

But Vivian kept thinking of the pigs. While Mr. Moon was barricading the little pigs from their mother, Vivian turned upon her companion eyes live with feeling. "But how *terrible!*" she breathed.

It was not terrible at that moment to look at Vivian. This was one of her moments which had made Horace write on the margin, "emotional." In such moments her eyes were darker and deeper and, in fact, rather wonderful.

She took it for granted that he, too, would think it terrible, so he disclosed no other feeling, though his own reaction to this defeat of mother-love by mother-nerves was not in truth an emotional one. For that matter, he did not think highly of emotional reactions—even though he did think highly of what those reactions made of Vivian's eyes.

He now followed those eyes to the faithless mother pig. She was still fretted by the squealing of her seven little pigs, but she had the look of one who is not, after all, unsustained. In her rolling eye was a light which seemed to say there was one perfect little pig. There was one little pig who was still; she knew just where he was.

That night, instead of going to sleep or instead of reading Sanskrit, Mr. Caldwell kept saying, "This little pig went to market; this little pig stayed home; this little pig—" What *was* it he had? Whatever it was, of it the next little pig had *none*.

Even Gertrude had been wrought up about the pig. She was strongly of the opinion that such things shouldn't be allowed. It was no way for a mother to act. No, not even a nervous mother—though she admitted mothers had enough to make them nervous. Ben said it was fortunate most sows weren't so highly strung—for pigs were too valuable to be eaten by other pigs. Vivian—Vivian said little. Sometimes she said, "It's so *terrible!*" and her eyes—well, Vivian was emotional—not a doubt of that.

The pig who ate her little pig turned Mr. Caldwell to reflections on life. As a matter of fact, he hadn't reflected much on life, for he had always been studying some particular thing. Of course, he was studying the particular thing in order to—well, in order to deepen his knowledge of life and therefore his understanding of it, but he had always been too engrossed in that particular thing to—to get out of it *to* life. He was terribly wary of life as a thing that would take him away from the thing

195

he was studying. This fear made him nervous. He admitted now that he was nervous. And the pig was nervous. That he and the pig should be the same thing somehow interfered with Mr. Caldwell's segregation, drawing him into that main body of life from which he was holding away in order to pursue the studies that would—well, that would deepen his understanding of life. He thumped his pillow. He told himself to go to sleep. If there was anything more ridiculous than a nervous pig, it was a nervous man! He was determined to stop thinking, for there was something *there* he'd think if he went on thinking. He *knew* it was there; he could fairly smell it—as a cat a mouse. Only he didn't know just what it was—and he didn't want to know! With great persistency he turned his thoughts to his sister Gertrude. Confound that pig! What did she mean by making him turn and look at people's lives like this? It was Vivian had brought this down upon him—bringing pigs into the house, so to speak. She was an interfering person—Vivian. But he didn't want to think of Vivian, either. He made another determined lunge at Gertrude. It was rather entertaining—what the pig made him think about Gertrude. He'd tell her!

But he didn't want to say anything to Gertrude until after he had done his day's work, for it might start a discussion that would not be good for the day's work. He decided he wouldn't say anything to her, and yet he somehow knew he would—vaguely knew that his decision had nothing to do with it. What was the *matter* with him—he who had always been so perfectly controlled in his thinking!

At the very instant that he was telling himself to get right into work, "Gertrude," said he, "why do you have this house?"

Gertrude stared, finished fixing her egg, then said, "What a silly question!"

"Can you answer it?"

"I certainly can."

"Then do."

Again she stared at him. "What's the matter with you, Horace?"

"Nothing. Answer."

"Well, I have the house to live in, of course."

He leaned forward. "Then why—" But Vivian was there, too—having the manner of leaning forward, whether doing so or not. He would *not* get into a discussion. A discussion that might—Heavens!—get emotional. He had *work* to . . . Quite indignant at whatever power it was that seemed expecting him to sit there and discuss life with two women, he rose and without his second cup of coffee shut himself up with the ancient Hindus.

He was harassed by a fear that things not ancient would come in at the window—as yesterday; harassed by a fear that she would, and beset by the fear that she wouldn't. Over by the roses he could hear a voice—not ancient. He would raise his eyes from time to time to the box of nasturtiums—but only nasturtiums fluttered there. But he had a well-disciplined mind—how did men exist who *hadn't?*—and so, despite it all (he didn't stop to classify "all"), he had a good day's work, and of this he was proud—as of something achieved against odds.

It was then, of course, quite reasonable to go walking with Vivian that afternoon. And when she said, in a laughing voice brushed with tenderness, "Don't you think we should stop and see the little pigs?" he responded, gaily, "I wonder how many will be there?" She said, softly, "Oh *don't!*" and he had the pleasantly indulgent feeling of the male for the emotional female.

Seven were there—and playing tag. "Oh, you happy little things!" cried Vivian. Solicitously she addressed the mother pig, "And you feel lots better, don't you?"

"Guess she's done all she's a-goin' to do," answered Mr. Moon, for the pig.

"Oh yes, I think so, too," agreed Vivian, in an all's-well-with-the-world voice.

"Probably it didn't agree with her, anyhow," added Moon.

"*Oh!*" shuddered Vivian. She turned to Horace. "Shall we go?"—turned to him as to one who would take her from unpleasant things.

It was to pleasant things they turned—soft little hills not too hard to climb, pleasant valleys and a broad river not far off. At last they sat down by a little river that was playing along to the big river. And there Vivian asked, "What was it you stopped saying at breakfast?"

"Gertrude is a nervous pig," he answered, promptly.

Vivian stared; apparently she thought of saying various things—things indignant and loyal, but instead she dimpled and played the game.

"And what does she eat up?"

"Living beautifully."

"*Living* beautifully?"

He nodded. "Living beautifully is the pig that is eaten."

After enjoying her bewilderment, he explained himself. Gertrude had a beautiful house. Why would one have a beautiful house? Why, that living might be beautiful, of course. But she stopped short at having the beautiful house. She got so nervous having the beautiful house in which one might live beautifully that she quelled the thing in her that could live beautifully, for fear it would squeal, or something of the sort. He lay on the grass and brandished his stick and elaborated on the case of Gertrude, the case of Gertrude which stood between him and himself. He supposed there were lots of Gertrudes. There should be some ugly things in every house—a law about it, if necessary. Then the house beautiful would be an unattainable ideal—and many little pigs would be spared.

"It isn't only Gertrude," he went on, as one who plays with fire, for if he went on long enough there'd be only himself left. "Take Ben," said he, daringly. "'When I make my pile,' says Ben. Then he's going to *live*. But he's got a pretty good pile already. Is he living? Not unless it's living to make a pile! Why, Ben would run a mile at the idea of living. Ben eats the pigs up as fast as they squeal. Everyone does—'most everyone. That's why there's so much indigestion."

Beset by the idea that he himself had indigestion, he got up and started briskly for home—as if walking away from something—indeed, quite rudely walking away from Vivian, who followed.

To get away from individual cases—they having a dangerous proximity to a certain individual, he generalized. "And then there are the countries that get so rasped having democracy that they eat up the squealing pigs to which democracy has given birth!"

He turned upon Vivian with suddenly inexplicable anger. "Think of eating up your *own* thing—the thing it's all *for,* because you get so rasped getting up to the point where you can *have,* what it's all for. Isn't it funny?" he demanded of Vivian, who failed to laugh. "It's the great joke on the human race! Getting so worn out getting ready as to exterminate the thing they've been getting ready *for.* Oh, well," he went on, swinging his stick in a sort of "I should worry" fashion.

Suddenly he turned round, as if to take by surprise. "You thinking about it?" he demanded of Vivian.

"I'm thinking of you," said Vivian.

This infuriated him. "Well, I'm thinking of *you*," he said, viciously, and stalked on.

"How's your indigestion, Ben?" he inquired, jauntily, of his brother-in-law as he and Vivian came up the steps.

"Never had indigestion in my life," said Ben.

"Don't you believe it!" called Horace from the hall.

"What's the *matter* with Horace?" he heard Gertrude ask Vivian.

She asked it again after dinner, for as he ate his roast pork Horace mused: "Perhaps eight is too many to have. Six might be better."

"What are you talking about, Horace?" asked Ben.

"He's talking about the pig," said Gertrude.

"No," said Horace, "I'm talking about civilization."

There was a pause. "I think you work too hard, Horace," suggested Gertrude.

"Civilization works too hard," replied Horace. Suddenly he announced, brightly, "War is civilization eating her own little pigs."

"I do wish you'd rest while you're here," said Gertrude, soothingly.

"I'm here to *work*," he declared with vigor.

And so he was!—and work he would! Just to show what he was there for, he'd work that evening—pigs or no pigs! All right—what if Gertrude and Ben *were* going over to the Logans'? Vivian could sit alone on the veranda. Did he exist in order to sit on a porch with Vivian Truce? If he thought of women at all that night, it would be Hindu women.

But it was queer; a woman would start out to be a Hindu and then turn into Vivian. Very well, then! He would banish Vivian by going out and telling her what he thought of her.

This apparently was just what she wanted him to do, for, picking herself up where he had left her that afternoon, she asked, "When you think about me, what is it you think?"

She had asked it quite simply and directly, but as he stood looking at her she seemed to grow confused. "I mean," she laughed, "what do *I* eat?"

"It's hard to say," he said, and they sat down, as before an undertaking.

At that he did not at once undertake it. "Nice night," he said.

"It is a nice night," agreed Vivian.

Then they just sat there, and the night went on being nice.

Presently he said, with a dissatisfaction staringly intense, "Feeling itself isn't enough."

"Enough—for what?" asked Vivian, with perhaps righteous exasperation.

"There is feeling that—gets somewhere, and then there is feeling that—goes round and round and takes it out in—being feeling."

"And you think I have the latter?" asked Vivian, after a wait.

He had at least enough gallantry to keep silent.

"I'd like to know how you're so sure of that," she came at him with spirit.

"Oh, it's what all emotional women are like," he told her.

"Is that *so?*" she challenged.

"I think so," he replied.

"I suppose," said Vivian, witheringly, "that you have had a large experience with emotional women."

He disregarded this. "You see," he said, "first we were apes."

She did not reply, so he looked at her, as if to make sure she was following—not sticking there in a morass of peevishness. "First we were apes," he repeated, giving her another chance.

"So I have been told," said Vivian, icily.

"And you were told right. And it's hard on us. Hard to have that groundwork of the apes we once were and yet to be that—that—"

"That *what?*" she pinned him down.

"That—what we might be." As he tried to formulate it he was swept into wonder at its beauty. "That thing we might be that has never *been.* The furthest edge of experience. The furthest reach of consciousness— further than it has ever reached before. The other—that's *old* stuff. Falling in love—living together, and all that—that's been lived and lived and relived. Well, all right. Suppose it has. That's what living is—reliving what has been lived. That is, in the main it is. But there's the new thing—the ever-extending edge—where we push realizing on a little further than it has ever been before. *There's* the thing that makes the eternal reliving worthwhile. To get up to that point where we—go further. What feeling might be is a road, and a road that makes itself as it goes. But is that what most people let it be? No—it's a swamp. A place where you *stick*. Emotion is a place to hide one's head. You just stay *there*. A personal experience—a passionate personal experience—it's a limiting thing. It's just something to engage you so you won't try to—realize."

He had been speaking with intensity. "So the poor super-ape," he finished, lightly, "eats that little pig which is the furthest reach of consciousness, and just feels and feels and *feels*—much too taken up with feeling to do any—realizing."

Vivian got up. She was angry—and quite splendid. "You have certainly made it plain to me," said she, "that you think me vulgar."

It was rather ridiculous not to kiss her. That would be the way of it. Just because he wanted to kiss her, and was determined not to, he told himself it would be the right thing to do—for that, of course, was the easiest way to keep himself from doing it. Oh yes, he speculated, probably a great many men had kissed women just in order not to appear ridiculous. Of course—there might be other reasons. True—there might be. He stood beside Vivian—and it was still a very nice night, and—to tell the truth, he wanted a limiting personal experience so fearfully that—apes must have laughed!

Why didn't Vivian go away? As she was so angry—why didn't she leave, instead of staying there to show how beautiful anger made her? He would have to kiss this beautiful woman who was very angry, this— emotional woman. Make her still more angry and then have all that feeling turn to passion for him, as he had a feeling it was ready to do—as he was so tantalized by suspecting it was ready to do.

A sound broke the night—or Mr. Caldwell's distance from the apes might have been shortened then and there—the sound of the returning motor.

Horace and Vivian continued to stand there. "Well," said Ben, "I suppose you two have been talking about pigs?"

"Apes," said Vivian, in an emotional voice.

"Apes?" repeated Gertrude. "Apes make me nervous. They look too much like us."

"But did you ever think, Gertrude," inquired Horace, "how much we look like them?"

She sighed. So he escaped before she could say he worked too hard. When he got to his room he looked in the glass—perhaps to see what resemblance he could find. When Mr. Caldwell looked in the glass what regarded him was pleasing. Perhaps the reason most scholars aren't good-looking is that the good-looking ones aren't permitted to be scholars. If you are very good-looking and determined to be a scholar—there is struggle in your life. There was struggle tonight in the life of Horace Caldwell. The reason he had spoken these harsh words about being emotional was, not so much that Vivian was emotional, as that Vivian made him emotional. And he wanted the decks cleared for study and reflection. Marrying Vivian would be eating his eighth little pig. He'd be *damned* if he would!

He sat down to his books. But he couldn't study—he couldn't study because he was thinking—usually he didn't have that interference. And his thoughts crystallized to this, "Where *is* your eighth little pig?"

So there he was—right up against himself! He had put Gertrude in between, and Ben, and Vivian—now his pigs had come home to roost—he didn't attempt to keep zoology straight. He had been in a rage because Vivian threatened the eighth little pig, but what was *he* doing to that unfortunate animal?

And after a while he was ready to admit that perhaps no one was as cannibalistic as the men who gave their lives to study. For they dealt with the very stuff out of which the life-sense must be born—and what did they do? They just stuck in a little pocket of learning—put their heads deeper and deeper and deeper in scholarship that there might not be anything of themselves left for—for moments of wonder out of which vision comes—for that greater sensitiveness to life which was man's one chance to justify man. Heads buried in learning as other heads were buried in emotion, or in money making, or in the house beautiful. And they had the *goods*, as it were. Here was he studying India—*India*, of all things!—and instead of this helping him to know what was in his own soul he—why, he just studied India! He was a nice one to talk to anyone else! Could frustration of purpose be more ignoble than his?

He went to the window and looked out into the beautiful night. "Well, *realize*," he said to himself, savagely. He got into a rage—that horrible rage of the thwarted. "*Realize*—you fool!" He could laugh a little at this—but it wasn't a laugh that helped much. What did he *want?* This was what he wanted. It was not speaking too highly of himself to say there was in him something of aspiration. He aspired to beauty. To the beauty that might flower from understanding. But, somehow, understanding was sterile. He was very much like the pig—very much indeed. He got so nervous in *having* it that he wasn't equal to it when it came. And he and the pig weren't alone in this—more was the pity of it. People got so frazzled by living that they didn't really have life. When they came up to the moments it was all *for*—they could do nothing but revert to the things which existed in order to bring them up to those moments. In other words, the mechanics of living ate life up. In still other words, stomachs were full of eighth little pigs.

He slept as badly as if his stomach were full of some such thing. He dreamed that Vivian was the queen of a zoo.

She acted a good deal like a queen next day—a displeased queen. She and he and Gertrude had lunch together. Fortunately Gertrude talked a good deal about how to make woodwork look like old ivory. He didn't know why it should look like old ivory, but he was glad someone was talking. Finally Gertrude stopped talking. Vivian did not talk. So he had to. As he couldn't think of any extraneous thing to say, he had to say what he was thinking. He frequently did this—and got blamed for it. Apparently most people didn't do it.

"I suppose," he said, "that we never should have left the trees. It—it's too much for us."

There was a long silence. Silence is really a peculiarly articulate thing. It can make you feel—as words never can—how you are being disapproved of.

"Horace," said Gertrude, at last, "I don't know whether you really *are* ill, or whether you are merely trying to rouse apprehensions."

"I'm not trying to *rouse* apprehensions," he hastened to assure her. "I'm trying to quell them."

He looked at Vivian. Certainly he had quelled nothing—least of all, rage.

About four o'clock he saw her starting alone for the walk they usually had together. She came to the crest of the hill and hesitated. Her hesitation was long. She didn't know whether to visit the pigs or to cut them!

This decision became of tremendous moment to the man who watched. So rapidly did it go on increasing in importance that it was as if his whole life hung upon it. Vivian was beautiful standing there before the poplars—the wind blowing her skirt out to one side as if she were poised to fly. She herself was slim and straight and strong—but lithe—oh, much lither than a tree. And—she was going to visit the little pigs!

He snatched his hat and followed.

He found her at the pigsty. And he found there a scene of contentment good for a spirit fagged by aspiration. The little pigs were sucking. *All* of them were sucking. They did enjoy it! Some could sit down, but others had to stand up—those which had to reach the upper tier. So they stood on their hind legs, front paws kneading their mother—going at it for all they were worth.

He and Vivian looked from the pig family to each other—laughed. No two people could stay cross at each other when seven little pigs were nursing!

Mr. Moon came along. "Well, she's made up her mind to it," said he.

And so she had made up her mind to it. It was a contented mother pig who gave suck to the little pigs. One of them finished his meal and came and played with her snout. She pawed him playfully. She *liked* her little pigs. There she lay, doing just what she should do, and happier than she could be doing anything else. Perhaps she didn't go quite so far as to make one feel God was in His heaven—but she made one feel that the good old earth was very good indeed.

He and Vivian walked slowly away.

"Vivian," he said, "I've fought a good fight and lost. I'm sorry to say I love you. Will you—*you* know—marry me—and all that?"

He stopped; his hands were on her shoulders, he looking into her eyes. It wasn't going to matter much what she said. For looking into her eyes—"she had made up her mind to it."

Though with words she resisted. "Marry you?" she choked, "and drag you down into my *swamp?*"

Feeling took him, then, with great mercifulness—so overwhelmingly that he had nothing to say about it. Vivian in his arms, he kissed her again and again and again—and knew nothing save that he was kissing her. "Yes—*drag* me there. I— Anything else is too *lonely*, Vivian. I— It's all right," he assured her, and incoherent things like that.

And it was all right. As they came back over the fields at sunset he had a moment of beauty such as had never been his before—a lift of the spirit—a widening. If he was going to be, for the most part, in a pocket, let it be a pocket of feeling rather than a pocket of learning! It wasn't so ridiculous. And nicer.

Of course, he was probably fooling himself. He wasn't so lost that he couldn't see he was probably fooling himself. But perhaps that was what we *had* to do!

Anyway, the sun went down and the sky was purple and gold and Vivian moved in a magical light. Things smelled good. A bird was singing.

And the neighbor's pig had eight little pigs. No—seven.

Originally published in *Harper's Monthly Magazine* 140
(February 1920): 309–20

A Rose in the Sand

CELIA CAME IN TO REMOVE THE breakfast tray, hesitated, decided Mrs. Paxton was not through with it. For the past week there had not been much way of telling whether she was through or not. Celia was very sorry for her mistress. How was she ever going to get along without Mr. Paxton?

She brought in the letters—perhaps that would rouse her. And when she returned she saw there was one letter which certainly had roused her. Celia stole away and told the cook maybe it was better not to have a man at all; then you wouldn't have this to go through, anyhow.

It was a stilted business letter which had roused Ellen Paxton. It was from William Josephs, grocer and real estate agent at Cape's End, the little fishing village where the Paxtons had spent the summer. He wrote to say the bid he had been instructed to make for them on the abandoned lifesaving station on the far side of the cape was the highest which the government had received. The station was theirs. The letter closed with a labored attempt at the amenities. He hoped they would see Mr. and Mrs. Paxton there next year; he hoped they would enjoy their new home. It was at that moment Celia had come in, and retreated with her observations on love.

Suddenly Ellen Paxton arrived at a decision. That abandoned lifesaving station was the place for her. She would go there at once and remain there. Ringing for Celia she told her to begin packing, telephone men to break up the apartment, put things in storage—no, offer them for sale. Anyhow, take them away. Pack a small trunk with her own plainest things and she would leave New York on the afternoon boat. Celia would have to find another place. She would leave money to tide her over.

At noon next day Mrs. Paxton reached the little town on the tip of the cape, the town which she and her husband had left in September. It had been a gay summer place then. It was different now, as everything was different. Though as a matter of fact she scarcely looked at it, eyes down, as they jolted by the cottage she and her husband had lived in the summer before, careful not to look out to see if anything was left of the garden she and Ned had planted in June.

Mr. Josephs was alone in his store, opening a box of canned things. Not heeding his stare of amazement, "Mr. Josephs," she began, "I have come to take the lifesaving station. I will sleep over there tonight."

He dropped his hatchet. "Why, Mrs. Paxton—you *can't*."

"Yes, I can," she said, but suddenly sat down.

She was so white and strange, so unlike the pleasant gentle woman who had come into his store all through the summer that he could only stand there staring.

"Is Mr. Paxton with you?" he finally asked.

"No."

"I suppose he's coming later," he ventured, seeking his bearings.

"No."

Mr. Josephs, when perturbed looked as if he were about to cry. "But you see you can't stay there tonight, Mrs. Paxton. There's no furniture."

"Get furniture."

"You can't furnish a house in an afternoon!"

"Just a bed, a stove, a chair. Oh, Mr. Josephs, do this for me!"

She had held out her hands to him. When at last he spoke, it was gently. "I'll do the best I can for you, Mrs. Paxton."

She would not leave the store, but sat in the back room amid barrels, dishes and oil-skins while he telephoned stove man and furniture store, teamster and coal yard. Yes, *yes*, he meant the old lifesaving station, he insisted again and again. Yes, across Snail Road. Well, they'd be paid for their time. But right away—yes, start right away.

He would go to the door and stand looking at the woman who sat with her back to him. At last he walked up to her. "Excuse me, Mrs. Paxton, but have you got somebody to work for you?"

She shook her head.

"You want me to see to that too?"

"I wish you would," she said, and looked at him, but quickly looked away.

"I suppose"—he thought it out—"that you want some good reliable woman who can just take hold and attend to everything?"

She nodded.

"And somebody that will, in a way, be company for you?"

"No!" she retorted. "Somebody that doesn't say an unnecessary word!"

He started away, but stopped, stood there looking at her.

"Mrs. Paxton," he began, as if overcome by his own courage, "does Mr. Paxton know you are here?"

She raised her eyes, and when he saw them, "Oh," he whispered. "He—died?"

She turned away, as if trying not to break down.

Grocer Josephs stood there helpless. Again he started softly away, again stopped. "It's awful lonesome here this time of year. It's even hard on us natives. I don't see how a city person could stand it. And over there at the station—way off across the sand, on the outside sea—why there's none of us would do that. You've no idea what the storms will be—and nobody around."

"I shall like it," she said. "Please see about the woman, will you, Mr. Josephs? And get a team to take us over."

He stood there, reluctant. "It don't seem right," he muttered.

Half an hour later he told her he had the woman to work for her. "Allie Mayo—that's her name. There's better cooks in town, but she's clean, and it's been twenty years since she said a word she didn't need to say."

Within an hour Ellen Paxton was on her way to her new home. She sat on the backseat of a wagon drawn by two heavy horses. Beside the driver sat Allie Mayo, a valise at her feet, a bundle in her lap, a little shawl wrapped round her head—a gaunt woman. They drove toward Snail Road in the face of a strong east wind. Once the driver ventured to speak. "Breezin' up, ain't it?" he said to the woman beside him. Her only reply was a nod. He did not try again and so in silence they left the harbor and turned in the woods—Snail Road, deep sand, a clearing just the width of a wagon. There was a mile or so of woods, queer dwarf

woods of scrub oaks and maples, pines which took strange shapes, dic-
tated by the whim of the sand. She and her husband had tramped those
woods in the summer and been fascinated by the queer stunted things
so valiantly growing in their plot of life between sand and sea.

Woods stopped and sand dunes began. To come out upon them was
like leaving life behind. These strange hills are valleys, forms there were
no names for were like a country in another world. She had never cared
for them; they were too bleak, too unlike life. She liked growing things,
things familiar. But now there was relief in leaving things familiar.

It was after four, already the sun was low, throwing an unreal light
across those weird forms of sand. It was a little caravan which labored
across the dunes to the abandoned lifesaving station on the outside shore.
In front of her was the bed on which she would sleep; behind her strained
horses drawing wood and coal. Over there against the sea she could see
the house which was to be her home, a place abandoned even by lifesavers
for the sea had washed in, making too precipitous a descent for launching
the boats. Smoke rose from the chimney of the new lifesaving station,
about three-quarters of a mile to the eastward. This was the only sign of
life, save gray sails of a fishing schooner rounding the cape.

An hour later the men had gone back to town. They had put the
stove in place, set up the beds. They were subdued, stealing looks at the
women they were leaving in the abandoned place. "It'll be a gay life,
what?" the man who had brought the coal whispered to his friend who
was wrestling with the stovepipe.

The Paxtons had bid on the place thinking it would be amusing to
bring friends and spend a couple of weeks over there from time to time.
It was a large well-built house which would go for little because of its
isolation; the way it had been adapted to its purpose could be attrac-
tively readjusted to theirs. The long "boat room," where the lifeboats
had swung, would become a lounge, a fireplace across one end. They
were going to do it over in gay colors—a camp where people would
have a good time.

But the readjustments were made by Allie Mayo, scarcely in the direction of having a good time. That first night she said, "There have got to
be more dishes and pans."

"Get everything we need," her employer answered.

Mrs. Mayo would go to the new lifesaving station and telephone in to town for a team. The lifesavers tried to question her:

"Is that woman crazy?"

"I don't know," she would answer.

"She ain't much more talkative 'an you are, is she?"

"What does that woman *do* over there?" a member of Allie Mayo's family demanded.

"She sits and looks," was the reply.

They had one visitor—a horse. On days not too stormy he would come stiffly across the sands from the new lifesaving station to this old one which had long been his home. She could see him a long way off—an old horse retired from service. He would walk round his old barn and sometimes stand there for hours. Occasionally a lifesaver patrolling the beach would stop: "You don't live here any more, Prince," and would get the old horse to follow him along the beach to the new station. One day she heard one of these lifesavers talking about Prince to a man who was putting on outside windows. "He ought to be done away with, but the ol' man don't like to do it. He had him more than twenty years, and he was the best horse he ever had. And do you know, to this day when he hears the signal for the boats, out *he* comes and hobbles alongside of the horses that's doing the work."

November, December, and January passed and Allie Mayo had not spoken an unnecessary word. She was as bleak as the place where they lived. She seemed to belong there. Yet sometimes Ellen Paxton would find this woman looking at her in a way she came to resent. "I'd rather she'd *talk* than do that," she told herself. Mrs. Mayo had high cheekbones and deep-set eyes. Her face looked as if unfavoring winds had blown upon her all her life long, but there were those times when her eyes had a look as if they could see *through*. After Mrs. Paxton found her servant looking at her like that she would watch the drifting sand, as if it could bury what the look had disturbed.

It was a busy winter for the lifesavers. Men died right out there in front of Ellen Paxton's new home. There were nights when it seemed everyone who was caught at sea must die. Those nights the old lifesaving station shook as if the sand upon which it was built must go from under it. There were nights when the sea battered her house on the one side and the sand on the other. The worst storm was late in January. That night it seemed Allie Mayo was on the point of speaking an unnecessary word. She kept coming in to attend to the fire; for three days it had been a fight to keep warm, and after she had done this she would stand there a moment before going out. The woman who sat before the fire, a rug around her, would not look up. No night before had been like this night. It was like something outside the world in which one was secure. The last time Mrs. Mayo came in and did not immediately go out again there was one moment when it seemed the two women must be driven together. Then Mrs. Paxton raised her eyes and met that look which to herself she tumultuously called impertinent. "Did you want something?" she asked, forced by the thunder of wind and sea to raise her voice but speaking in a studied tone of everyday things. Mrs. Mayo shook her head and turned away, but her lips—it seemed almost as if there was an impulse to smile.

Next morning, the sun shone and the dunes gleamed in their strange beauty. It mattered not at all to them who may have died the night before. It was that fascination the dunes had for her which finally took her out of doors. They were something outside life. She was attracted by the forms they took—forms like nothing else. The natives called that part of the cape the Outside. She too thought of it as outside, but she did not mean what they meant.

One day she walked over to the line where dunes met woods. There was a high hill with which they threatened the woods, and from that hill of sand she could see all sides around—the woods, and the town at the edge of the woods, and at the edge of the town the harbor—where men were safe; turning the other way were dunes and outer sea, the Outside.

She formed the habit of walking over to that place where the dunes encroached upon the woods, where the Outside threatened life. She was unable to keep away from that line of death. She could see tops of trees which the sand had covered; the buried things gave the sand its form. Upon returning home from these pilgrimages she would find Allie Mayo's eyes upon her, that look which seemed an intrusion.

One day she must go over to town to sign a paper at the courthouse; there were business readjustments had to be made now that she was alone.

It was the first time she had left the Outside since leaving life behind in November. The man who drove over for her was a man who did some work around the house. There were windowpanes to be replaced; wind and sand were always breaking them. So Mrs. Mayo was to drive Mrs. Paxton over to town and the driver stay there and work while they were gone. It was Mrs. Mayo's arrangement. Her mistress was not attracted to it, but made no comment.

The two women drove at the enforced snail's pace across the mile of sand. It was just before they reached the line of the woods, as they came up to the little outposts of vegetation, that the thing happened. Allie Mayo stopped the team. The horses had rested just a little before so the woman who was being driven now looked at the driver in inquiry. Allie Mayo broke the precedent of twenty years. She spoke an unnecessary word.

She pointed to the woods. "*They* fight too," she said in a queer scraping voice, then reached for the whip and sharply touched the horses.

They drove through the woods faster than the horses wanted to pull. Ellen Paxton was struggling with tears, angry tears. She did not look at her companion.

On their homeward way they had reached that line where woods give way to dunes, before another unnecessary word was spoken. It was spoken this time by Mrs. Paxton.

"They may fight," she said in a high trembling voice, "but they lose!"

Mrs. Mayo shook her head.

"Why, they certainly *do*," she insisted angrily. "Look! That was a tree. The woods were farther over. The woods are being buried."

Again—somberly—Allie Mayo shook her head.

"That's simply childish!" cried Mrs. Paxton.

"They lose," said the other, slowly heavily, "and then they fight, and gain again."

"To lose again!"

Slowly, stubbornly, the woman who had been silent for twenty years shook her head. "They get back what they lose," she said in a firm mournful voice. "They may lose it again. Then gain it back. Things take root in the sand, and when there's enough growing there—they've *got* the sand. It's anchored." She pointed to the great bank that threatened the woods. "You come here in a couple of weeks, when things have begun to grow. You'll see them beginning to climb that hill."

Two weeks went by and she had not returned to the line where woods and dunes fought their battle. She remained where the Outside had its way, wandering in weird hidden places where life was not—strange inlets, wide sweeps of desolation.

Allie Mayo had returned to her silence.

One day, on her way to the inlets where life was not, something passed over her face like a message. Spring. April had come. People were planting things.

As she stood there, not knowing what to do, she saw that Prince, the horse life had no use for, was standing beside a pump at the side of the house. Suddenly she went over there and pumped a bucket of water for him. Then she felt as if her knees were going to give way. It was some time later that she started slowly towards the woods.

After that she went each day. She would start in the other direction, towards her refuge in desolation, but no matter what way she went she would be drawn to that line where dunes threatened woods and woods fought dunes. She came to know this battle line along a stretch of several miles, came to know all the queer things the woods put out to meet the dunes. That conflict seemed to have made a life all its own, weeds and vines and bushes she had never seen before, a rude vegetation; things sorry enough in themselves, but at times, looking at milkweed or cat vine, tears brimmed her eyes. Often she hated them, and again they seemed to her the most wonderful things in the world; she would sit for hours just looking at them. They were meeting the Outside, fighting the fight for all the richer life back in the woods. There were places where she could see it was a losing fight, where her moving about was enough to send down sand to bury the advance guard of the woods. There were days when she could no longer see the rude stubby little things she had seen the day before; but there were many places where life was taking hold, and no places at all where it was not fighting. She knew there were flowers in the woods, but she did not go to find them; she remained on the edge, that poor fringe of life that fought for what it had lost, waging war to hold its own—to hold life's own. It tired her; she always turned back to the Outside with relief; she wanted to remain there. But again and again she was lured back to the disturbance that was life.

Returning one day to her home on the Outside she was stopped by a sound from within the house, a sound that made her pull back as if something had been flicked before her eyes. It was a laugh. It was a *child's* laugh. She had started to retreat when Mrs. Mayo came out of the house.

Before either woman could speak the child herself appeared in the doorway, a little girl with rosy cheeks, eyes soft brown and fair curly hair. Mrs. Paxton stepped farther back.

"Who brought her here?" she whispered.

"I did," said Allie Mayo.

"You?"

The baby girl had sat herself down on the sand. She was playing with the sand.

"Her mother died this morning," said Mrs. Mayo. "She's got nowhere to go."

"But she can't stay *here*."

"She's got to stay somewhere," said Mrs. Mayo doggedly.

"She can*not*." There was an interruption. The little visitor had produced an avalanche and was laughing at the sliding sand. Mrs. Paxton hurried past her into the house.

Night fell on desert and sea, but within, in the abandoned place which was her home, she could hear that little girl running about and laughing.

After Mrs. Mayo had fixed the fire for the night she stood a moment with the empty coal bucket in her hand. "I couldn't send her home tonight," she said.

"Then send her tomorrow!"

But the woman did not go. "I thought," she ventured, "that maybe we could keep her here till they get somebody to adopt her."

"This is no place for a child," was the low response.

"She'll have to be adopted," Allie Mayo went on in her monotonous voice, "and it may be hard, for she's not legitimate, and there's a good many don't like that. But she's a lovely baby, and her mother was a lovely girl. She and Walter Evans had been wanting to get married for a long time, but he had his mother to do for and she hers, and so—well, anyway he was in one of the *Lady Jane* dories lost January two years ago, and Esther was born that next summer. This morning the mother died. And here's this little girl, so lively and nice-looking—"

"Now that will *do*, Mrs. Mayo!"

Next day, after the child had been taken away, she walked the five miles to Mr. Josephs' grocery store. "Mr. Josephs," she began, "can you get somebody to work for me?

"I want somebody that doesn't talk," she continued.

"Why, I didn't know Mrs. Mayo had left you."

"She hasn't left me. But I want her to leave. I simply can't stand her talking!"

He stared. "Mrs. Mayo's—what?"

"I simply can't *stand* her talking! You—you will have to get me someone else!"

But Mr. Josephs seemed incapable of word or action. "Why, Mrs. Paxton," he finally stammered, "this—this is certainly a great surprise to *me*."

She told Mrs. Mayo she would not want her after that week. "Mr. Josephs is going to get me somebody that doesn't *talk!*"

"Somebody that talks less than I do?" asked Mrs. Mayo mildly.

"Yes, he is!"

"In Cape's End?" inquired Mrs. Mayo dryly.

"Now this is no joking matter!"

"No," replied the other woman, "it isn't."

"They told me you didn't say an unnecessary word!"

Allie Mayo, who had been mixing bread, looked at the woman who reproached her. "I don't know as I do," she said.

Neither of them said an unnecessary word the rest of that week. It was Saturday night when Allie Mayo came to Mrs. Paxton's room. "Then I'm to go tomorrow?"

Her employer only nodded.

"You—you've got somebody else?"

She shook her head.

"But I can't leave you here alone."

Slowly, unwillingly, Mrs. Paxton looked at the woman before her; after she had seen her face she was not able to look away again.

The woman who had been asked to leave came nearer and sat down. Neither of them seemed to have any sense of strangeness in this. There was something else—something they had touched and could not draw away from.

"For twenty years," Allie Mayo began, "I did what you're setting out to do."

Mrs. Paxton raised a hand to stop her. The hand fell to her lap. Her eyes did not leave the woman's face.

"And I can tell you," rose the bleak voice, "it's not the way."

She did not look at the woman she addressed; her eyes were as if looking through something. "We had been married two years." It seemed she could not go on. "Two years," she made herself repeat. "He had a chance to go north on a whaler. Times were hard. He had to go. It was to be for a year and a half. Two years we'd been married.

"I'll not try to tell you," she said, slowly, "about the day he went away." She stopped. "Nor I'll not try to tell you—about the days after he was gone.

"Through the first six months I heard several times. The last letter said he might not have another chance to write till they were starting home.

"Another six months went by. Then another. I did not hear." She was still, as if again waiting. "Nobody ever heard.

"I used to talk as much as any girl in Cape's End," she took it up at last. "Jim used to tease me about my talking. But they'd come in to talk to me. They'd say, 'You may hear yet,' or 'Suppose you was to hear tomorrow.' They'd talk about what might have happened. One day a woman who had been my friend all my life began: 'It would be a satisfaction if you could just *know*.' I got up and drove her from my kitchen, and from that day to this I've never said a word I didn't have to say.

"I froze." Her voice fell to a whisper. "The icebergs that caught Jim—caught me."

Now it was as if the fog from an iceberg had indeed settled around her.

At last she turned her eyes to Mrs. Paxton. "It's not the way," she said, simply, but as if coming from far off and for only a little time. "I wish you'd take that little girl, and let her—let her show you how to *laugh* at the sand."

Suddenly she changed. "You're not the only woman in this world whose husband is dead!"

"*Dead!*" cried Ellen Paxton. "My husband's not *dead.*"

The other woman stared. "He's *not?*" was all she could say.

"Did you think—" she began passionately, but could not go on. Raising flooded eyes to Allie Mayo she implored, "Please go."

The woman who had broken the silence of twenty years stood there awkwardly. "I'm sorry," she said, helplessly, then went.

That night undid everything she had done. Her idea had been to keep quiet; she had known women who had not been dignified, who had made a vulgar fuss and cried out for men who did not want them, whimpering so that everyone could hear. When the hour came that the life was struck out of the world for her, terrified by things she had an impulse to do, she said to herself, "Keep still." Over and over again she said it. It had been her word to herself. It had been her way.

She hated this woman who lived in the house with her, who had stolen in upon her and forced her to know that she was not dead—even now, that she was alive and unhappy. Because she did not want to stay in the house with Allie Mayo she went out of doors next morning, but not to that line where the woods fought for what they had lost. She remained on the Outside. But even on the Outside there was no evading spring. The world was warm and tender. It was the first time in many years that she had not made a garden in the spring. She and her husband had always planted things together. She sat alone on the barren sands and thought of the years they had planted things together. Tears fell, and then tears stopped; the last two years, making a garden with her, it was love for another woman had been the living thing in his heart. That thought was to her the iceberg this woman talked about. She had been standing in the way and had not even *known.*

They had been married for ten years. They were happy in a serene sort of way. At least, she had supposed they were happy. Her husband, the night he told her he did not love her and wanted to leave her—wanted to leave her because he loved Madeline Osborne—in his irritation at her because he was forced to hurt her, had told her she was stupid. She should have seen. And then, more gently, "You live contented in your little spot and do not see very far around you."

Years before, analyzing her in love instead of resentment, he had said, "You're like a plant, Ellen." In that first year he often told her, "You'll make a lovely mother." But she had not had children. And—no longer a growing thing, but pulled up and tossed aside—comes this insolent woman suggesting that *now* she take a child! Sitting in one of her inlets of desolation she tried to laugh. But she did not laugh. She cried.

They were unhappy weeks that followed through the month of May. She told herself soft air could never hurt her like this again. She would be farther away another spring. . . .

She did not go to the woods to find the flowers. The only growing thing she saw was the harsh beach grass. The wind bent its long sharp spears, making them describe circles in the sand. She would sit looking at these circles as if caught into them. There was indeed likelihood spring would never find an open way to her again.

She walked slowly towards home late one gentle afternoon. Prince, the horse who was no longer needed, stood by the pump. She pumped a drink for him; she had fallen in the way of doing this. She started towards the house, but had done only a few steps when she stopped abruptly. She told herself she must be mistaken. She looked all round in a frightened way. Then slowly, unwillingly, she again looked down at her feet. In a stiff frightened way she bent and smelled. Next instant she was kneeling on the sand. For when she smelled she knew she was not mistaken, knew that a wild rose was indeed blooming in the sand.

But what she never knew was whether it was minutes or hours she knelt before the little rose bush with its single flower. It had nothing to do with time. It was the whole of life. The wind brushed her lifted face. Off somewhere a bird was singing. The wind and the birds—carriers of life, extenders of boundaries. She looked down at her feet; a little patch of sand fertilized by the visits of a horse who had outlived his "usefulness," water spilled in drinking; and to a woman too stricken to go to the roses comes this one wild rose, a messenger. There it bloomed in the sand, alone and undismayed, fragile and authoritative. The whole Outside could not daunt it, for back of it was something more powerful than the Outside. Back of it was the will to grow. Back of it was the way of life.

She went into the kitchen where Allie Mayo was getting supper. "Tomorrow," she said, "I would like to go over and get that little girl."

Originally published in *Pall Mall Magazine* 1 (May 1927): 45–51